when all else fails

NOV 19

# when all else fails

### a novel by
### Rayyan Al-Shawaf

Interlink Books

An imprint of Interlink Publishing Group, Inc.
Northampton, Massachusetts

First published 2019 by

Interlink Books
An imprint of Interlink Publishing Group, Inc.
46 Crosby Street, Northampton, MA 01060
www.interlinkbooks.com

Library of Congress Cataloging-in-Publication data:
Names: Al-Shawaf, Rayyan, author.
Title: When all else fails / by Rayyan Al-Shawaf.
Description: Northampton, MA : Interlink Books, an imprint of
    Interlink Publishing Group, Inc., 2019.
Identifiers: LCCN 2018061372 | ISBN 9781623719777 (pbk.)
Subjects: LCSH: September 11 Terrorist Attacks, 2001--Fiction.
Classification: LCC PJ7902.L215 W44 2019 | DDC 813/.6--dc23
LC record available at https://lccn.loc.gov/2018061372

Printed and bound in the United States of America

*For my parents and my (late) maternal grandmother,*
*without whose support this book would not have been possible*

# PART I
# SEPTEMBERLAND

## 1

On the morning of September 12th, 2001, I set off by car from northeast Orlando, where I lived, for Winter Park, a suburb to the west, convinced I had to see Hashem— though I wasn't sure why.

It had found me. The mini-Moloch that used to chase me around Lebanon had followed me to the States, except now it was all grown up and really pissed. How could this happen?

One minute, you're taking a leak, your tendency toward idle contemplation in such instances leading you to ponder why James Earl Jones's baritone voice is so often described as "commanding." And the next minute, you're sitting in front of the television watching CNN. Not because of James Earl Jones's commanding way of saying "This…is CNN," but because, while flipping through the channels, you come across a vaguely familiar high-rise building with a large hole in it, from which smoke is billowing.

I knew it was an attack as soon as I saw that building, despite the fact that the people on TV kept going on about a "tragic accident." I also knew, instinctively, who—or pretty much who—had carried it out. The first thought to enter my mind concerned my former friend Khaled. *You fool, if only you'd waited, you'd have found yourself in precisely the situation you longed for.* How not, with Arabs and Muslims in the States surely about to enter an era in which the burden of proof would fall on them to prove their humanity?

When the second plane hit, thoughts of fleeing, of just grabbing a bag and jumping in the car and driving away like some sort of fugitive, invaded my mind. But I had nowhere to run to. No Ashrafieh if skirmishes broke out in Hamra, no Brummana if Ashrafieh blew up. America was thousands of times larger than Lebanon, but because it was a real country as opposed to a patchwork of distinct and feuding localities, and because the now giant Moloch, as ravenous for human life as ever, had devoured so many people with just one bite, someone like me, whose appearance betrayed a shared geographic if not ethnic origin with the bloodthirsty ogre, could not hide anywhere.

As it happened, I was a pretty jittery and suspicious guy to begin with. When my buddy Lewis and I had gone to the Korean restaurant on East Colonial Drive for dinner one night a few weeks earlier, he suggested we try the "Bi Bim Bap." I convinced him otherwise, insisting that the dish didn't actually exist. "Trust me, man, these Koreans only put 'Bi Bim Bap' on the menu so that we say it so that they laugh at us," I explained.

Now, driving toward Winter Park, I consulted the rearview mirror every so often, as was my habit, so that if I glimpsed any sort of untoward developments, I could take appropriate action. However, the development I anticipated on this occasion was not the otherwise expected Mossad agent materializing in the backseat to assassinate me, but rather a police car with flashing lights indicating that I should pull over—which I desperately wanted to do, so that I could surrender (even though I hadn't done anything) and put an end to this nightmare. Yet to my consternation, every time I checked, no police cars appeared in the mirror. In fact, the streets were virtually empty.

My wheels were new. A few months earlier, midway through my junior year, I had bought a used 1997 Geo Metro (a compact hatchback) with some money de Monet my parents had kindly wired me for the purpose. I made the acquisition for a simple reason. In olden times, a man had to slay a dragon to win a woman's favor; today, he needed an automobile. My fortunes in the romance department hadn't changed since I scored the car (which made me consider trying to get my folks to also spring for a sword, so that I could seek out any aged, doddering dragons busy foraging for leftovers in dumpsters behind fusion cuisine restaurants), but at least now I could zip over to the University of Central Florida campus and back to my apartment complex, rather than spend half an hour hoofing it each way, or waste time waiting for the shuttle bus. I could also go to Winter Park.

Normally, on a drive like this, I'd admire the scenery, a lush, verdant landscape stippled with shimmering teal blue lakes that exemplified Central Florida's natural beauty. On the approach to Winter Park, I enjoyed trundling down one road in particular, the oak trees overhanging both sides forming an umbriferous canopy that shards of sunlight sliced through here and there, giving me the impression I had entered a tunnel haphazardly illuminated by jagged ceiling lamps.

As I'd roll into Winter Park itself, a town gobbled up by the ever-expanding metropolis of Orlando, my attention would shift to street scenes. Here you'd see people bustling about, ducking into and out of boutiques, restaurants, and

11

coffee shops, infusing the place with a city vibe. Orlando was big but sprawling; outside the downtown area, you couldn't find much building density, and the population was thinly spread. In fact, whole swaths of territory lay vacant save for the occasional strip mall, which usually included a Publix supermarket, a Blockbuster video store, and a few other assorted commercial establishments. (Oftentimes, you'd have two such malls on either side of the same stretch of an otherwise empty boulevard. For some reason, these always seemed to have drugstore giants CVS and Walgreens facing each other.) Surveying the ground below from the airplane when I first came over from Beirut via London, I couldn't spot any signs of urban concentration.

Little Winter Park, on the other hand, was compact and overflowing with people. Park Avenue, the brick-cobbled main drag, brought to mind some of the streets of Rome, where I had lived before we moved to Beirut. Although I liked the chocolate-box look of this affluent town-cum-suburb, I hesitated to express this to other UCF students for fear of being seen as a bourgeois wannabe.

None of this was on my mind now, with horrifying images of desperate people flinging themselves out of the burning Twin Towers' windows—exchanging one kind of certain death for another—having displaced almost everything else. Driving from northeast Orlando to Winter Park, I felt the impact of what had happened in New York City, Washington, DC, and rural Pennsylvania the day before more forcefully than anything that had taken place in Florida since my arrival nearly three years earlier. Nothing even came close.

Indeed, following the presidential election in 2000, I watched the news programs on the chaos unfolding in the Sunshine State as though it were occurring in another country. This was true of most UCF students, whose political apathy during the election predictably held firm in its aftermath.

And a year before that, when the cops arrested Khaled, I felt that they had surgically removed him from our midst without so much as grazing the rest of us, his (precious few) friends and acquaintances. We were left shocked both by what he had done and by the speed of his very much deserved punishment. But this thing yesterday hadn't simply shocked me; it had vivified and broadened my consciousness, so that I became aware of the absence of any natural law governing societal reactions to disruptions large and small. Nothing had guaranteed that, with Khaled's arrest and trial (a minor incident in the grand scheme of things), or the Supreme Court's ruling on the presidential election (a pretty big deal whichever way you looked at it), hotheads emotionally invested in either case wouldn't make trouble. That they didn't in fact stir anything up made me complacent, so that I took it for granted that courtroom verdicts resolved conflicts and crises. Now, I was forced to think. What I came up with was hardly comforting: Even if the United States apprehended and tried the planners of these attacks, or went so far as to kill them, things still wouldn't return to normal. *And before any of that happened… well, who knew how bad it could get?*

I needed to talk to Hashem, having convinced myself that he could help me make sense of the situation. Not that he proved especially insightful on the phone when I had

13

called him the evening of the previous day—but I attributed that to the sense of dread that crept up on us at the same time. After we said our (awkward) hellos, the conversation went something like this:

Me: That was pretty bad, huh?

Hashem: Yes, terrible.

Me: Looks like it was…you know…terrorism.

Hashem: Oh, I'm sure of it.

(A pause pregnant with meaning—as well as a sudden shared suspicion of the presence of something nebulous and undefined, but very, very attentive.)

Me: You know, I condemn terrorism in the—

Hashem: I have always condemned terrorism very—

Me: Strongest terms.

Hashem: There are no terms stronger than the ones I have used.

Me: Unless you consider what I've said on the subject.

Et cetera.

In reality, Hashem, whom I had known for a couple of years, didn't really fit the bill as the sort of reasonable guy able to provide the sober analysis I craved. He was too conflicted and captious. A Lebanese who had come to the States from his country to pursue an MA in liberal studies at Winter Park's Rollins College (which the actor Michael Nouri, an Iraqi like me, had attended), he loved the freedom, security, easygoing culture, and physical vastness of America. But in addition to his many criticisms of US Middle East policy (some of which I shared), he also harbored a deep-seated urge to carp about unsavory aspects of American society, especially lesser-known ones, an activity from which he derived much satisfaction. He read up on the history of racism in Florida and enjoyed bringing its formerly prominent public role to the attention of those who didn't regard the state as culturally Southern. Naturally, he knew all about the Rosewood race riot of 1923, the popularity of the local chapter of the Ku Klux Klan—which assassinated early Civil Rights activist Harry T. Moore and his wife Harriet Moore—in the 1940s and '50s, and the decades-long career of notorious lawman Sheriff Willis V. McCall. In my view, this ugly history was important, but I cringed at Hashem's claim that white Floridians were still racist even if they rarely translated their fanaticism into action, and that white American society (from which he drew most of his friends) remained sick to its core.

In general, I took Hashem's anti-Americanism in stride, reasoning that people from our part of the world sometimes needed to suppress the vague but insistent feeling that we now lived in a land that, by its very tranquility and stability, mocked our countries' lack thereof, and challenged us to find some—any—fault with it. Still, a couple of things about him did disturb me. The first admittedly became an issue only when I took an Introduction to Judaism class at UCF: *How would Hashem explain his name when the fateful day arrived and he was faced with the righteous opprobrium of the exalted, hierarchy-obsessed, and hypersensitive HaShem?*

The second matter concerned his reverence for Saddam Hussein. He was genuinely saddened that I, an Iraqi, didn't share his esteem for the bloodthirsty dictator. Hashem maintained that, were Saddam to rule chaotic and unstable Lebanon, he'd turn it into an ordered and well-run country. I wondered if his preference for Iraq's Saddam over Syria's

Hafez Al-Assad stemmed from sectarian reasons—Hashem, like Saddam, was a Sunni Muslim, while the Syrian dictator and his son/successor were Alawite—or because Assad had helped to destroy much of Lebanon during its ruinous civil war, which lasted from 1975 until 1990, and proceeded to make it a Syrian vassal state.

At any rate, my friend's fantasy suffered from a major inconsistency. Hashem yearned for the Iraqi president precisely because the latter was iron-fisted and brutal, yet in his alternate reality, Saddam the president of Lebanon never deployed these signature traits against him or his family and friends. The chimerical Saddam, though endowed with his real-life counterpart's murderousness and sadism, would unleash such savagery only on people who had wronged or taken advantage of Hashem in some petty dispute or other. This Saddam didn't demand a cut of Hashem's father's business, never sided with anyone against him, and didn't lead a political party some of whose local officials came knocking on his family's door demanding to marry his unwed sisters or draft them as "secretaries." He existed only to please Hashem and advance his interests.

When I arrived at the handsome white-brick Park Avenue building where Hashem lived, he was practicing getting deported. The exercise consisted of giving himself five minutes to gather together those of his belongings he considered indispensable, cram them into one suitcase and one carry-on bag, and finish by standing on the sidewalk, luggage in hand and head bowed, waiting to be shoved into a police car. To make the rehearsal more realistic, Hashem, who lived alone in a two-bedroom apartment on the second floor of the two-story walk-up, had instructed his neighbor, Mrs. Gutiérrez, to stand in the stairwell, thwack him a few times with her bulky handbag, and curse him in Spanish as he rudely tumbled past her with his overflowing luggage. Mrs. Gutiérrez, a stately and refined matron who taught physics at Winter Park High school, took to the task with vim and vigor.

I understood from Mrs. Gutiérrez that they had already rehearsed this deportation several times. Hashem now decided to place himself at a disadvantage, stripping down to his boxers—because "they" might come for him while he's asleep—and, after depositing his luggage on the sidewalk, bounding back up the stairs to retrieve something before the all-important five minutes had elapsed. (What if they gave him fewer than five minutes? I wondered.) The introduction of these elements pleased Mrs. Gutiérrez greatly, as she could now smack his bare, wobbling flesh with her hand in addition to slamming his ass with the handbag, and even enjoy a second and third chance to do this during a five-minute period, because she'd still be on the stairs when he dashed back up to retrieve the "forgotten" item and then tumbled down again.

Standing on the sidewalk with Hashem hopping around beside me as he tried to get into his jeans before the latest five-minute deadline expired, I assumed the air of a therapist trying to coax a delusional patient back to reality. "Do you really think we'll be deported just because we're Arab?" I asked him—despite the fact that, as a Chaldean, technically I wasn't Arab. Of course, I was afraid that even worse things were coming, but seeing my friend in such a neurotic state had a somewhat calming effect on me.

17

Although, deep down, I shared his anxieties, I preferred to project an image of stolidity rather than the ridiculous appearance of a hunted animal he was treating me to.

"Well, I think those of us who consider a cross more than just a cross don't have quite as much to worry about, if you know what I mean," he said, looking up from his little jig so as to briefly make eye contact, a cold smile flitting across his lips.

The possibility of relief—however imaginary—from the fear that had consumed me since yesterday ensured that I didn't take offense. But then I felt like a coward for momentarily taking succor in the notion that my Christian identity might shield me from Americans' wrath. "You didn't answer my question," I said without addressing his snide remark. "If we're not guilty of anything, why should we be afraid?"

Looking very grave now, even with an empty pant leg swaying to and fro in the warm fall breeze, Hashem replied, "My brother, we are all guilty. There can be no more explanations, no more excuses. It's finished."

The first thing that surprised me about this answer was that he delivered it in Arabic. My Arabic wasn't bad, but the few times we spoke in that language, he'd lose me the moment he reverted to old Lebanese proverbs. The fact that several of these revolved around farming and other aspects of rural life probably meant that I wouldn't have understood them in the Iraqi dialect of Arabic or even in English.

Hashem and I usually spoke in English, partly because it was my mother tongue, but also—I reasoned on the rare occasions I thought about it—because we lived in an English-speaking country. For me, his hybrid variant of the language was the source of no end of amusement. Not just the mangled idioms, American in origin yet delivered with a distinctly Lebanese twist—such as "Cut me the crap"—but the contrast between the textbook English he had learned in school back in Lebanon and the more colloquial brand he picked up from movies and music and more recently life in the States. This contrast sometimes manifested itself in the same sentence, to comical effect. When we'd play a one-on-one game of basketball on the outdoor court at Rollins (which he pronounced "R-R-Rollins," rolling the "R" as diligently as you would the finest Colombian cross joint), he'd trash talk in his distinctive manner, saying something like, "I very much fear I shall be obliged to take you to school," before huffing past me toward the basket as I doubled over in laughter. Good times. If only today could have been the same.

"How can we all be guilty?" I asked him. "I mean, if we didn't take part in the attack, what are we guilty of?"

Hashem (still in Arabic): Everything. And in our heart of hearts, each one of us knows it.

Me (suspicious of my heart): Oh.

Hashem: You're familiar with Kafka, I'm sure. Have you read *The Trial*?

Me (brightening): Oh, yeah. In fact, in this one class about modern European influences on English literature that I took as part of my major, we read quite a bit of stuff that came out of the Austro-Hungarian Empire. I mean, I know *The Trial* was only published after—

Hashem: The thing about *The Trial* is that nobody pays attention to the ending. All they ever talk about is how creepy it is that the main character is charged with something but that the charge is never revealed to him—and that's why whenever something like that happens in real life, they call it Kafkaesque. But it's the story's ending that's important. You remember the ending?

Me: Uh, they kill him, right?

Hashem: They don't just kill him—

Me: Those two guys in the funny top hats.

Hashem (irritated): Yes, those two guys kill him. But he actually helps them by not resisting. He colludes in his own execution. See?

Me: Okay.

Hashem: What do you mean, "okay"?!

Me: Well, I don't know. I guess—

Hashem: He realizes his guilt! His original sin, see? And so, despite his lingering resentment, and even though he won't go so far as to plunge the knife into his chest for them, he lets them do it, because he knows deep down inside, in his heart, exactly where that knife is supposed to go. He knows he's guilty!

Me (frustrated): Guilty of what?

Hashem: The charge, brother, the charge, whatever it is!

After that, I decided Hashem wasn't in a frame of mind that would enable him to help me much. To be sure, I found his interpretation of *The Trial*, which he'd probably cribbed from some literary critic or other, intriguing (though I had read somewhere that Kafka sought to write stories that resisted interpretation). But I wasn't as eager as he was to metamorphose into Josef K., and despite my fears of a popular and political backlash against my kind, I couldn't bring myself to practice getting deported. I'd have to find somebody else to help me figure out this mess.

## 2

Were it not for his phone call, I'm pretty sure I wouldn't have succeeded in bringing myself to see Lewis until several days later. But he called on Thursday while I was in the bathroom and left a message on my answering machine, one so ordinary it almost set me at ease: "Hey man, it's me. What're you doing tonight? Unless you're pulling one of those marathon TV-watching sessions like everybody else, gimme a holler. We could have a drink at Knight Lights. Colleen told me the sign on the door said they're gonna be open."

It was close to a perfect message, given my jumpy and anxious state. He didn't ignore what had happened—which would've made me feel even more pressured to tackle it if and when I called him back—but neither did he address it directly. He alluded to it, liberating me from the quandary of how to go about broaching the subject, and he did so in the context of something he made clear he considered more pressing: grabbing a drink.

Of course, I shouldn't have needed such reassurance that everything was still fine between us. After all, Lewis was a good guy, and I had long known this. That he, an American, had befriended me in my freshman year despite knowing that I was Iraqi shouldn't have seemed special. To me, though, it was; I had never quite overcome the trauma of being one of only two Iraqi kids at my American school in Rome, where we lived for several years before moving to Beirut.

I hadn't grown up in Iraq, as we left for Abu Dhabi, capital of the United Arab Emirates, not long after my birth in Baghdad in 1979. My parents, members of a small liberal democratic party, had had to go underground that year, when the already powerful Saddam Hussein assumed the presidency of Iraq and began consolidating his authority—which entailed murdering potential rivals and using the Baath political party to crush all others. Two years later, we managed to make our way to Abu Dhabi, where my father went to work in the oil sector and my mother taught Middle Eastern history at a local English-language high school, just as they had done in Iraq. This was our home for the next 10 years.

In the summer of 1989, my parents and I, their only child, moved to Rome, Italy, where my father had landed a job with a company in his field that was eager to expand its reach into the Arab world. A couple of months later, I was a student at the American Community School, or ACS. That first year proved agonizing, as virtually all my classmates, who were Americans or Americanized continental Europeans, ridiculed my British-inflected accent, the result of my having attended an international school with British teachers and no American students back in Abu Dhabi, as well as the influence of my parents, whose English bore traces of British Mandate-era Iraq. (I made a diligent effort to change the accent, and by the following year sounding like my classmates came naturally.) To make matters worse, I was younger than everybody else; educational standards at my school back in Abu Dhabi were higher than those of this one, especially in math and certain sciences, so following my entrance exam I was placed in fifth instead of fourth grade.

There were good things about the move, but they didn't involve school. The bigger of the two redeeming virtues of my being uprooted from the town in which I had spent my childhood and plunked down in this unfamiliar place was that the destination in question was Rome. I loved the layout of the city, especially the piazzas, where people congregated just to hang out even if they didn't have the money or inclination to sample what was on offer at the coffee shops and restaurants or buy stuff at the stores. After all, they could always flirt or listen to street musicians or just people-watch. The architecture of the piazzas' buildings, rich and intricate even when not imposing, was unlike anything I had ever seen. And then, of course, there were the Vatican Museums, which my parents took me to several times, initially despite my protests. As a Chaldean, I came to feel a surge of pride in counting myself part of a larger Catholic family, certain of whose members with convoluted Italian names had created the magnificence I saw in the paintings of the Sistine Chapel and the exquisite sculptures and statues in the other museums, all things you could never find in Abu Dhabi or anywhere else in the UAE.

The other benefit of moving to Italy was MTV and a Rome-based oldies radio channel. Previously, my exposure to music had been haphazard and unguided, consisting largely of what the radio stations in Abu Dhabi were playing, which I later realized had included a lot of sterile contemporary pop, as well as records my parents had lying around, which contained mainly music from the 1960s. MTV and the oldies radio channel opened up new vistas, exposing me to the impressive breadth music had attained since the middle part of the century. This kind of entertainment at home and in the car also equipped me with knowledge that came in handy years later in college, as I tried to follow the references Khaled would make to a song or artist when driving home a point. But before all that, music helped me pull through tough and lonely times during our stay in Rome.

My nemesis at school was a freckle-faced, pointy-eared gnome named Danny, whose obvious inferiority complex, doubtless born of his diminutive stature and unsightly looks, elicited terrific hustle and heart on the basketball court (he played point guard), but also unprovoked violence against random targets, and a dedication to sniffing out fellow students' vulnerabilities. This last trait enabled him to maintain a blackmail-scented advantage over his friends as well as torment kids he disliked, thereby shielding his aesthetic blemishes and his physical "shortcoming" (a fitting description if there ever was one) from unwanted attention.

At the time, I failed to detect this whole psychopathology, and was so wrapped up in my own concerns that I often thought Danny reserved his ridicule and hostility for me alone. Evidence to the contrary never ceased to surprise me. For example, at first I couldn't comprehend his savage mockery of a new kid's North Carolinian drawl. Surely this was a misunderstanding, I thought. North Carolina is in the US, just like Danny's native New York. If the new kid is American—as opposed to "foreign," like me—why does he persecute him?

The other thing I found counterintuitive about Danny was his ability to intimidate bigger and almost certainly stronger kids, sometimes without even trying. I never saw him square off with anyone for a fist-fight or some such. In fact, that probably never happened; he was too crafty to allow anyone to lure him into the type of traditional physical confrontation that would place him, with his limited reach, at a clear disadvantage. Instead, he'd seize the initiative by punching his adversary in the balls or twisting his arm and locking it in a physically improbable and always excruciating position. I didn't know it, but I had an appointment with this particular brand of pain and humiliation—which was considerably worse than the verbal taunts, ear flicks, and knuckles grating back and forth across my spine that I usually had to put up with.

When Saddam occupied Kuwait and signaled a willingness to fight off the entire world in order to hang on to it, my parents were furious. Not me. I swooned over the promise an Iraqi politico-military victory held: a chance for me to shed my abject nature and enrobe myself in the glory of a mighty country, *my* country. Iraq's subsequent crushing defeat in Desert Storm would resensitize me. With my bubble burst, I took a fresh look at the situation, and found it easier to sympathize with people Saddam had slaughtered or persecuted over the years, but whom I hadn't cared about.

At the time, however, all that lay in the future. So, despite my being apolitical, I rooted for Iraq. Even though I didn't do so openly (I had no death wish), things got pretty bad. My first year, it had stung a bit when students informed me—sometimes politely—that I wasn't white, which they and I seemed to tacitly concur was the best thing to be. In Abu Dhabi, I hadn't considered lily-white people a separate race (superior versions of me, perhaps, but not altogether different), so discovering that they thought otherwise proved disappointing. But the second year, what with the Iraq crisis, direct insults were quite often hurled at me. Sometimes, simmering down a bit after silently boiling with rage at taunts such as "raghead," "sand monkey," and "camel-fucker," I puzzled over the fact that they weren't Iraqi-specific. After all, Iraqis shared these presumed characteristics with their neighbors, including those with whom they were now at odds—and whom the West was supporting.

Well, there was no need to exacerbate matters, so I batted away my classmates' questions about whether I supported my country by professing not to care about the conflict. In reality, I actively nurtured the fiery pro-Iraqi sentiment lodged in my breast.

The crisis had turned me into a news junkie, and the newspaper articles I read predicting massive Coalition casualties thanks to the Iraqi military's formidable air defense systems and its troops' fighting prowess (honed during war with Iran from 1980 until 1988) increased my confidence in the likelihood of the desired outcome. These news reports also helped me build up the self-discipline necessary to quietly endure the withering assaults on my dignity (and occasionally my person) by my classmates, especially the Americans, with Danny the worst offender. To assuage the pain and humiliation, I'd revisit those articles in my mind. I didn't have to respond to my tormentors in kind in order to regain my dignity; Iraq's upcoming victory against their country would do that for me. This conviction, more than my belief in the teachings of Jesus Christ, ensured a forbearing, Christian response on my part—though the knowledge that any attempt to defend myself would result in my receiving an ass-kicking, which was just what those bastards wanted to give me, also served as a restraining influence.

I did sometimes wonder what my life would look like if my classmates resembled those of Maysoon, who was the only other Iraqi at the school. My first year, when she was in eleventh grade, I was astonished to discover that Maysoon's peers respected and even liked her. The fact that they didn't ostracize this Iraqi girl even after Iraq's invasion of Kuwait the following year impressed me further.

Our small school, like many American ones located outside the US, consisted of kindergarten all the way to grade twelve, so I got the chance to observe the older students during lunch break and reflect on how they differed from my classmates. Two things stood out: less sniping and showboating between the guys, and the romantic attachments some of them formed with girls. In the midst of this congenial group whose members didn't voluntarily practice gender segregation, and whose top dogs didn't run roughshod over the runts, stood the dazzling and popular Maysoon, with her pineapple-style hairdo, that perpetually sun-kissed look many southern Iraqis are blessed with, and a fearless approach to sports, including those—such as softball—for which she demonstrated no aptitude. She was rumored to possess countless talents that I couldn't confirm, like the ability to crunch numbers like a calculator and belt out a soul extravaganza like Aretha Franklin. During my second year, when she was a senior, people put it about that the struggling school band had taken to begging her to join them as a singer.

Just how much of Maysoon's popularity was made possible by her Americanness—she was born and raised in Los Angeles—I didn't know. Would her classmates have behaved the way Danny and company did toward me (maybe minus the physical harassment because she was a girl and because they were older and more mature than my antagonizers) if she spoke English differently and had no ties to the States? Did her politics matter? I assumed that she supported the war—most Diaspora Iraqis, like my parents, opposed Saddam, and Maysoon was American to boot—but didn't know for sure.

If anything, I considered myself fortunate to have a passing acquaintance with her. It was probably inevitable that our mothers should've found each other and developed the habit of exchanging visits to "take afternoon tea," a favorite pastime of middle-class Iraqis, who picked it up from the British during the Mandate era. Anything but inevitable, however, was Maysoon's decision, thanks to these little tête-à-têtes, to greet me whenever our paths crossed at school, whether in the hallways or in the courtyard. (Most of the older kids never did that even with their own siblings, the only indication I detected of any coldness or snobbery on their part.) I found it difficult to reciprocate in kind, not just because of the difference in age and status between us, but because she was a girl, and a pretty, busty one at that. Looking at her without allowing my gaze to drift to her bosom—with which I was eye-level my first year—proved impossible. But I'd try, and although I failed every time, she never seemed to take offense.

We'd had a test that morning in biology class. As soon as you finished, you could leave the classroom. I'd just done so, and was shuffling around the textbooks in my bag and locker in preparation for the classes to follow morning recess, due to start in a few minutes. Doing this now rather than during the 15-minute break, when people swarmed the area, seemed a good idea. Our lockers, located in the court-yard outside the main building and situated side by side, weren't mere cubbyholes, but small closets standing at my height. Some students had outfitted theirs with additional shelves (so that they'd have more than the readymade one constructed about a foot beneath the ceiling) with the help of the school's resident carpenter, but I hadn't bothered. As I bent down to put my extra sneakers for P.E. class on the floor of the locker, having retrieved the books I needed from the shelf above and unburdened myself of the others, a kick to my backside sent me tumbling forward. My face smashed against the interior back wall, my nose fizzed up, and my eyes welled with tears.

"Hey, dingleberry, got a question for ya," someone sneered.

I stepped back and turned around. Danny stood before me, flanked by a couple of henchmen taller and more mus-cular, but (like everybody else in our class, it seemed) not as possessed of brawling prowess. "What!" I barked.

"Oh, he's all angry now!" snickered Danny. The other two laughed.

"Hey Hunayn, are you crying about I-raq?" someone asked as he joined them.

Danny now noticed my tears. Pointing at me even though I was only a few feet away from him, he jeered in delight, "Oh my God, you fucking dweeb, you really are crying!"

They all erupted in laughter again, quite boisterous this time.

Seething with rage, I stood mute, except for the snorting necessary to stanch the flow of blood from my nose, which had begun to trickle down to my mouth. (I had no tissues in my pockets and didn't want to soil a shirt sleeve.) The snorting aggravated the pounding in my head.

"So, my question is," Danny began again, "if you're I-raqi, why don't you get on a magic carpet and fly back to your shitty country so you can help those faggots try to shoot down one of our planes? Huh?"

"Because it's not necessary," I replied. "As soon as the real fighting starts, we will kill all your soldiers."

Danny's face went blank, foreshadowing his loss of all poise a split second later. He let out an effeminate, banshee shriek and flew at me. I covered my face with my hands, turned to one side, and doubled over in anticipation of a frightful wallop.

This kick proved much more powerful than the first; it sent me crashing into the locker. And then they were upon me, Danny punching furiously, the other guys helping out as much as they could. The blows landed almost everywhere, accompanied by cries of "We're gonna kill *you*," "Fucking Saddam butt-boy," and "Who's doing the real fighting now?" as I sat in the position the kick had left me in—upright in the locker with my back against its interior wall, trying to bury my head in my chest while cradling it with my hands. I couldn't pull up my legs, the length of which stuck out of the locker, because at least two of my assailants were sitting on them as Danny, almost inside the locker, pummeled me.

The recess bell rang. Danny stopped hitting me. "Quick, get him in the locker," he panted.

The others got off my legs, and they all lifted me to my feet. Without them propping me up, my legs would've buckled. My torso was still inside the locker, sagging back against its interior wall. My head was crammed just below the shelf. They grabbed my legs and tried to push them over the tiny step into the locker, but I flexed in resistance. Then, summoning all my strength, I lurched forward, so that my upper body emerged from the locker.

Danny punched me in the stomach. I crumpled—and understood that more resistance would mean more pain. So I allowed them to push me in, and then accommodated them further by standing to the side with my knees bent and my head pushed up against the bottom of the shelf. This enabled them to slam the door shut and hook the combination padlock into the hasp, trapping me without locking me in.

I thought that, having achieved his goal, Danny would open the locker a few moments later. But nothing happened. I could hear the chatter of students flooding the hallways and streaming outside. My classmates began to converge on the area. I didn't make a peep. Yes, here was an opportunity to make my situation known to people who might be inclined to help, but I couldn't bear the thought of publicizing this ignominious defeat at the hands of Danny and company, emerging from the locker a spectacle for everyone to gawk at.

Minutes, long ones, elapsed. I began to feel faint due to the lack of oxygen. Meanwhile, outside, everything seemed to have gone quiet.

Suddenly the door swung open. I almost didn't notice Danny's malicious smirk, as my attention was caught by the eager faces of the kids—most from my class—gathered in a semicircle around me, with many more from the lower grades behind them standing on tiptoes and craning their necks, or else jumping up and down for a better view. Seeing me, they all burst into euphoria, hooting and pointing to their hearts' content. I remained in my near-crouching position, mortified, and didn't even step out. In fact, I was praying that Danny, beaming as he showed off the cowed and cowering Iraqi he had bloodied and corralled, would shut the door and everybody would just go away. But of course he didn't do that, so eventually I forced myself to step out, and, buffeted on all sides by gales off raucous laughter, staggered through the rambunctious crowd until I reached the sanctuary of the restroom.

Now, years later, as the hour of my meeting with Lewis approached, dread that the same kind of humiliation was in store for me began to build. I sat in my sparsely furnished, one-bedroom apartment, my mind gravitating—despite my best efforts—to a quip I had made in a conversation with Lewis several months earlier, and replaying it in a continuous loop. When, as we walked through the UCF Communications Building's parking lot after a film class, I showed him the Geo Metro I had just bought, he commented on its diminutive size, lack of power steering, and inability to attain a speed worthy of a young man out to impress women. Shaking his head in mock pity, he placed a consoling hand on my shoulder and said, "I'm sorry you have to drive such a shitty car."

"Me too," I replied. "It's just that my other car blew up your embassy in Kenya, so what can I do?"

My friend let out a hearty laugh, and I grinned, delighted with my quick-witted comeback, which helped soften the sting that he found my car, which I was quite proud of, so unimpressive.

But now I couldn't get the exchange out of my head. I began to fret that it was preoccupying him, too. That he was watching amateur video footage of the other day's attacks on the World Trade Center, which all the TV channels were replaying, and taking the opportunity to revisit what I had said several months earlier. Not that he would suspect me of involvement in either the recent atrocity or the bombings of the US embassies in Kenya and Tanzania in 1998, but that, looking back, he might now adopt a different perspective on my irreverent attitude to terrorism against American targets. Should I remind him that tasteless humor rarely, if ever, bespeaks an actual political inclination, let alone a moral outlook? To ground such pedantry in an illuminating anecdote, we might consider my take on those very '98 attacks, from which I had recoiled, even though I later opportunistically used them as fodder for a nasty joke. *Or did none of this matter, because it was too late already, and he and his real friends were preparing to ambush me?*

After a good deal of deliberation, I decided that snubbing him would, if anything, arouse his suspicion. Best to agree to meet him, but to proceed with caution. Besides, if it turned out that he was still my friend, he might guide me through this morass of terrorism and mass murder and airplanes toppling buildings, something Hashem had failed to do. As I couldn't bear to call him and didn't have a computer at home, I sent him an email from the UCF library confirming receipt of his message. I explained that I was writing him because when he called I was too busy to answer, subsequently forgot to call back, and only now remembered the matter. And I told him that I could meet him at Knight Lights at 8:30 p.m.

Lewis was the first friend I made in Orlando, which I had moved to in large part because I wanted a laid-back atmosphere, a climate as warm as Beirut's, and an abundance of skimpily clad women. I had read positive reviews of UCF's academic record, so I applied to it along with a few other Florida colleges, got accepted by UCF right away, and enrolled.

My initial few months in the city were uneventful, except for near-daily discoveries of my domestic incompetence. If you had happened to enter my single room at CVI—the "Collegiate Village Inn" studio apartment complex just off the UCF campus—one morning shortly after my arrival in the States in the fall of 1998, you'd have found me sitting at a ramshackle desk and cracking open a succession of eggs, all of which produced a gooey substance that didn't meet my liking. I couldn't understand it. So I went back to the Chevron gas station to complain to the owner that he had sold me foul eggs.

After some confusion, the guy, an Indian American who had struck me as reserved and somewhat glum, broke into a guffaw. In between continued bouts of laughter, he explained to me that in order for the eggs to come out "right," which is what I had termed the outcome I desired when describing it to him, they had to be boiled. I was so embarrassed I could have died. Instead, I just pretended that he hadn't understood me properly, turned on my heel, and flounced off.

I never returned to that gas station. This complicated my life considerably, as the nearest alternative was a convenience store some distance away; the area around UCF was, like much of Orlando, anything but built-up. It was a pretty long walk to the store, and I had yet to purchase a car, but I couldn't bear to face that guy again.

No matter, I reassured myself; I may not know much about eggs, but I possessed a latent greatness perpetually on the verge of breaking out. (In reality, the only noteworthy thing about me was that, were I to be measured according to every academic, social, and other available standard, a statistical anomaly would emerge: a precisely average score in every category.) Out of curiosity, I took an officially administered IQ test. Several other students sat for it alongside me, as UCF was encouraging us to give the test a try in hopes of finding, and then publicizing, geniuses on campus.

When our time was up, an administrator ushered us out of the classroom and into the building's foyer, only to discover that there weren't enough seats for all of us. She counted off a group and took us to another room. I entered last, by which time everyone had sat down and no seats remained available. The administrator, smiling way too ingratiatingly, motioned for me to follow her, and led me to a small, empty office a short distance down the hall. She told me that no one was using the room and, since wheeling out the swivel chair would require moving the heavy desk in front of it, I might as well just maneuver myself between the desk and the wall, kick back in the comfy chair, and wait until the test results came through. "There's a few magazines on the desk, so you just make yourself right at home, honey," she said in her folksy manner before turning around and walking out.

By this time, I had grown convinced that machinations were afoot. Though the exam administrators had taken great pains to make the dispersal of the students look as if it were caused by spatial issues, their true intention was to sequester me in that office. Why? Because they had already tallied the results and learned that I was a genius. If I sat in that chair and duly waited, a few minutes from now a hunched-over geezer in a white lab coat would shuffle in. Then, almost breathless with excitement, he'd announce in a thick German accent: "Ze time has come to conduct some sehr special examinations."

I had recently learned the term "Schadenfreude" in Intermediate German I: to derive pleasure from someone else's pain. (How fitting, I had marveled while sitting in class, that the Germans should have such a word.) Standing in the empty office that day, I fretted about giving Mengele's twin, surely about to appear at any second, the opportunity to experience it at my expense. So I bolted... and never received confirmation that I was a genius.

Around this time, though I was hardly in the best frame of mind to socialize, what with my trouble acclimating to Orlando and UCF, loneliness began to gnaw at me. Of course, the fact that I had no roommate at CVI—by choice, as the motel-style room was tiny—and felt disinclined to join any of the student clubs on campus didn't help.

One day, during a short break in the middle of a longish

American government class, a guy came up to me as I stood outside and told me that he had found my comment on the reference to "unalienable rights" in the US Constitution thought-provoking. In a self-consciously clever but not altogether frivolous interjection during the professor's lecture, which had tackled the wording of certain passages in the famed document, I said that describing "rights" as "unalienable" was redundant, as a right was such by definition. (For good measure, I added that this was precisely what distinguished a right from a privilege, which could be revoked.) I thanked the guy and said that, although I wasn't American, I'd taken an interest in the Constitution ever since I was introduced to it back in school. He asked me where I was from. I told him Iraq, but that I had lived in Lebanon before coming to the States.

"Oh, West Beirut!" he exclaimed.

Surprised, and feeling to a certain extent caught out, I replied, "West Beirut, that's right, that's where I...how'd you know I was from West Beirut?"

"No, man," he chuckled. "*West Beirut*'s a movie. You haven't heard of it?"

I hadn't. The guy, whose name was Lewis, explained that he had watched the film at Maitland's Enzian Theater, which often screened foreign and independent flicks, and thought it very good. We got to talking about the civil war in Lebanon, which *West Beirut* depicted, and where things stood since the end of hostilities in 1990. I told him that the situation was more stable thanks to the otherwise stifling phenomenon of Syrian political hegemony, but included periodic flare-ups of violence between Israel, which occupied south Lebanon, and Hezbollah, the Lebanese Shiite

"Party of God" that fought the Israeli army and its local militia ally.

Over the next few American government classes, Lewis and I would meet up at the vending machine during the short break and chat for a while. It turned out that he was majoring in the same subject—English language and literature—as I was. Lewis, like me a slim and reasonably athletic fellow, but with a mop of unruly seal-brown hair instead of my closely cropped jet-black variety, was a mischievous sort who possessed a raunchy sense of humor and a complete disregard for political correctness of any kind. He could be snarky, but his whole "I'm not easily impressed" persona—though constructed with obvious care—failed to conceal his charged and faintly desperate lust for life. The way he barreled toward any and all opportunities for adventure, sex, and the slightest whiff of some serious partying put me in mind of those giddy Black Friday shoppers shrieking hosannas as they scooped up one armful after another of the exquisite products arrayed before them.

He also wanted to broaden his horizons. Growing up in the small Detroit suburb of Utica, he had experienced the suffocating—rather than the pleasantly numbing—side of suburban boredom. Living near downtown Orlando and attending UCF in another part of the city offered him more stuff to do, along with milder weather and the related bonus of encountering plenty of beautiful, sun-bronzed women. Otherwise, the state of affairs couldn't excite him for long. The idea of travel, of gallivanting around the globe, had already seduced him. That's why he was studying for a degree in English; he wanted to journey throughout the world teaching the language. Naturally, he was quite taken with the fact that I had attended American schools in Beirut and Rome, and an international one in Abu Dhabi, expressing his envy more than once and telling me that he intended to do much the same when he became a teacher.

Lewis and I took to hanging out on campus between classes. Sometimes, we borrowed videos from the library to watch back at my one-bedroom residence at the pretentiously spelled "Arbour" Apartments on Alafaya Trail (which I moved into because it afforded a good deal more space than my digs at CVI), or in one of several small study-rooms the library had equipped with TV sets and VCRs. Lewis lived with his parents and depended on them for his ride home, meaning that we couldn't go out in the evenings except on those occasions when we'd agree beforehand that he'd crash on my couch that night. Throughout this period, Lewis's social situation, almost as lonely as mine thanks to his family's recent relocation from the Detroit 'burbs, solidified our bond.

My friendship with Lewis was what I tried to focus on while driving over to the University Shoppes plaza to meet him at Knight Lights. The exercise didn't do much to allay my fears. Before entering the popular student haunt, I cased it from afar. Having made certain that my possibly revenge-seeking friend hadn't posted any look-outs in the parking lot, I peered in surreptitiously to check for shifty characters playing cards and puffing on cigars in strategic spots near the door, or by the restroom, or at either end of the bar, or tucked into a booth—or anywhere, really…

There were none; the place was empty save for a couple seated at the bar some distance from Lewis. I approached him.

"Dude, check out the smokin' barmaid," he said in a low voice without averting his gaze from the leggy young woman placing two drinks before the couple at the bar.

Still standing, I quickly ran through my prepared list of gentle rejoinders to all anticipated accusations of guilt by association, before realizing that I had no need for any of them. "Uh, I don't think you can say that."

Lewis (distracted, still ogling the woman): Whaddaya mean?

Me: "Barmaid." It's almost like saying "wench." I mean, imagine if someone came in and said, "Hey, that saucy wench is just what I'll need to go with this here cask of ale I'm about to knock back."

Lewis: Hmm, good point. Now try this: Imagine if some of my boys hijacked a few airplanes and flew them into your politically correct ass.

Me (racking brain for correct response): …

Lewis: Ha ha ha!

Me (feeble attempt to join in): Oh, yeah, ha, ha, ha.

Lewis (mock relief): Boy, we sure are lucky Islam's a religion of peace, though, huh? I mean, just think how many more people would've been killed if it was a religion of war and violence!

Me (nervous titter): Right.

Chuckling, he told me to "sit down already." In an obedient mood, I did.

He kept right on talking: "Man, you should've seen Jenny on Thursday. I had class early that morning, so I'm on campus, and since I have a few minutes to spare, I go to the library to check my email. And everybody's standing like in a clusterfuck in that large area that's to the right after you walk in. So I go over and see that they've rolled out a big-screen TV, and everybody's watching and gasping, and there's like this fake camaraderie between them."

I didn't know if this was a test of some kind, so while he spoke I just kept nodding and mumbling "Yeah" every so often, as though I were hanging on every word.

"So now I'm watching the screen too, and all of a sudden I feel a hand on my arm. So I turn and she's right there, Jenny, just staring up at me, eyes all Bambi-like and shit."

Me: Uh-huh.

Lewis: So now I'm looking back at her, and I don't get why she's just gazing up at me and not saying anything. I mean, I get that she's expecting something from me—she was always expecting something back when we were together—but I can't for the life of me figure out what she wants me to do about a damn plane hitting the World Trade Center. Not that if I knew, I'd necessarily do it, but I mean I'm getting really curious, right, so much so that, instead of turning back to the screen, I'm still looking at her and wondering what's going through that "I'm used to being coddled and I'm gonna get mine" brain of hers.

Me (mindful of the need to engage): Yeah, like maybe, "Hey Lewis, so what did we discuss about emotional attentiveness?"

Lewis (explosion of mirth): I know, right?!

Me (strained, tinny tee-hee): One of *those* looks.

Lewis: So it's obvious that she's sad because of what's happened, but at the same time she's still managing to be manipulative, like , swatting my nuts with that ping-pong paddle vibe that says, "You'd better stop your tomfoolery and start connecting with the people around you on a deeper level."

Me (mustering a lackluster laugh, but uneasy with the guy's flippancy): Ehe, ehe.

Lewis: So then, after like a couple of seconds of me being all impassive, she bursts into tears, grabs my shirt and buries her face in it, sobbing. And I'm standing there awkwardly holding her shoulder, which she thinks is me hugging her but which is actually me trying not to lose my balance and fall over, and the whole thing becomes clear. What she wants me to do, what she *expects* me to do, is console her! Can you believe it? *Console* her, like she just escaped from that burning building!"

A short while later, I was back at home, lying on the sofa with the TV on mute. Lewis had stayed at Knight Lights in order to wait for Colleen, the girl he had started seeing shortly after breaking up with Jenny. By this time, I had begun to despair of extracting anything useful from my friends. I couldn't quite pinpoint what I wanted, but suspected that any sort of insight or seemingly plausible prognostication would go a long way toward mooring me, so that I'd get some purchase on a piece of ground still subject to predictable, terrestrial laws. Contemplating the possibility of a cosmic realignment of fortunes, so that everything the US was previously immune to would now become the norm, induced vertigo so powerful that even hours after it had subsided, a nauseous taste remained in my mouth. I needed somebody to give me an idea of where things stood, and free me from the ordeal of trying to figure it all out by myself. Soon enough, my thoughts turned to Khaled again, this time with a resentment bordering on rage. Had he not behaved in such a selfish and brutal manner, he'd be here now instead of in his native Jordan, and would almost certainly know what to do.

Blond and fair complexioned, Khaled, a descendant of those Muslim Circassians who were expelled from or fled their ancestral region in the Caucasus in the late 19th century as the Russians pushed the Ottomans farther south, might have seemed a perfect fit for the States—thanks to his whiteness as well as his background as a student at the American school in Amman, which he had attended from kindergarten until graduation. But he could never attain anything even approaching serenity. Always a bundle of nerves, when he sat in the same spot for even the briefest length of time his legs would start to bounce up and down as though readying to gallop off without him at any moment. He fidgeted with his hands and glanced about furtively even if otherwise very much involved in talking to you. His physical appearance lent itself to the image of a feral beast trying to break free of the life-size wax figure trapping it. Intricate, crisscrossing networks of lurid bluish-green veins seemed poised to rend asunder his taut, alabaster skin, enabling the real Khaled to burst forth and take on the world.

Often socially inept, and self-absorbed to the point of mental estrangement from his immediate surroundings, Khaled had another, more significant quirk: He connected with people's feelings—joy, sorrow, and everything else —through songs, especially their lyrics. Now, I didn't discount music's usefulness in helping one attain a deeper understanding of matters. (Khaled told me that he knew

George Michael was gay as soon as he heard "Wake Me Up Before You Go-Go," even without having seen the Wham! video, and years before the singer came out of the closet.) But it unsettled me that, for my friend, music functioned as a conduit to—not merely an enhancement of—perception and emotion. Worse, it was his only such conduit.

Sometimes, this made for an awkward situation. When he drove over to pick me up one night so that we could hang out, and I told him of my acute disappointment at having had my (tentative) advances rebuffed by a girl I liked, he blurted out, "Oh, I have the perfect song for that!" But he didn't *feel* with me. He would have to listen to the song (during which time I was not permitted to speak). If, as he surmised, it awakened his sympathy for its jilted protagonist, he would find himself able to extend such sympathy to me.

The song, he informed me, was Leonard Cohen's second version of "Hallelujah," from the album *Cohen Live*. Listening to the lyrics, I thought the choice unsuitable; it seemed like the protagonist had had at least some sort of relationship with the woman before she shunted him aside. At any rate, the lugubrious verses, which Cohen delivered in a croaky, funereal basso profundo, made me seriously consider jumping out of the moving car—and I had promised myself that the only time I'd do that was when the long-awaited Mossad agent turned up to assassinate me.

Looking back, it often occurred to me that, had I not stupidly clung to the notion that because Khaled's predicament was both self-generated and artificial, it didn't qualify as serious, I might have sympathized more with him and even tried to help. But I never shook the impression that this guy, with his sexy and intelligent girlfriend doting on him during the day and giving herself to him at night, couldn't have any real problems—at least insofar as said girlfriend was concerned. His feeling of guilt, I told myself on the few occasions I thought about the subject, stemmed from faint but persistent stirrings of self-doubt of the kind I'd also surely have were a grown woman to take up with me as opposed to any of the guys all around me who were far more suited to her affections.

I remained so enthralled by his life, replete with those imagined fuckfest nights, that I failed to grasp the implications of things he told me. Once, sounding distressed, he said, "You know that stereotype that every man wants a woman who's a whore in the bedroom, a cook in the kitchen, and a lady in the living room, right?"

Me (interest piqued): Oh, is that the stereotype?

Khaled: Yeah. Pretty accurate, I think.

Me: Huh.

Khaled (intrigued): Why, are you looking for something different?

Me (dreamy): Well, I wouldn't mind if she was a whore in the living room too, you know? As long as it's just me and her, that'd be just fine. I got a couch, couple armchairs. She'd be more than welcome to make use of them for her whorish little things.

Khaled (irritated): Fine. Whatever. The point is that I have that with Mindy, all right?

Me (eyes widening): Really? What kinds of things does she do in the living room specifically?

Khaled (losing patience): Forget about the living room, would you? For God's sake, I'm trying to tell you that I

45

have what every man is supposed to want!

Me (chastened): Okay.

Khaled (earnest): But it's not enough; I want more!

Me (titillated but also a little frightened): Yeah? Something...more?

Khaled: Yes!

Me: What?

Khaled: The feeling that I deserve this. Having done something I can point to that proves that I earned this. Really, Hunayn, look at our situation. Foreigners, *Arabs*, who come to this country and, without having to do anything, are given everything. Even their women. Can you imagine? We're fucking their daughters!

Me (brought low by this whole conversation, demoralized enough to confess to having never attained manhood): I'm not doing much fucking, to tell you the truth. In fact, to be perfectly honest, I haven't done any at all.

Khaled (oblivious to the personal nature of what I've revealed to him): Uh-huh, and what are they doing about the fact that we're fucking their daughters? Instead of lynching us, they're inviting us over for dinner! Mindy's parents want us to join them for Christmas vacation!

Me: Actually, they call it Winter Break here.

Khaled: Yes, Winter Break! They're going to put me in a room with their daughter so I can fuck her under their very noses! During *Winter Break*!

I should have understood that Khaled's feeling that he didn't deserve an American woman's affections—at least until he had passed through a series of trials and tribulations—would poison his relationship with Mindy. Without knowing it, he wanted to be the black guy in a

46

movie about an interracial romance in a small town in the Jim Crow South, so that he'd suffer all kinds of indignities and possibly violence. Then, through some heroic act or other (rather than simple love for his girl), he'd convince everybody that he was okay after all and deserving of their acceptance.

He never got his wish, and instead of having to fend off aggression, he became its perpetrator. On Mindy. In a beating following an argument about something trivial. She was left bruised and heartbroken. Yet, tough and resilient girl that she was, she didn't let her emotional turmoil or physical pain stop her from reporting the assault to the police. And Khaled, who probably did what he did due to a subconscious desire for a social handicap, which his American colleagues wouldn't provide him with, was arrested that very night.

This nauseating saga ended with a remorseful Khaled, who wanted to plead guilty, taking his lawyer's advice and doing so only after they had extracted a deal from the district attorney's office: a six-month jail sentence for assault causing bodily injury, followed by his voluntary departure (in lieu of deportation) for Jordan. Now, after the terrorist attacks, the irony of the whole situation hit me hard. If only he had refrained from committing his grotesque act and instead waited a while; here was the long-awaited atmosphere of suspicion and hostility against which he could strive to prove his worth.

As for me, I had to reorder my priorities. A few short days ago, snagging a girlfriend was my main goal in life. Now, I bumped it down to a distant second. The first was to figure out what the fuck to do. Of course, if Khaled were here, he'd tell me how we might reaffirm our humanity in the eyes of those (just about everybody, I suspected) who now viewed us as potential terrorists. We'd work to redeem ourselves and in the process regain a measure of self-respect, which the hijackers had—with the sleight of a boxcutter-wielding hand—carved right out of us. But Khaled had disgraced himself, and was long gone.

## 3

On Sunday, I drove from my apartment complex to the UCF campus and parked my car in one of the many vacant lots, having decided that I'd try to make sense of my place in the America 9/11 had made while power-walking through tranquil, leafy surroundings—replete with merry sparrows chirping away and frisky squirrels gamboling about.

Here was my concern: Terrorists had attacked America. Not just American interests abroad, but America itself. And not just any kind of terrorists, either. Not, for example, the homegrown, lone-wolf, Timothy McVeigh kind. Foreign terrorists, quite a few of them, suicidal and (worse yet) homicidal, with nearly 3,000 charred corpses to prove it. And these foreign terrorists—who belonged to the same organization that had attacked a US warship off the coast of Yemen a year earlier and the US embassies in Kenya and Tanzania a few years before that—were Arab Muslims acting in the name of their extremist version of Islam. I had an Arabic name and came from a predominantly Arab and overwhelmingly Muslim country, so one might easily mistake me for an Arab Muslim.

The fact that the place was almost deserted proved even more conducive than usual to contemplation. Of course, the UCF campus always provided a serene environment on Sundays, though whatever meditative exercise you engaged in was liable to face the occasional interruption by roving pairs of students-turned-proselytes once a week. These guys, often newly religious, were aware from their own recent experience as friendless sad sacks that every Sunday they could become fishers of solitary young men wandering aimlessly around campus, bereft of romantic partners and any semblance of a social life. I had had several encounters with such missionaries, who struck me as harmless but rather cynical and opportunistic, laying on the gregariousness thickly so as to better woo the lonesome and lovelorn.

With time and practice, I came to dispatch them with aplomb, especially those who had the misfortune of proselytizing on behalf of a group that was obviously and incorrigibly deviant. For example, when the folks from the Unification Church asked me why I wouldn't even consider reading their literature, I explained that this was because their founder and leader for life was called Sun Myung Moon, and I simply could not trust anybody who had both "Sun" and "Moon" in his name. It was unnatural. In fact, not only did it go against nature; it contravened cosmic law. Sure enough, this cogent argument silenced them. Rather than engage in a futile attempt to refute my impeccable logic, they shook their heads in abject defeat and plodded away, having failed to unburden themselves of a single measly pamphlet.

But the first time was different. On that occasion, two guys waylaid me as I tried in vain to convince an obstinate vending machine to surrender the bag of chips I had paid for, pressing buttons maniacally and letting loose a verbal stream of cajolery seasoned with the occasional obscenity. At first, they just stood nearby without saying anything. When it became clear to them (but not yet to me) that the robotic junk-food-and-soda-dispensing miscreation had won, they seemed genuinely disappointed and became sympathetic, saying "Darn" and "That's a shame."

I nodded in appreciation and murmured "Yeah," glancing at them out of courtesy before returning to the task at hand with brio.

Soon enough, the older of the two, a buttoned-up yet still obviously young gentleman with a kind face who put me in mind of an eager-to-help guide on a journey he'd painstakingly mapped out for scores of people in my position, addressed me directly. "Say, friend, have you heard of Jesus Christ?"

The absurdity of the question immediately made me suspect some sort of ploy. I turned to my side and eyed them warily. They stood immobile, bodies tense and leaning forward, breath bated, eyes bulging out of their sockets. In short, frightfully sincere. This convinced me, unaccustomed as I was to the phenomenon of Sunday campus missionaries, that my behavior must have given them reason to believe I was crazy and in need of some sort of counseling, the more paternalistic the better. Could they have taken my remonstrations with the vending machine at face value? Didn't they realize I was just trying all means at my disposal to get what I had paid for, and that I didn't actually expect the thing to answer me?

I proceeded to tell them, in as even a manner as possible, that yes, I had indeed heard of Jesus Christ, and was in fact Christian myself.

Their faces brightened. "We are, too!" cried Life Guide, looking at his companion and then back at me in awestruck joy, as if there were practically no statistical chance that adherents of the world's most popular religion could ever find one another on a college campus in the American South.

"I used to be a Catholic," the other guy now piped up. With his beach-blond spiky hair, turquoise sleeveless T-shirt featuring a black sketch print of a sailboat, and flip-flops one size too large for his feet, he struck me as a sort of Florida surfer-for-Jesus dude. "But now I'm a Christian," he added.

I wasn't quite sure what this meant, but noted with some annoyance that he had situated Catholics (whose number included Chaldeans like me) outside the Christian fold. Then Life Guide asked me what part of Florida I was from. I told him that I had lived in Lebanon before coming to the States for college. My answer seemed to please both of them greatly. "Awesome!" said Surfer-for-Jesus. "So they have Christians there?"

Me: Yes, they do.

Life Guide: Is that because the French were there for a while? 'Cause I remember someone saying that they came in—

Me: No, it's because of Jesus Christ.

Life Guide: Oh.

Surfer-for-Jesus: Cool!

Me: I'm actually from Iraq. But I lived in Lebanon before I came here. There're Christians in Iraq too, also pretty much from the earliest days of Christianity.

Surfer-for-Jesus: Iraq, huh? You're probably a member of a tribe then, right?

Me: Absolutely, a tribe called Quest.

Surfer-for-Jesus: Kwest, wow! And are you guys, like, close?

Me: Big time. You should see us when we get together

and just kick it. Somethin' else, man, lemme tell you.

Surfer-for-Jesus: That's great. Really great.

Life Guide (contemplative): Is that with a "q," because of that letter you have in Arabic? Quest?

Me (taken aback): Yeah…that's actually…correct.

As the conversation continued, some of what I said dampened their initial enthusiasm. Apparently, my adherence to general Christian principles was insufficient to secure my salvation; a "personal relationship" with Jesus was required. Worse yet, my tendency to emphasize his moral teachings over his divinity pained my sensitive interlocutors, who regarded it as little short of blasphemy. They informed me that we do not exist for the mere purpose of behaving morally, but to prepare for what comes next. Surfer-for-Jesus leaned forward again and said, "Don't you see how important that is?"

Me: Well, to tell you the truth, I—

Life Guide: Tell me, friend, what do you live for?

Me: Not sure, really. The weekend, I guess.

Life Guide (aghast): The weekend?!

Me: What can I say? Friday I'm in love.

Now, as I crisscrossed the campus on my speed-walking and deep-thinking binge, I grappled with something much more serious. There beckoned the prospect of improving my standing, and perhaps even ensuring my safety, merely by dissociating myself from others. At issue was the question of whether I should try to escape vilification at the hands of people who now surely loathed Muslims and Arabs by using my status as a Chaldean Christian to distance myself from both.

What some folks—such as those two clueless missionaries—might have found surprising was that my Christian and Iraqi identities were intertwined. In fact, my parents had named me after Hunayn Ibn Ishaq, the famed ninth-century Iraqi Christian physician and scholar who translated major works of Greek philosophy and medical science into Arabic and Syriac, and became one of the key Christian figures who enabled Islamic civilization, the center of which at the time was Baghdad, to imbibe Greek thought. As director of Baghdad's legendary House of Wisdom, an institute dedicated to accumulating and disseminating knowledge, Ibn Ishaq served under several caliphs and trained an entire generation of translators, including his son. My parents' mantra all through my childhood was that the Christians of Iraq always contributed to their country, irrespective of its dominant religious or cultural identity in any given era, regardless of whether it constituted an independent state or was part of a larger political entity, and despite the fact that the advent of Islamic rule in the seventh century consigned us, along with other non-Muslims, to second-class dhimmi status in our own homeland for hundreds of years.

I didn't know it at the time, but my parents' values would influence my own a great deal. This first became apparent to me following an encounter my classmate Samer and I had with a couple of unsavory characters one night back in tenth grade.

In the summer of 1994, my father took a job with a joint Lebanese/Iraqi Kurdish private surveying firm looking to pinpoint the location of oil reserves in Iraqi Kurdistan, the northern region that, as of the Gulf War, no longer answered to Baghdad and was now primed for an economic boom. We left Italy, where I had spent five excruciating years and become a poor student in all subjects but my favorites of English and history, for Lebanon, whose civil war had ended in 1990. My father began shuttling between Lebanon and northern Iraq, usually flying from Beirut to Turkey or Syria and then crossing overland into the Kurdish-administered north before reversing the process on the way back. Meanwhile, my mother got a job teaching Middle Eastern history at the International College, or IC, a high school with both English and French sections. I sat for the entrance exam at ACS Beirut, part of the same worldwide network of schools as ACS Rome. My performance was only good enough to earn me admission to ninth grade. That's what I had just completed, but I didn't mind; now I'd be the same age as everyone else in my grade, instead of a year younger.

Samer, with his somewhat stilted manner of speech and a penchant for grammatical precision of the kind generally dispensed with in everyday conversation, was odd, but in a droll sort of way. He loved words, and his logophilia enabled him to forge a deeper relationship with them than the rest of us, so that if he read that someone was "discombobulated," he'd laugh out loud—a rarity—at the sheer bounciness of the term.

Yet even I sometimes had my doubts about his curious brand of humor. When we were in tenth grade, in response to a question about how he viewed the subject of having a threesome with two girls, he remarked, "I imagine it would require a fair amount of coordination." He actually said that. Still, when I thought about it, I conceded he might have meant it as a self-deprecating sort of quip. And then, when I considered his follow-up comment, "I'm afraid my sexual preferences are rather pedestrian," I finally figured him out.

Pedestrian, eh? Sounded ridiculous; I wouldn't be caught dead saying that. So went my initial reaction. Yet a closer look proved revelatory. Apparently, Samer thought he could convince everybody that he had already gotten laid. Not quite with two women at the same time, but, because of his decidedly pedestrian tastes, just one. I didn't know about the other guys in our class, but that's when I grasped what he was all about: With Samer, it was self-deprecating wit *and* a canny bid for an upgrade in social status, the latter piggybacking on the former. And that's when, in the middle of tenth grade, my second year at ACS, I decided I liked the guy.

We told the cab driver to drop us off at Sassine Square in the heart of the Ashrafieh neighborhood of east Beirut, across town. It was a Friday night and Samer and I were looking for something, anything, to do. Normally, we would have just wandered around Hamra, where we both lived. Alternatively, we'd have gone down to Bliss Street, where the American University of Beirut, or AUB, was located, popping into a pool hall every now and again for a game or two, or grabbing a bite to eat at one of the fast food joints frequented by college students. That was pretty much all the entertainment on offer in our general vicinity, save for a few dingy bars (or "pubs," as most people called them in Lebanon, where "bars" generally referred to brothels). However, neither Samer nor I had developed a taste for alcohol—despite the fact that we had every opportunity to do so, given that bartenders rarely cared that you might have yet to reach the legal drinking age of 18, and a couple of spots were known to cater in part to older high-school kids.

Of course, we had both been to Ashrafieh before, though never together or at night. The previous year, my first in Lebanon, my mother had taken me around with her on little excursions every Sunday so that we might familiarize ourselves with different areas of Beirut. Ashrafieh had even less to offer in the way of entertainment than Hamra did, so I put it out of mind for a good long while. But on this particular Friday, I suggested to Samer—who also hadn't gone there in some time—that we hop over and see if anything had changed. The taxi crossed the Fuad Shehab bridge, which connected Hamra to Ashrafieh. To our left lay the downtown district, destroyed during the infamous "Battle of the Hotels" in the early years of the civil war—and still in ruins. We continued to Sassine Square, where we got off.

Not a lot to see, really. The area hadn't changed much. A couple of cafés stood where none had been before, but they were closed because it was getting late. We walked around a bit, feeling stupid. And then I had an idea. Part of what made Sassine a busy place during the day was its function as a major intersection, with streets connecting it to other points in Ashrafieh and beyond. I picked the one I thought led to Saint Joseph's University, told Samer to follow me, and began striding purposefully in that direction. He asked me where we were going.

"This leads to Saint Joseph's," I answered, "back toward the beginning of Ashrafieh. Let's see what the area's like on a Friday night."

He didn't say anything, but I could tell he wasn't enthused.

"Come on, man, we came all the way here," I pressed. "We can't just get a cab and go back home without having done anything. Let's see what their version of Bliss Street is like."

Several minutes later, with me leading the way and Samer grumbling that we should've known better and just had the cab driver take us to Saint Joe's in the first place, we went down a side street I told him would get us to our destination faster, even though I knew no such thing. But I had seen a light and concluded that a grocery store might still be open, meaning that I could obtain accurate directions.

It turned out to be a small auto body repair shop, the sole guy on hand (most likely the owner or his son) refurbishing the chassis of a 1960s Mercedes Benz—the car most cabbies drove—which took up most of the space in the grimy garage. I said a brief good evening and asked him if we could get to Saint Joseph's University by continuing down this street and then making a left and walking some more. I wanted Samer to get the impression I was simply confirming something that was almost certain.

The man, in his mid-to-late 20s, clad in a white undershirt and blue jeans with a Chicago Bulls hat atop his head, just stood there open-mouthed, as though dumbfounded. Something was wrong, but I didn't know what. I decided that instead of expressing my puzzlement at his surprise and possibly receiving a discomfiting explanation, I'd do better to reformulate my question so as to deflect the man's attention from whatever it was about me that had disoriented him. Samer had by now joined me in the garage and was poking around without much interest.

"Yeah, we were just wondering," I began again, "if you might be able to tell us whether we're still far off from Saint Joseph's University," figuring this was an easier question for him to answer than the earlier one.

Nothing doing; same bewildered expression, mouth still hanging open. I began to think we'd stumbled upon a guy who was very good at feeding on air plankton and messing around with car parts, but not much else. I glanced around the shop, wondering if I could think of an admiring comment to make about his work. When I turned back to him, he was wiping his greasy, blackened hands with a tattered old rag. From the looks of his fingernails, you'd think he spent his free time bashing them in with a hammer.

"Saint Joseph's University?" he finally replied, pronouncing the words in a slow and deliberate manner as he continued wiping his hands.

Immediately, I realized what had thrown him. I had employed the Arabic—instead of the French—name of the institution, which was seldom used by those who lived in its vicinity. (Now it occurred to me that my having used the Arabic equivalent of the more popular French "bonsoir" when I greeted him probably also struck him as odd.) So I said, with as much nonchalance as I could muster, "Yeah, you know, Saint Joseph's; it's not far, is it?" this time using its French name.

"Not far, no."

"Okay, thank you," I said, turning around and indicating to Samer with a motion of the head that we were leaving. I hadn't gotten an answer to my original question about whether I had the right idea about how to get to our destination, but that wasn't a big deal. The guy gave me the creeps, and I wanted to put distance between him and us.

"Are we having fun yet?" said Samer a few moments later.

"Dude, just relax, all right? We'll be there soon."

"We shouldn't have wasted our time on that moron," he muttered.

We hadn't covered 200 yards before we heard a harsh whistling call behind us and a "Hey, you!"

Samer and I both spun around.

"Yeah, you two, come here!" Two guys were striding toward us, the one in front motioning with his hand for me and Samer to approach. We took a few tentative steps forward out of an instinctive desire to demonstrate goodwill, and then waited obediently.

Several seconds later, the two stood before us. Both were taller than we were and appeared to be in their late teens or early 20s. The one who had called out to us was wiry and sported a necklace with a large gold cross outside his T-shirt, one with a diagonal cut at its base. It was much bigger than my modest crucifix, which I kept inside my shirt at all times. His pudgy friend, face all sweaty and lips extruded to form a sullen, pouting expression, stood to one side of him, legs planted apart and arms crossed as he stared us down like a rap artist posing for an album cover. The wiry guy looked me up and down and said with a slurping sound, as though trying to prevent gobs of extra spit sloshing around in his mouth from flying out, "Who are you guys and what do you want with Saint Joseph's?"

*Shit. Air plankton guy must have gotten busy right after we left him and sent a smoke signal to the neighborhood watch group he presided over. Sicced the two junior sentries on us to find out what's what.* "Nothing," I replied. "We were just going to go and see what it's like, you know? To see if there's…see what it's like."

Slurper: Why's your accent so fucked up? Are you Palestinian?

Me: Uh, no, I'm Iraqi.

Wannabe Rapper (sneering): Liar.

Slurper (shouting, spluttering uncontrollably): Cowards! Admit that you're Palestinian!

Samer (calm): We're not Palestinian. He just told you he's Iraqi. And I'm Lebanese.

Slurper: What are you doing here?

Samer: We live here.

Slurper: Not here you don't. Maybe on the west side of town, but not here. That I'm absolutely sure of.

Wannabe Rapper (shaking his head in disgust): Fucking scum.

Slurper (turning to me again, temper rising): You didn't answer my question. What do you want with Saint Joseph's?

Me: Nothing. We just wanted to see the—

Slurper (apoplectic, foaming at the mouth): Girls?! You wanted to see the girls?!

Me (startled): What? No, we just wanted to see the area, because…

Slurper (narrowing his eyes, lowering his voice to a growl): You sleazy Muslims are always looking for Christian girls, and we know the stupid ones are starting to go out with you.

This flabbergasted me. I was so taken aback by the notion that female students at Saint Joseph's, or any university for that matter, might deign to give us the time of day should we try to win their attention, that I didn't know how to respond. Thinking about how to alleviate our interrogators' anger and extricate ourselves from a worsening situation, I considered revealing to them that I was Christian. And since they already knew about my being Iraqi, not Palestinian, I'd be in the clear. (Palestinian Christians were still half bad, because they had fought alongside their Muslim compatriots against the Lebanese Christians during the civil war, whereas no such stigma attached to Iraqi Christians.) This was the time to pull my crucifix out.

I couldn't bring myself to do it. For one thing, I had Samer to worry about; he was Muslim. They might cut him some slack because he was with me, but then again they might not. And if they didn't, I'd never forgive myself for what I'd done. So I kept silent. *Was this the right decision?*

A moment later, it was too late for me to change my mind. The first blow I received took me by complete surprise. Stupid, really, as I had just seen Samer get decked by Slurper. But that was so sudden and jarring I didn't register that my turn was next. I took a punch to the side of my face from Wannabe Rapper and another to the flank from Slurper, and fell to the ground beside my friend. They kicked us while we were down. Lest Samer think his Lebanese identity might make them go easier on him, Slurper spewed "Lebanese Muslims are just as bad as foreign ones; both of you ruined our country!" before giving Samer's ribs a vicious wallop. The two also let fly a torrent of French words—curses, presumably—which neither Samer nor I understood.

Not that this meant they were proficient in the language. Although most Christians, especially working-class folk, never mastered it, and despite the fact that fluent-speakers included upper-class Muslims, the Christian community as a whole tended to consider the language part of its distinct heritage. As a result, even those Christians who could manage only a smattering of French often employed it in public as a cultural marker to distinguish themselves from Muslims. The guys who beat us up didn't seem the kind who had attended private French-language schools. They had that ruffian look about them; leave those two on a street corner long enough and they'd find a discarded, empty Coke can to play soccer with.

About a minute later, with the two of us curled into fetal positions, our hands held before our faces to shield ourselves, Slurper stopped kicking and instructed his partner to do the same. Yanked us back up, slapped us a couple of times, pointed us in the general direction of the Fuad Shehab bridge, which we had crossed on our way over from Hamra, and told us to git. Samer and I staggered a bit and then shuffled forward a few paces as they swaggered off in the opposite direction.

After a few moments, with the two of them out of sight and earshot, we stopped to take stock of our situation. As far as we could determine, the damage wasn't major. Cuts and moderate bruises-in-the-making. Samer would turn out to have a cracked rib, but he didn't know it at the time. Neither of us could see the other clearly, owing to the darkness, so we couldn't tell just yet how we looked, but that was hardly a concern.

Somewhat reassured, we set off again, this time feeling firmer on our feet. Samer said we should have fought back. I told him I agreed, though in reality I believed that that would have just made things worse. At one point, I wondered aloud why they hadn't mistaken me for a Syrian when they heard my strange Iraqi-Lebanese accent.

"Too young," Samer replied. "The Syrians here are almost all grown men, like the construction workers and other laborers you see everywhere, or the soldiers. But the Palestinians in the refugee camps, they're all ages."

"Hey, did I ever tell you the joke about Bashir Gemayel and the Palestinians?" I asked, referring to the head of the civil war-era Lebanese Forces, a Christian militia infamous for its hatred of Palestinians. Gemayel was elected president in 1982 but assassinated before he took office. "I heard it from Ghassan, who sits right behind me in chemistry class; he told me it's popular with Palestinians, and a British or American journalist even included it in a book he wrote."

Samer: No, I don't think so.

Me: Well, Bashir is at the gates of heaven, waiting in line to be admitted.

Samer: That guy got into heaven?

Me: Just wait. So standing in front of the gates are Moses, Jesus, and Muhammad, right? And to pass through the gates and enter heaven you have to shake the hand of each of them. Naturally, all those waiting in line start whispering about Bashir, whose turn is coming up. You know, like, "Will Bashir, the hardline Christian, shake Muhammad's hand?"

Samer: Uh-huh.

Me: Now, there's a Lebanese Forces guy in line, and he gets really indignant at all this speculation. "What's wrong with all you people?" he asks. "Don't you know that Bashir was never anti-Muslim? He was a Lebanese nationalist opposed to sectarianism in all its forms!"

Samer (scoffing): Yeah, right!

Me: So now it's Bashir's turn. He walks up to Moses and shakes his hand, and then, to everybody's amazement, walks right past Jesus and stops in front of Muhammad, whose hand he shakes firmly and without hesitation. Everyone in line falls into a stunned silence—even the Lebanese Forces guy. But then someone pipes up, "Hey, what's so surprising? Didn't you guys know that Bashir would never shake the hand of a Palestinian?"

Samer: Ha, that's very good—makes perfect sense!

We both wanted to walk, and seemed to know this about the other. And so even when we reached the Fuad Shehab bridge, we didn't hail any of the few cabs that rumbled by every so often. Instead, we continued our way on foot, skirting the bridge—which had no pedestrian walkway, making it dangerous to slink along even when traffic was scant—and cutting through the edge of the downtown district. With the hulks of previously imposing buildings littering its forlorn landscape, the area exuded a creepy sense of abandonment. In the daytime, things wouldn't have felt much different. It was as if the Lebanese, by tacit consensus, had agreed to avoid the center of their own capital, so disturbing was its ravaged state. They would wait until it had been rebuilt—talk of reconstruction was in the air—and only then cease circumventing the area during cross-town excursions. For now, downtown lay thoroughly deserted; even squatters avoided it.

As we stumbled through the maze of destruction, Samer told me how he had almost revealed to our tormentors that I was Christian, but stopped himself at the last moment. "I figured it would probably get us out of trouble. But I was afraid that on Monday you'd come to school with a large cross around your neck; you know, the Lebanese Forces kind that's sawed off at the bottom like that guy's back there? Except even bigger than that. And during lunch break, you'd dunk that sharp tip in bacon grease, and then impale me with it in front of everybody while shrieking blood-curdling war cries the whole time," he said without cracking a smile.

I told him he was right, sounding more confident than I felt, and laughed for added effect. He chuckled a little. It occurred to me then that the reason he was attuned to my unstated but apparent prickliness on this whole subject stemmed at least in part from his own situation. Samer was a Shiite who disliked Hezbollah, which was otherwise wildly popular among members of his sect, from which it had sprung. He couldn't abide its religious fanaticism or the campaign of systematic murder the then-upstart group had unleashed against long-established leftist Shiite rivals during the civil war. Samer would never have claimed any favors, or even attempted to get his due, by portraying himself as a supporter of Hezbollah, or even just trading on his Shiite affiliation. I felt good about myself as we walked and talked all the way back to Hamra that night, and about the fact that my friend and I understood each other.

Recalling the Ashrafieh episode the Sunday after the 9/11 attacks, my dogged march through the deserted UCF campus having slowed to a tired trudge, an idea began to take shape. I still wore my crucifix every day and could easily make it visible to all. That would dispel any suspicions I was Muslim when people inevitably found out about my Arabic name and Iraqi nationality. For good measure, I might also inform everyone that I wasn't even ethnically Arab. Nothing dishonest about all this. Might even be the smart thing to do. After all, it would almost certainly make my life easier.

But no. A recognition of what was right crystallized in my mind, and a conviction took hold. I had had the right idea back in Ashrafieh that night with Samer, thanks in large part to the way I was raised, and now the real test was at hand. I resolved not to detach my Christianity from the Iraqi whole of which it was an integral part, even if that would smooth my dealings with people who thought I was Muslim and detested me for it. And, my necklace with its modest crucifix tucked as ever into my shirt, I would steer clear of seeking any sort of acceptability by association. No trumpeting of my Christian affiliation and non-Arab ethnicity as a means to set myself apart from, let alone above, Muslims and Arabs bound to suffer demonization and worse. Not because of a romantic attachment to them on my part, or some martyr-like desire to share in their pain and suffering; I just wanted to continue trying to earn people's respect through my own actions.

Of course, I wouldn't hide my identity if revealing it was relevant to a particular discussion. (And not just with dimwits like those two missionaries; I had always taken

pleasure in unveiling my religious affiliation before igno-
rant Muslims who, because they were non-Arab or hailed
from Arab countries long devoid of a Christian population,
assumed that because I was Iraqi I must be Muslim.) But
should the fact that I was Christian come up with people
liable to attribute some sort of civilizational or "us versus
them" significance to it, I would explain that that part of
me remained bound up with my Iraqiness and my connection to the surrounding Arab world.

*This, then, would be how I'd face the America 9/11 had made.*
Despite my apprehension that the country was turning
into something unrecognizable, a place of suspicion and
intolerance one might call Septemberland, I would refrain
from volunteering that I was Chaldean if it meant receiving treatment in any way preferential to that accorded the
despised of our new era. My decision was final.

4

At Knight Lights, Lewis seemed preoccupied—and not just by the cute bartender. As we talked, it became clear that he was in philosophical mode, at one point remarking, "You have to admit, though, Hunayn, that if you just put morality and the whole humanitarian aspect aside for a minute, that footage of what happened in New York was probably the most spectacular thing you've ever seen, right?"

I immediately reactivated my subterfuge-detecting antennae. *Was this the test, the one that didn't happen that earlier night at this very bar?* Had his behavior on that occasion —kidding around the whole time—served as a ploy to get me to lower my guard so that now, when he asked me this suspicious question, I'd agree with him about the attacks having been spectacular, and he'd pounce and shred me to ribbons? The possibility exercised me to such a degree that, when I finally allowed myself to contemplate his actual statement/question, I couldn't determine whether I agreed with it. My concern with giving him the "correct" answer was so overriding that it blotted out everything else, including my actual impressions of the attacks.

At length, I responded. "I admit that the scale of what happened," I said slowly, "and the method...the plans... were beyond anything I've seen, but using the term 'spectacular' could give someone the idea that..."

Lewis: What, that you support it?

Me: Well...yeah.

Lewis: Oh, come off it, man, wouldja? Can't you look at something, like, I don't know, a mansion or something, and say that it's impressive in size, even though when it comes to the architecture, it's a travesty?

Me: Sure, if you put it that way, it's clear what you think. But if you leave out the travesty part, then it's not so clear.

The bartender now ambled over. She wore a black button-down shirt the two front ends of which she had tied into a bow above an exposed midriff, in the center of which glittered a pierced navel. And she looked more dolled up on this occasion—with burgundy lipstick, black eyeliner, and a touch of rouge on her cheeks. A few more days were between us and the attacks, classes at UCF had resumed, and people seemed more comfortable with doing what they normally did. With a plastic smile, she asked us what we wanted to drink. I settled for a pint of beer (on tap) bearing the name of an apparently local microbrewery I hadn't come across before: 321, which had become the new area code for Orlando after all the 407 numbers had gotten used up. Lewis requested a Jameson on the rocks, "but not too rocky."

Bartender: Well, how many ice cubes would you like?

Lewis (frowning in mock concentration): Hmm…half.

Bartender: Half a glass?

Lewis: No, half a cube.

Bartender: Half an ice cube. You're serious?

Lewis: Indubitably.

Bartender (irritated): And how do you expect me to get you that half?

Lewis (brightening): Easy! First, bite the cube in two. Then, spit one half into my face. Do it with passion, though, okay? Finally, take the other half out of your mouth, smear it with your lipstick, and plop it into the glass.

She shook her head in disgust and walked away. This seemed to delight Lewis. "That's it, attagirl!" he called after her.

Then he turned to me. "What was that you said last time? I wanna tell her that. You know, the keg of ale, and how she's a sissy winch or something?"

Me (panicking): No, no, please don't say that!

Lewis: Why not?

Me (with all the resolve I can muster): Because then I'll leave.

Lewis (good-natured): All right, fine, spoil the party; I'll cut it out. Anyway, what was I saying?

Me: Well, I had just finished saying that if you say it's spectacular, you want to be careful not to leave out the evil part, because people might—

Lewis: Oh, yeah! So listen, I'm trying to say that it's spectacular *regardless* of what you think.

Me: That's the problem. At a time like this, what I think about the attack—

Lewis: Or what *I* think, if you're so touchy about language here.

Me: I'm just saying that—

Lewis: What *one* thinks, all right? Is that better?

Me: Yeah, it's better, but if you'll just let me finish. It still doesn't get rid of the problem. Like I was saying, at a time like this, what you think of the attack is what matters most. That's what everybody wants to know.

Lewis: That I don't support it? You gotta be kidding me. I don't think anyone's gonna suspect me of supporting the attack just because I say it was spectacular!

Me: Maybe not you. But if I went around saying—

Lewis: Or even you, man!

Me: You might be right. Still, it's almost like I'd…like you'd be asking for trouble.

And trouble was very much on my mind. Even as I altered some of my habits so as to avoid arousing suspicion (no longer taking out the trash in the middle of the night, for example, which the news analysts said should have alerted people that their Arab neighbors were up to something fishy well before they hijacked the planes), I nevertheless expected the worst. Specifically, popular mass movements taking shape and lashing out at Arabs and Muslims. I relied on the TV to tell me about this. You might not need a weatherman to know which way the wind blows, but you do need a newsman to know which direction the mob that wants to kill you is coming from.

With time, however, it seemed that I could breathe easy. Sure, hate crimes took place against people perceived— sometimes wrongly—as Arab or Muslim, resulting in a handful of deaths, but these were isolated attacks carried out by individuals who were swiftly apprehended by law enforcement. The much-dreaded and more dangerous group action failed to materialize. Perhaps by butchering such a large number of people at once and consuming their bodies completely (in many instances leaving only tattered scraps of clothing), Moloch had forever satisfied his appetite for our flesh and slaked his thirst for our blood.

As the specter of public lynchings and Rosewood-style mass expulsions receded, and the campaign in Afghanistan progressed (it looked as though Bin Laden and company, having suffered military defeat, now faced imminent capture), debates over US policy toward the Middle East began to capture my attention. Amid the swirl of conflicting opinions on TV, one stood out: the argument that the US, far from cementing its ties to autocratic Arab regimes in the interest of forming a united front against Al-Qaida, should pressure them to democratize, as they were very much part of the problem. The possibility that we had entered an era in which American philosophical ideals of combating tyranny and spreading liberal democracy dovetailed with US national security interests gave me a jolt of exhilaration.

One aspect of the new discourse, however, disturbed me. These guys all held Israel up as a paragon of Western-style democracy, often contrasting it with its Arab neighbors. But what about the Palestinians? In preventing them from establishing a state of their own, yet simultaneously not offering them Israeli citizenship, Israel had foisted upon the Palestinians an existential limbo. If a democratic country conquers another people and relegates them to statelessness, all the while subjecting them to martial law, confiscating their land, and providing them with less water than the illegal settlements it establishes in their territory, does it still qualify as a full-fledged democracy? The guys on TV didn't seem to care. Ironic, in light of their professed support for human rights, freedoms of all kinds, and, of course, democracy.

Other than my watching more TV, life for me went on pretty much as normal. Every Sunday, my parents called, as they had done since my move to the States, except now, my mother—who spoke to me for longer than my father did—would begin every conversation by inquiring about my safety and security. Much of the rest of the call would revolve around this subject. Were people harassing me? Did I know that 911 was the number to call the police? Was I being foolhardy and going out alone at night?

Far from annoying me, these questions came as a welcome break from her usual, pre-9/11 interrogation, which always began with an eager "So, do you have a girlfriend yet?" Back then, I would fib that I was leisurely dating here and there. She'd give me tips on how to turn one of my "lady friends" into a steady romantic partner. "Pick the one you like most," she'd advise me, "and show her how lucky she'd be to have someone who understands her young country and its culture. But also try to show her that you come from a country that is the product of some of the richest and most ancient civilizations in the world." She always sounded so earnest.

I came out of the bathroom, plopped back down on the couch in my living room, and used the remote control to change the TV channel, which was showing the Detroit Red Wings playing the Colorado Avalanche. Lewis immediately complained. With his slack-jawed Michigan accent, he sounded something like this: "I was kænda wætchin' the hæckey game."

I apologized unconvincingly and didn't return to ESPN, telling him that I was looking for the news or a discussion of some of the latest developments in Afghanistan.

"Forget the news, dude," he said with a dismissive movement of his hand, as though lazily batting away a mosquito.

As it happened, I had to do just that, because although

I tuned in to a channel running a report on life in newly liberated Kabul, Lewis launched into an enthused account of the growing chemistry between him and Colleen, and the various manifestations—especially on her part—of such a welcome development. I had briefly met this Colleen, whom Lewis set his sights on after things didn't work out with Jenny, when he asked me to join the two of them for lunch at the Student Union, where we got ourselves Dirty Hoagies and waffle fries from Wackadoo's.

Colleen turned out to be a petite, lissome babe with a ready smile and a habit of tilting her head to one side and cooing "Goooooooood" when friends of hers dropped by our table and asked how she was doing. She drove a sports utility vehicle, to which Lewis and I walked her after lunch, as she had to go somewhere and he and I had nothing to do. Following her departure, we agreed that there was something inescapably sexual about a wee woman grappling with such a mammoth machine. We failed to pinpoint the elusive source of this undeniable truth, but Lewis told me he came tantalizingly close every time he observed her clambering into or out of the driver's seat while struggling with tremendous valiance but little success to prevent the deceptively idle behemoth from bunching up her T-shirt, pulling down her shorts, or swallowing one of her flip-flops.

Anyway, she was bubbly and garrulous—a perfect fit for Lewis's manic disposition (though making me appear somber and reticent by contrast). I was happy for him. The only issue that caused me some discomfort was her questioning me repeatedly during lunch about whether anyone was discriminating against me, and her doubtful look when I assured her that I hadn't experienced the slightest trouble.

Now Lewis was telling me about an on-campus swing dance the two of them had just attended, one which featured a selection of songs from the genre's heyday back in the 1930s and '40s plus the recent retro trend that started in the late '90s. "Yeah, you should've seen her, man," he enthused. "It's like neither of us really knew any swing moves, so we were doing all this other stuff, kinda just wingin' it. And then more than once she came up close and shook her shoulders at me, so that her small but perky tits were tryin' to bust out and be like, 'Hey, boy, make a couple a new friends,' you know?"

Me: Uh-huh.

Lewis: I'm tellin' you, that chick is bangin'. Got it totally goin' on. And check this out, yo, she knows someone.

Me: Oh, no, really, man. That's okay. It's not my style. I mean—

Lewis: Hold on, just listen, all right? This girl, Kendra, from out West somewhere, she's smart and into politics and stuff, just like you. Plus, she's got that whole curvaceous thing going on. And I told her all about you, and get this: She totally wants to meet you.

I paused for a moment. Though scoring a girlfriend, or at least losing my virginity, was still my number two goal, and had long occupied the number one slot before my quest to make sense of 9/11 and its aftermath displaced it, I didn't want any favors from anyone, not even a good friend. Nevertheless, I reflected, this might constitute my best shot at hooking up with a girl. Perhaps, in order to retain my pride, I could make as though I were put out by

Lewis's attempt at matchmaking and pretend to go along with it for his sake, not mine, so that if it didn't pan out, I wouldn't look pathetic, and if it did, I'd have a girl on my arm without having to express gratitude to him.

"Well, look, if you're gonna keep nagging me about it," I said, "and if my going along with this is the only way to make you shut up, I'll do it. But if I don't like her…"

"You got nothing to lose, Hunayn. If you don't like her, you can just drop the whole thing—but I know that's not gonna happen; this girl's your type, bro."

A few days later, Lewis brought the girl in question to Apollo's Lyre, the campus music store where I worked part-time, blithely disregarding the fact that I was on duty—even if I didn't have my employee shirt on, which my boss Jeff had told me to cease wearing because "HUNAYN" was emblazoned across it. As Jeff hovered about, frowning all the while, Lewis introduced me to Kendra, a zaftig strawberry blonde whose Lycra T-shirt's elastic strained against a prodigious bosom, and whose scrumptious little nougat nose struggled to keep a pair of pink horn-rimmed eyeglasses from slipping off her face. Striking a surprisingly debonair gentleman-leaning-on-piano pose (the cash register substituting for the piano), and employing a smooth facilitator-of-romantic-dreams tone, as though he were a dinner host both gracious and beneficent, Lewis proceeded to tell Kendra that he was sure I could offer some advice about the event she and fellow members of the Progressive Students Organization were planning, and then turned to me and said he was sure Kendra would appreciate my words of wisdom.

I wondered what this was about as I motioned for them to mosey along with me to the Avant Garde & Experimental Rock section several feet away at one end of the small store, where we wouldn't run the risk of obstructing any browsing customers at this early morning hour. We now stood in front of the Frank Zappa collection, among others. I tried to ignore Jeff—whom I noticed was still eyeing us suspiciously—the better to concentrate on the conversation. "What's the event?" I asked Kendra, while thinking that if, as I presumed, it had something to do with the attacks, I wouldn't feel comfortable speaking to her about my still raw feelings of fear and confusion, much less try out the tentative analysis I was trying to formulate.

"Well, together with the Muslim Students Association, we're getting this guy to come to campus in a few days and give a talk," she said with a good deal of excitement. Then, sounding reverential, she added, "He's a *Mufti*."

"That's quite a coincidence," I replied. "I'm actually in mufti right now. Yeah, check this out," I said, tugging the bottom of my UCF Knights T-shirt. "Street clothes, and yet I'm on the job even as we speak."

I caught Lewis, who by this time had stepped back a bit, shaking his head, a look of genuine pity come over his face. This didn't offend me. In fact, I was pleasantly surprised that he might have understood the reference. Kendra certainly hadn't; I could tell by her puzzled expression. So I said to her, "Anyway, you were saying?"

Kendra: Yeah, so we're getting this Mufti from a mosque to come and talk to us about how the real Islam is peace and how the terrorists are perverting it.

Me: Uh-huh.

Kendra: His name is Ahmad Abdullah. We address him as Sheikh Abdullah, out of respect. Do you know him?

Me: No, can't say that I do. The only Mufti I know personally is Sheik Yerbouty.

Kendra: Oh.

She seemed disappointed, though I couldn't tell if this was because I didn't know Sheikh Abdullah or because she didn't know Sheik Yerbouty. Lewis excused himself, saying he had class, and left, shooting me a stern "Don't fuck this up" parting look. Kendra and I continued to talk. She told me, lowering her voice and sounding reverential, that Sheikh Abdullah had a "zabeebah." I recognized the word as Arabic for "raisin," but didn't understand what she meant. When I asked her, she seemed taken aback, but explained that Sheikh Abdullah's raisin was in fact a blotchy spot on his forehead from prostrating himself on a rug five times a day in prayer.

"You know, I used to have one of those myself," I told her.

Standing on tiptoes despite her height, and scrutinizing my forehead, she said, "Really? So it's not there anymore?"

Me: No, mine must've been different. I took a shower one day and it just vanished. Poof! Just like that. Poof! Then again, I was depressed—new at UCF, no friends—and hadn't bathed in a while.

Kendra: Oh, right, ha ha.

Me: Anyway, what else are you guys gonna do?

Kendra: Well, we're screening a film. *The Message*— you know it? It's about the life of Muha...the Prophet Muhammad. Anthony Quinn's in it.

Me: Yeah, I've seen it.

Kendra: Really? I can't wait to see it. I just found out about it from the Muslim Student Association guys. It's from the '70s. So, what's it like?

Me: Different. For one thing, in both versions, the English one with Quinn and the Arabic one without him, Muhammad doesn't even appear because of the whole Islamic prohibition on depicting the prophets. You know, so people don't fall into idolatry and all that?

Kendra: So…how do they tell his story?

Me: With great difficulty. I suppose it's kind of a feat, artistically speaking, but that's part of the reason the movie ends up being boring.

Kendra: Both versions?

Me: Yeah, both versions, 'fraid so. What's interesting is that even with the filmmakers reassuring everybody that they wouldn't portray Muhammad and also that they'd make the movie totally hagiographic, they still ran into trouble. The king of Saudi Arabia, who was later assassinated, had issues with the project, so he got the Moroccans, who had allowed filming to take place in the deserts of Morocco, to backtrack and forbid it.

Kendra: Who assassinated the king?

Me: Well, the filmmakers did, naturally. As you might imagine, they were pretty miffed at the old coot for scuttling their project. Yeah, I think they used the lighting equipment, or maybe it was the camera dolly—for the steady hand. And then they went off to Libya to film the rest of the movie, 'cause Gaddafi jumped in and gave them permission to.

Kendra: Wait, you're kidding again, right?

Me: Absolutely not. You know what they always say

about him, right? "Mercurial." Not merely unpredictable, mind you, but positively mercurial.

Kendra: No, I mean about them assassinating the king.

Me: Oh, that. Well, yes, I was.

Before she left, Kendra pressed me to attend the up-coming event (I demurred, explaining that it wasn't my scene), and said she had really enjoyed our little talk, gushing, "You know, I just can't get over the fact that you have no accent!"

It took me a moment to remember that most Americans believed they spoke English without an accent; if you spoke the way they did, you also didn't have an accent. Meanwhile, she added that we should get together soon, maybe with Colleen and Lewis. In one sense, I wasn't thrilled about the idea, given her overall ingenuousness and her rose-tinted view of Islam in particular. But I did find her physically attractive. We exchanged contact information and agreed to stay in touch.

I watched her walk toward the exit, her Rubenesque figure forcing an inadvertent sashay. This served to demonstrate the far-reaching effects of her callipygian attribute; the individual letters "UCF," emblazoned in gold on the back of her tight black shorts, each wigwagged independently of the others with the purposeful movement of her buttocks. Meanwhile, her hefty and for the most part exposed thighs struck me as powerful yet supple, capable of strangling a mighty Burmese python down at Everglades National Park one afternoon and doing the Hanuman splits in a yoga class back on campus the next morning. A pair of ovally rounded bare calves—muscular definition noticeable but not obtrusive—enhanced her gams' exquisite shape, and were so succulent-looking they made me salivate as I imagined sinking my teeth into them.

My reverie ended with Jeff, a burly-cum-obese black Alabamian, placing his bulk squarely before me. He was huffing and puffing. I resigned myself to being reprimanded as soon as he collected himself. "Yeah, sorry about that," I said, trying to pre-empt him as I wiped my drooling mouth with the back of my hand and attempted to look contrite. "She just kept talking, and I didn't want to be rude, you know?"

Jeff, his wheezing having subsided, seemed alarmed. "What did she want?"

Me: Uh, well…to get together? Maybe have a drink?

Jeff (contemptuous): Have a drink, huh? So that's how they be playin' it these days. Must think you got no sense.

Me: (bewildered): Who?

Jeff: The government. Y'all probably the next Tuskegee guinea pigs, still unsuspecting as shit. You just be sure you stay on the ball when all this boozing goes down. Don't let her serve you a drink at her house; meet up at a bar and get it straight from the bartender. And don't take your eyes off the glass for a second, 'cause that's when she'll slip the drug in.

Me (concerned he's lost his mind): I don't think she's planning anything like that, Jeff. It's totally innocent. In fact, I think she has a bit of a thing for me.

Jeff (tut-tutting): Oh, come on now, man! Of course she acts like that; how else she gon' lure you in? And as far as the planning thing goes, it's not up to the girl what strategy to use. Her handler tells her what to do, and she does it. Simple as that.

Me: Her handler?!

Jeff: Yeah, the guy who brought her here and set this whole thing up.

Me (confident I can resolve this misunderstanding): Oh, I see what you mean. No, there's nothing to worry about. That guy's my friend Lewis. He's been here before; you might've seen him.

Jeff (undeterred): All the more reason you should watch out. He's the best guy for the job. After all, he knows all about you. They put him on the case and he recruits exactly the kind of girl you're weak for, thick and bulging everywhere it counts like all them fatass Egyptian belly dancers, but also white and blond for that "opposites attract" factor. And then you ripe for the pickin'.

The next day, when I met Lewis for lunch on campus, he grilled me about my encounter with Kendra, demanding to know whether I agreed to attend the event she had informed me about. I told him that I hadn't, explaining that even though I understood Muslims' desire to absolve their religion of responsibility for the blood-soaked barbarity of a few months earlier, I tended to find Islamic apologetics insulting to my intelligence. He rolled his eyes. I continued, "And the other thing is that this sort of event diverts attention from the victims of the attacks. What do the families of the dead care if the terrorists' actions violate Islamic law or not? I just think it's really selfish for anybody to concern himself with Islam's image at a time like this, when our attention should be on the victims and their families."

This sounded a trifle sanctimonious when I heard myself say it, and I felt a twinge of embarrassment recalling that my first thoughts following the attacks were themselves selfish, concerned as they were with my personal safety. Nevertheless, the sentiment behind what I said was genuine; I really did consider it insensitive to prettify Islam at such a time. Yes, Muslims facing harassment deserved protection, and Americans inclined to consider them guilty by association deserved censure and a basic educational lesson on the illogicality of their view. But guaranteeing the civil rights of Muslims was a world away from making Islam look good, or even just shielding it from criticism.

"So what?" replied Lewis, exasperated. "You don't have to agree with everything they say. Anyway, even if you don't go, try to make things happen with her. She's into you, man."

Kendra called me a few days later to tell me that the screening of the English-language version of *The Message* and the subsequent short lecture delivered by Sheikh Abdullah, during which the attendees received confirmation of their belief that Islam was all peace and flowers and that the terrorists weren't real Muslims, had gone swimmingly. She asked me when I'd be on campus next, and we agreed to meet the following day for a coffee between classes.

Sitting in the coffee shop section of the UCF Barnes & Noble bookstore, sipping our coffees—decaf for her, latté for me—she again sang the praises of both the film and the speaker, adding that I should have come. I steered the conversation toward her, wanting to find out whether we might have anything in common, though her irrepressible breasts, which neither her demi-cup cock-tease of a bra nor her flimsy diaphanous dress proved able to restrain as they jiggled in accompaniment to her animated speech, made me wonder if the issue was all that important.

"Oh, it's great!" she effused in response to my question about what she thought of Orlando. "I mean, it's December, and look what I'm wearing."

This immediately caused my gaze to revert to her bustling boobs.

"Where I come from," she continued, "it gets really cold this time of year. But Orlando, right now, it's like summer back home." She explained that she was from Portland, Oregon, which she planned to return to for the Winter Break that began in a few days, and admonished me—before I had the chance to err—to pronounce the name of her beloved state just as she did, with the ending a clipped "gən," as opposed to "gone."

It occurred to me that I could happily live the rest of my life without pronouncing "Oregon" any kind of way, but I refrained from revealing this, instead pointing out that I had come to the States from a country whose name was also pronounced two ways. "I say 'Lebanon,' with the final syllable coming out the same way you pronounce it in 'Oregon,' but it doesn't really bother me when people say it the other way," I told her. Intrigued, she asked me a few general questions about Lebanon, having been unaware that I had lived there; she'd assumed that I had grown up in Iraq.

Before long, we had found our way to the thorny subject of Middle Eastern politics. When it came to what roiled the region, making it such a dismal and dangerous place to live in, Kendra's outlook proved a bit simplistic. She'd issue several broad statements of opposition to this or that US foreign policy, such as unconditional support for Israel, the coddling of pro-American dictatorships, or sanctions on Iraq, and then ask my opinion on the matter. She seemed to consider me an authority on the Middle East. I tended to agree with her initial statement, and didn't have any qualms about criticizing specific US actions, but felt a mite uncomfortable with her tendency to blame America for all the region's ills; she reduced Iraq's problems to its victimization at the hands of US-spearheaded sanctions, seemed to believe that the US caused—not merely exacerbated—the Arab-Israeli conflict, and maintained that US support of oppressive regimes served as the only impediment to democracy in that part of the world. When she told me that she hoped to get together again after Winter Break, I said sure, but told myself that I'd do best to refrain from pursuing any sort of relationship with her.

With the start of the vacation a few days later, I found myself with little to do. Lewis and his parents drove up to Detroit to see family and friends, making several stops on the way. Kendra flew to Portland, apparently unafraid that anything would happen (thanks to her anti-imperialist politics, perhaps?). Meanwhile, I wasn't about to fly to Lebanon—or anywhere else, for that matter. Not just for fear of the plane getting hijacked and then used as a missile, meaning that more people would perish in flames and I'd die a virgin, but because airport security officials might subject me to a host of physically invasive procedures before letting me board. Hashem was over in Winter Park, of course, but I felt uneasy about the prospect of seeing him, as he might well make the unprecedented and still somewhat daunting situation we all found ourselves in appear even worse.

When Christmas rolled around, I felt lonely. The previous two Winter Breaks, I had traveled to Beirut. Got a chance to see my folks—and, on Christmas Eve, attend Midnight

Mass with them at the Chaldean church in Hazmieh. Also hung out with Samer.

But I wasn't lonely just for the obvious reason that I was alone; Christmas in Orlando, and apparently in much of the States, wasn't really Christmas. This was due in part to the law prohibiting federal and state buildings from displaying religious symbols of any kind. But the weird thing was that department stores and private establishments often operated as though the law applied to them as well. Just being politically correct, I supposed. As a result, no Nativity scene was to be found anywhere other than churches and the odd front yard of a private residence. Even Christmas trees remained scarce. Just as bad, the anodyne "Happy Holidays" had replaced the meaningful "Merry Christmas" for everyone but fundamentalist Christians. It wasn't the Grinch that stole Christmas, but overzealous secularists.

I felt a pang of nostalgia for Christmassy Lebanon, recalling how, heading for home in the evening after basketball practice at school, I'd often alight from the shared taxi at the beginning of Hamra Street and walk the remaining distance. That way, I'd have something to listen to; throughout Saison Noël, Christmas carols played over loudspeakers affixed to lampposts lining both sides of the street. They were in French, but that was fine. The sky tenebrous and overcast, vast and oppressive. Shutting out heaven above, cackling in anticipation of the chance to disrupt our lives, and savoring the anxious looks on our faces every time it momentarily dartled its dark self with streaks of lightning. Its amorphous gray minions jostling each other for dibs on soaking us, the bigger clouds shunting aside their smaller counterparts so that they'd win the prize of unleashing a deluge of icy water on this buzzing quarter of the city, causing chaos among the pedestrians.

To walk down Hamra Street, my oversized gym bag slung across my scraggy shoulder, beneath all this wrong-side-up Hadesian hubbub, and to hear the tender yet rousing carols commemorating the birth of Jesus Christ, who sacrificed his life to expiate our sins, and to know that I was in the bosom of a neighborhood whose mostly Muslim residents embraced Christians and shared in both their joys and sorrows, convinced me that we were here to stay. To stay, to witness, and to celebrate. And nothing could rain on our numerically diminishing yet continuous and still exuberant two-millennia-old parade—not even the rain itself. As our tormentor above roared with cruel glee and the baleful clouds finally burst, drenching all and scattering many, the dulcet and deceptively restrained carols mounted in volume, carried upward, and punched through the obstructionist Cimmerian sky, making the welkin ring and surely pleasing God in heaven. And all the while, I strode onward.

Kendra called and left a message on my answering machine as soon as she returned from Portland, which was just after New Year's and still a few days before the end of Winter Break, proposing that we have dinner soon. I didn't want to do the rude thing and say no or not call back, but neither did I wish to place myself in the vise of going out on a date with a girl I wasn't seriously interested in, but whose very appearance before me stirred my loins better than an ambidextrous prostitute's handjob (presumably) could. Roping Lewis and Colleen into it might have extinguished any expectations of romance on Kendra's part and simultaneously kept my impulses, however alcohol-fueled, in check. Unfortunately, though, Lewis had yet to return to Orlando, and I didn't want to suggest that we invite Colleen only for Kendra to tell me that she wasn't back either, leaving me with no option but to settle for the two of us. So I devised another plan; I would set something up with Hashem and his girlfriend Amanda.

Hashem, whom I hadn't seen since the day after the day everything in the States changed for the worse, seemed a bit surprised to get a call from me (we had arrived at a tacit understanding to avoid that medium of communication, given our shared paranoia, and instead kept in touch via the occasional email), but otherwise indicated that he was cool with the four of us grabbing a meal. We agreed to meet at Fiddler's Green, an Irish pub and eatery in Winter Park, the evening of the following day. I called Kendra and presented her with this fait accompli, asking her whether she'd like to go with me. She said yes.

Standing before the bathroom mirror, I noticed that my crucifix had somehow slipped free of the jump ring at the end of my necklace. Couldn't find the thing anywhere, so I left without it and picked Kendra up from her apartment complex, which, like mine, was near campus. She looked very pretty in a white halter blouse, blue skirt, pantyhose, and white leather flats, but I refrained from complimenting her so as not to encourage forward behavior—or, even more problematic, an advance later that evening that I'd have to stave off.

When we got to Fiddler's Green, instead of the planned casual encounter alleviating some of the pressure I felt, it plunged me into an awkward situation of another kind. Hashem and Amanda had already arrived, and she was in a swivet. In between sobs, she told us that her thesis advisor at Rollins had insisted she change the thrust of her argument or risk having him sabotage her push for an MA (in education). Apparently, she had stood her ground and debated him, but by the time she met up with Hashem, the tension had caught up with her and she suffered some kind of delayed reaction, sobbing uncontrollably. This unsettled me, accustomed as I was to the self-assured, confident Amanda. For Hashem, it was an absolute nightmare. The poor guy had no idea what to do. Shrinking into a corner, eyes bulging and mouth agape, revealing teeth that—to complete the picture—should have been chattering, he looked like a petrified hamster, and didn't so much as even try to comfort her.

Amanda, a tall and slim yet shapely redhead, was a serious and scholarly girl who also had a wild, uninhibited side she manifested in risqué dances at nightclubs and house parties—it was at one of the latter that she met Hashem. Apparently, from the way she shook her booty, you'd have thought old KC himself had driven up from Hialeah and told her it was her duty. I didn't know Amanda well, though after Hashem got together with her earlier that year, he and I began to have lengthy discussions about women, which he pronounced phonetically as "whoa-men," reminding me of what an uncle of mine who had moved to London—home to lots of Iraqis—was fond of saying: "Even if none of us can understand women, at least some of us can pronounce the word correctly."

In Hashem's case, he also had no idea how to soothe

one when she fell to pieces, as was happening now. He just sat there rigidly, stricken expression on his face, while she cried. So Kendra took it upon herself to commiserate with Amanda, leaving me and Hashem looking like insentient dolts as we remarked on the quality of the finger food and the continued pleasantness of the weather. I wanted to make a run for it as soon as possible.

By the time we finished eating, Kendra had succeeded in calming Amanda with blandishments accompanied by tea and Irish oatmeal biscuits. I seized the opportunity to pry her away, and we said our goodbyes and left. Because the two of us were still hungry, we decided to go to Broadway, the New York–style diner in the University Shoppes plaza, for a bona fide dinner. Kendra and I scarfed down our veal marsala sitting just a few feet from the now eerie wall-length poster of the Twin Towers glinting at night. She then asked me if we could go back to my place for another drink. Hoping that we might end up getting it on (lust and alcohol had combined to batter my defenses), I hesitated for only the briefest of moments before saying yes.

What was about to happen, I reflected on the short but quiet drive back to my apartment complex, as Kendra massaged my thigh, was just about perfect. *We're going to my place, where no one lives but me, and I'm the only person with a key.* I even noted with something approaching a sense of triumph that because her car wouldn't be parked outside, anybody out there who for whatever reason didn't want the two of us to get together wouldn't even know she was at my apartment. No repeat of the incident I'd experienced in Zahle, back in Lebanon, was possible. All that remained was for me to perform when the time came—which, by the looks of it, was soon.

Half an hour later, we were making out on the narrow couch in the living room, both of us having stripped down to our underwear, with Kendra taking the opportunity to slip off her bra. Quickly getting my fill of kneading her ample tits, I slid a hand southward to her nether regions, discovered the difference between pantyhose and the far more complicated matter of stockings—which is what she had on—and brought my other hand into play for some help. Nothing doing. I was pawing away at her still buckled and seemingly intricate garter belt, simian febrility no match for ursine clumsiness, when she undid the buckles with two deft little hand maneuvers and then pulled off the whole kit and caboodle in one go, clearing my path to her pussy. A few minutes later, I had put on a condom and we were on the carpeted floor fucking in the missionary position. I had done it. Goodbye forever, virginity, you have lost your hold on this boy who will soon come his way to full-fledged manhood!

Having assumed a modified push-up stance (knees on the floor), and encouraged all the while by her warbling, I began to establish a pretty solid rhythm with my pelvic thrusts. That's when it happened.

A few moments earlier, she had arched her back and closed her eyes, legs interlocked over my hairy ass as it bobbed up and down, hands squeezing what precious little flesh padded my hips, fingernails digging into my skin. But now her head lunged forward and her electric blue eyes popped open. With the sort of urgent, desperate rage you might expect of a grievously wounded soldier trying to convince an anguished and wavering comrade to finish him off and end his suffering, she snarled in a guttural, menacing voice, "Fuck me hard, you strong Muslim man!"

There comes a time in your life when you must decide whether to defy your conscience in pursuit of comfort and pleasure, or do the right thing irrespective of the consequences. Of course, I had anticipated as much in the immediate aftermath of 9/11, with the dilemma revolving around whether to repudiate my ties to Arabs and Muslims and thereby forestall any trouble, or stand shoulder-to-shoulder with them and endure whatever indignities I was subjected to as a result. The Sunday after the attacks, walking through campus and thinking about it all, I made my decision.

But now the dilemma had very nearly reversed itself. *Should I reveal that I'm not Muslim, and cut short my getting some? Or pretend that I am, and get more than some?*

As it turned out, my body pre-empted my mind and provided the answer. Before I even absorbed what Kendra had said, her sheer ferocity shocked me, and I froze mid-thrust. When her words sank in a moment later, my immobile but throbbing dick, still in the tight grip of a pussy loath to relinquish it, began to go limp, even as her gimlet eyes, now aflame with impatience, shattered the lenses of her eyeglasses and bore into my rapidly constricting pupils, and her fingernails threatened to tear away portions of my lower back.

Trying to wriggle out of her, I sputtered, "Hold on... hold on a second."

With a mixture of alarm and annoyance, she grunted, "What's the matter? What's wrong?" as she unlocked her legs.

Having safely extracted the insertive portion of my manhood from the clutches of her snatch, which I feared would sprout piranha-like blade teeth and chomp it to bits if I revealed the disappointing truth about me before retrieving it, I said, "Well, here's the thing…"

And, back on the couch, with the two of us facing each other at either end of it and my small rug with its map of Iraq hanging just above us on the wall, I proceeded to explain the situation. Not just my being Christian, but, for good measure, an overview of the history of Christianity in Iraq. Also, the communities that adhered to the religion—Chaldeans, Syriacs, Assyrians—and, of course, how we were ethnically one people and in turn an integral part of the multi-ethnic and multi-religious Iraqi nation. The voracious virago before me, by now rather subdued, listened to all this with an expression of distaste, lips downturned and nose crinkled. Every so often, she cast a doubtful glance at my now condomless, shrunken, and shriveled (yet free) willy, clearly wondering how she had deluded herself into thinking that this tiny, sponge-like protrusion—from the body of nothing more than another Christian schmo—could ever have given her pussy the badass, jihad-style dicking she so craved.

Half an hour later, she was dressed and ready to go. I told her I'd drive her home, but she said no, she'd just use her cellphone to call a friend, whom she'd ask to pick her up at the apartment complex's entrance. Our goodbyes included a peck on the cheek, notable only for its awkwardness, and a non-specific apology from me, which she brusquely acknowledged ("It's fine") without returning the favor. And then she left.

## 5

Following the Kendra debacle, despite feeling that I had acquitted myself reasonably well (both in doing the right thing to begin with and afterward in providing a brief history lecture in the buff), I plunged into a deep and unrelenting depression. Which of course sapped my energy and left me unwilling to make even a minimal mental or physical effort to do anything. This included seeing Lewis, who returned to Orlando a few days later. Though, to be honest, when it came to that issue there was more than depression at play.

To begin with, I hadn't crafted any sort of lie to explain why things hadn't worked out between me and Kendra. And I knew that whatever I came up with would sound pathetic if he had already gotten the skinny from Colleen, who'd have gotten it from the horse's mouth. My hope was that Kendra had felt too embarrassed about the whole incident to give Colleen a truthful account of it.

Yet at certain moments I wondered whether the lie she came up with—if it was indeed that—not only portrayed her in a positive light, but made me look ridiculous or even worse. What if she was so aggrieved by the whole experience as to want to punish me, and as a result decided to tell Colleen that I had failed to perform? (Which, come to think of it, wasn't that far from the truth.) And there was another reason I didn't want to see Lewis, though it stemmed from a childish line of reasoning; I couldn't help but think that this whole fiasco with Kendra wouldn't have happened had he not sicced her on me in the first place.

So I avoided him when he tried to get in touch with me following his return from Detroit, which was shortly before the Spring Semester began. He left a couple of messages on my answering machine, and then sent me an email asking why I hadn't called him back and also suggesting we meet up for a drink or a bite to eat. Although I didn't want to see him and end up talking, as we inevitably would, about Kendra, neither did I want him to think that I had sunk into depression over the fact that things hadn't worked out with her (which, I figured, was the very least Colleen had told him). So I replied to his email with a brief one of my own saying that I had entered lockdown mode in order to ensure that two demanding courses I was taking that term got off to an auspicious start. Once I felt confident that I was in the groove, I reassured him, I'd get back in touch and we'd plan something. This, I figured, would give me some breathing space.

It did, but peace of mind wasn't forthcoming. Every day, sitting alone in the apartment and trying to watch TV, my attention would wander back to what had happened, and I found myself unable to follow the news programs I had made it a point to catch. I regretted apologizing to Kendra, especially as she might have thought it was to do with my turning out to be Christian, as opposed to my failing to fuck her right. Of course, that didn't merit an apology either, given that continuing to fuck her even after it became clear she had opened her legs for me on the assumption I was Muslim would have constituted a form of deceit on my part.

At least my crucifix turned up. Unlike the guy who

found Jesus and explained that He had been behind the couch the whole time, I felt something between the seat cushions when I absent-mindedly slipped my hand down there; sure enough, it was the missing necklace. So that was good, and I had a spare jump ring that closed more securely than the old one.

When I received a terse email from Hashem informing me that he and Amanda had broken up and asking if I wanted to come over for a few drinks at his place that night, I immediately said yes. Still preoccupied by what happened, and still disinclined to see Lewis, I felt this was just what I needed. Even though I didn't intend to reveal everything to Hashem, he and I could engage in some mutual commiseration. So I drove over to Winter Park with high expectations for an angry and inebriated guys' night.

The building's entrance was unlocked. After I walked up the stairs to his apartment, I realized he had left it that way on purpose; a note stuck to his door read, "On the roof—join me."

A minute later I was sitting in a deck chair beside him as he contemplated, without much interest, Park Avenue traffic. I, on the other hand, looked at him; he was a sorry sight, and things got worse when he started talking.

Leaning back in his chair, belt unbuckled, pants button undone, white tank top freshly stained with whiskey, he spoke in a gravelly, enervated voice I hadn't heard before, his words a string of garbled lamentations over the loss of a good woman. Interspersing this English-language threnody—one undergirded by a strong and obvious feeling of guilt—with Arabic proverbs about men who behave alternately as stupid donkeys and egocentric bulls, he seemed a new and unique breed of bluesman. I half expected him to pull out a guitar from beneath his chair and take to howling in melodic grief to the accompaniment of an elegiac but infectious tune.

I knew that he loved Amanda. And I remembered him saying to me, in a conversation a couple of months after he had gotten together with her: "Southerners are more like us, especially the ones from small towns." (Intriguing notion, I had thought, but if his earlier-stated conviction that Southern whites were racist bigots at heart was true, what did that say about us?) Narrowing his eyes and rubbing together his index finger and thumb, as though savoring the exquisite feel of an oh-so-smooth-and-delicate fabric, he added, "And Amanda, well, she is truly exceptional."

I asked him that day where this Amanda, whom he had introduced me to briefly on an earlier occasion, was from. Based on her drawl, I'd have said Georgia or Alabama, but he told me she hailed from some hamlet or other in Florida's northwestern "panhandle" region. When I thought about it, this made sense; looking at Florida from the vantage point of Orlando, the farther north you went, the more culturally Southern it got.

A clearly smitten Hashem, doubtless still thinking of Amanda, then told me, "If I ever marry an American, she'd probably be Southern."

Because I knew all this, when I read Hashem's email about the breakup, I assumed that she had been the one to end the relationship, and decided for self-serving reasons that she dumped him because she had found a more Lebanese Lebanese or Arab Arab or Muslim Muslim. So I got all amped to sympathize with my friend over his objectification at the hands of a leftwing American simpleton (a rightwing American simpleton wouldn't have gone out with the likes of us to begin with), after which I'd inform him that he should consider what happened for the best and tell him a little about my recent experience with a similar woman. And I came to his place to do just that.

Only that's not what happened. Up on the roof, once I got him to start making some sense, he explained to me that Amanda hadn't wronged him in any way, let alone dumped him. In fact, it was the other way around. He had demanded that she dress more conservatively. When she refused, he brusquely informed her that that was the end of their relationship.

This proved disappointing, but I could handle it; if I had planned not to reveal everything about the Kendra incident to Hashem, now I'd just have to refrain from revealing anything. And we'd still have stuff to talk about, because even after he made clear who had broken up with whom, I remained taken enough with my larger assumption to want to convince the poor guy that Amanda had objectified him, and he was better off without her.

What enraged me was that he wanted to reverse his decision. This sent me into a tizzy. I began enumerating the reasons he shouldn't try to woo her back. Of course, I was thinking of Kendra and myself, not Amanda and him. But that didn't stop me. And the alcohol spurred me on, infusing me with a determination to see this through. "She doesn't really love you, man; you know that, right?" I told him. "If she's in love with anything, it's your identity package. Lebanese and Arab and Muslim and Oriental and exotic and something she's fetishized for a long time."

"What're you talking about?" grunted Hashem. He sounded both annoyed and offended. "Have you been reading *Season of Migration to the North* again? Is that what this is all about?"

Surprised, but happy to keep the conversation revolving around literature, rather than allow it to edge toward my personal experience, I replied, "No, fuck that, man. Yeah, I'm thinking of a book, but a totally different one."

Hashem (curious): What is it?

Me: *Song of Solomon*, by Toni Morrison.

Hashem: Don't know it.

Me: Toni Morrison.

Hashem: Yeah, I—

Me: She won the Nobel some years back.

Hashem (teeth clenched): Yes, I know who *she* is; it's just that I haven't read any of her work, including this Solomon song's book.

Me: *Song of Solomon*.

Hashem: Whatever. Anyway, what made you think of it?

Me (pleased): So check this out. In the book, there's this black guy who has a white wife, right? Well, one day he comes home early from work. Guess what he finds?

Hashem: What?

Me (breathless): Another black guy…in his bed…with her. That's what.

Hashem (indignant but self-controlled): Amanda never cheated on me—with an Arab or anyone else!

Me: That's not the point. She didn't have to, because you were always there. And if you win her back, it'll be the same, as long as you're available when she wants you. But what happens when you're not around one day? I'll tell you what. She jumps into bed with the next Lebanese or Arab or Muslim guy who comes her way. That's what.

Hashem (quiet, angry): You don't know what you're talking about. Just because you're bitter about something or jealous of me doesn't give you the right to talk about her that way.

Me (nearly hysterical): *Jealous* of you?! Are you kidding?! The last thing I want is to be in your position! I'm trying to save you from that bitch!

Hashem (still quiet): Watch it.

Me (almost pleading): She doesn't love you, believe me. I know what these women are like. As far as she's concerned, you're interchangeable with all the others. She's a groupie going through the male members of her favorite ethnic group one at a time.

Hashem (voice rising): That's enough, Hunayn.

Me (heedless): Now that you've stepped out of the picture, and her bed, if I stepped in, she'd totally wanna fuck me.

Hashem (shouting, pointing toward the roof's exit): That's it; get out!

Me (self-cast spell not yet broken): And after that, if you came back into her life, she'd hook up with you again. But not because she loves you. She doesn't. She loves the monkey in you, understand? The monkey, the monkey!

Hashem: GET OUT OF MY HOUSE!

At least my little outburst proved cathartic. In the days following the ugly incident at Hashem's house, my anger was in the main directed against myself for what I had said to him, displacing some of my anti-Kendra-and-her-kind sentiment. Also, the anger wasn't all-consuming; I found myself able to do other stuff again. Not calling Lewis just yet, but certainly paying more attention to books I had to read and assignments I needed to complete for class. And I regained the patience to watch TV.

A good thing, too—otherwise I would have missed an impressive and inspiring appearance by a spokesman for the Council on American–Islamic Relations. This rotund and jovial (white) convert, a honey-tongued CAIR bear of a man with a full beard and elaborate wraparound headwear he doubtless considered "Islamic," duly condemned the latest string of terrorist outrages committed by Muslims in various parts of the world. Then he launched into a monologue about the peaceful nature of his religion.

I was familiar with his estimable nationwide organization, which focused on American Muslims' civil rights and the general image of Islam in America, because I received its daily newsletter via email. Was never sure how I got on the mailing list—I hadn't subscribed—but I suspected it all went back to my articles for the *Central Florida Future*, UCF's pompously styled campus newspaper. The Arts and Culture editor had taken me on as an occasional film critic; I reviewed movies playing at the theaters. This way, I honed my writing skills and also netted a 40-dollar honorarium for each review, which generally ran about 750 words. The paper required its writers to provide an email address to be published alongside their byline, so as to facilitate "conversations between members of the UCF family." The only conversation I got came in the form of CAIR's newsletter, a daily digest whose compilers, perspicacious religio-cultural interlocutors and implacable opponents of stereotypes that they were, must've concluded that my Arabic name indicated a Muslim religious affiliation.

That wasn't the first time something of the sort happened. Earlier, I had begun to receive snail mail from an outfit calling itself the Islamic Society of Central Florida, doubtless because those folks at the "Society" tasked with community outreach had also lighted upon my name somewhere and cannily sought to lure another hapless Muslim into their clammy communal embrace. They sent me their monthly circular, which apprised readers of upcoming events, including the popular (according to them) "Islamic picnics." How had they gotten hold of my name and mailing address? Through a stroke of luck? Resourceful snooping? I had no idea. But what I really wanted to know concerned those Islamic picnics: *Were the genders properly segregated?* After all, we couldn't have the guys cavorting about with the girls, especially if some of the latter were bareheaded.

But back to the CAIR bear on TV. To prove his claim about the peacefulness of his religion, he related one historical anecdote after another in which Islam's Prophet Muhammad says the nicest things and behaves with the utmost consideration and kindness in his dealings with adherents of other religions, some of whom are his adversaries. At first, I found it selective and self-serving on the CAIR bear's part to cite only these stories and omit those concerning the prophet's less savory and even belligerent words and deeds. But as the smiling, smooth-talking guide to the world's most misunderstood religion continued his jaunt through epigrammatic outtakes from Muhammad's life, he began to win me over. Islam's prophet now seemed not only harmless, but delightful and warm. Cuddly, even.

As the interview with the CAIR bear drew to a close, and I was left with his wise words about the prophet, another member of the family Ursidae sprang to mind. If I had a teddy bear, I mused, I would call it Muhammad. How come nobody had ever done that? I mean, what better name could you give something so adorable and snuggle-worthy? This realization in turn prompted me to imagine myself entertaining female company some evening at my apartment.

The scene begins with the two of us sitting in my living room. The teddy bear, whose name I've spread far and wide to demonstrate to as many people as possible that the Prophet Muhammad deserves to be venerated in this affectionate way, enjoys pride of place on the couch: the seat between me and my special lady friend. The Iraq rug, of course, hangs on the wall above us. Hearing the hullabaloo just outside my apartment, the people pounding on the door and hollering "Allahu akbar" and "Jihad," I'm not fazed in the least. After all, I know that Allahu akbar means "God is greatest," a slogan that would find many a taker among non-Muslims, including yours truly. And jihad? Why, that just means "striving," as in striving for the advancement of society, or striving to ameliorate the plight of the poor, or striving to improve the lot of women—all of which is fine by me.

So I excuse myself, leaving my trusting companion to curl up with Muh the teddy bear for a moment as I skip my merry way to the front door. It tickles me pink that the people banging on it and chanting "Jihad! Jihad!" want to come together with us and clasp hands for some collective striving. If anything, this mob of excitable men—and perhaps a few women suitably cloaked in a modest and tasteful tent-like garment—will complement the vibe I've got going with the dishy distaff object of my interest, and join Muh in keeping us company on the couch. (Good thing I've stocked my refrigerator with delicious non-alcoholic beer in case of just such an auspicious occasion.) They'll help me and my special lady friend strive for a better date—more romance, perchance a little action once they've gallantly taken their leave of us and I've tucked little Muh in for the night—and, ultimately, a better life. I'm tingling with joy and anticipation, and can't wait to let them in.

I pulled into a parking space in the lot under I-4, and Lewis and I disembarked. Church Street Station, downtown Orlando.

I had always liked this part of the city. Intriguingly, Amanda had informed me that the original, smaller model for it was Seville Quarter up in Pensacola, which I had never visited. Sure, Church Street offered up a mishmash of places with disparate themes and music, but several charmed you well and good, what with the innovative interior design and bona fide historical artifacts. Lili Marlene's, an "Aviator's Pub and Restaurant," was adorned with aviation memorabilia from both world wars. Phineas Phogg's Balloon Works, a nightclub, featured items associated with the first solo hot-air balloon crossing of the Atlantic Ocean, undertaken by Florida native Joe Kittinger in 1984. (The two-story nightclub, which usually played disco hits, boasted the additional distinction of having had NBA star Charles Barkley chuck someone through a large glass window following an altercation—good thing they were on the ground floor.) Sometimes, what caught my eye wasn't necessarily of historical value, but just as interesting nonetheless, and even rather imposing. Say, the taxidermied grizzly bear and the pair of buffalo heads at the Cheyenne Saloon, or the beautiful stained-glass windows and gigantic brass cappuccino machine atop a marble mezzanine in the Orchid Garden Ballroom.

Rosie O'Grady's Good Time Emporium, the rollicking nightclub famous for its Dixieland jazz band, can-can girls, and 800-pound brass chandeliers, had long served as the centerpiece of Church Street Station's thriving entertainment scene. But it had closed in the summer of the previous year. Crowds had begun thinning out in 1999, when Universal Studios opened its own nighttime entertainment district on the southwestern side of town. Given the existence of Downtown Disney, another such quarter in yet another part of Orlando, the competition proved too much for Church Street to bear. Shortly after Rosie's closed in 2001, Lili Marlene's and the Orchid Garden followed suit. Club Confessions, a nightclub with a church's confession booth that had earlier replaced Phineas Phogg's, suffered the same fate.

Most of the establishments still holding out seemed to approach the disheartening developments all around them with a stoic attitude born of a deliberately myopic view of the future. In these places, the party continued unabated. But this went on in a self-conscious, almost studied way, with employees putting on a brave face and donning a party hat, joining the patrons for drinks or dancing, and in general acting as though they were the happiest people in the world.

Also, the music was too loud, possibly another indication of the willful obliviousness on display. The bars had worse soundproofing than the nightclubs and were never located a few steps underground (as was Tanqueray's, for instance), so their stereo systems mounted a sustained aural assault even on folks sitting at tables outside. And because some of these bars were bunched up together, what you heard outside was either a cacophony of widely dissimilar music or—should the songs merge instead of clash—continuous undifferentiated noise.

We could have ducked into Apple Annie's, a Victorian-themed bar and courtyard with music soft enough that you could hear yourself talk (unless a live bluegrass band was playing). But it was located in the same forlorn complex as the shuttered Rosie's. So we walked to the old train station—which stood alongside the new one—instead. The tracks were still in place, as was the decommissioned train, Old Duke. In the late 1970s and into the '80s, Bob Snow, the legendary entrepreneur who transformed this once decrepit downtown block into a renowned entertainment district, spent part of every year living in Old Duke's Pullman cars, which he converted into an apartment. Staff holdovers from that golden era would recall seeing the mustachioed, potbellied, and ever-sunny Snowman promenading about in a tattered bathrobe with a comely babe draped over each arm, Orlando's answer to Hugh Hefner. Now, rumors swirled among the desperately optimistic staff that Snow, who'd long since sold his Church Street properties and moved on to other business ventures elsewhere, would sally back out here on a majestic white steed (or maybe just shuffle up in his ratty old slippers) and announce an ambitious project to rejuvenate the quarter. But that seemed unlikely.

Lewis and I decided on something simple and inexpensive for dinner, even if it wasn't distinctively Church Street: Uno Chicago Grill. We went in, slid into a booth, and ordered one large pizza and a couple of beers from the waiter. Then, eager to resume our conversation, I began, "So, about what I was saying, we just weren't on the same wavelength. I mean, Kendra…"

"Yeah, I should've seen that," he cut in during my pause. "And I know you didn't really think much of her intellect. Which is understandable, 'cause—"

"No, it's not that," I interrupted him in turn, wanting to dispel any notion that I was a snob. "But when it comes to the issue of respect, it's just difficult to respect someone if they say one thing, and then behave another way. And with Kendra…"

Without divulging details either salacious or embarrassing, I proceeded to explain that despite the girl's supposed interest in Islam, Arabs, Iraq, Lebanon, and US foreign policy, all she really wanted to do was hook up with a Muslim guy. And how, naturally, once I discovered this, it spoiled things between us. Lewis listened to my account with great attentiveness, clucking his tongue and shaking his head at the disappointment Kendra had turned out to be. "How could she not know an Iraqi could be Christian?" he muttered when learning of that bit of rank ignorance. He even apologized for encouraging me to pursue things with her, and for having introduced us in the first place. I told him not to sweat it, though I felt vindicated—and grateful for such a considerate statement, especially as it involved uncharacteristically critical self-examination.

At one point, I circled back to the issue of respect,

reiterating that it wasn't a case of my deeming myself smarter than Kendra (I did, though that was merely incidental), but of her revealing that she wasn't worthy of my respect. "You know what I mean?"

Lewis: I sure do. I'm sort of having a similar situation with Colleen.

Me (surprised): Really?

Lewis: Yeah, well, maybe not as dramatic, but kinda like how, on the face of it, she's totally into feminism and all that, and expects me to, like, conform to her guidelines of what to say and how to behave—'cause otherwise she'll be all offended. But then she does stuff that, I don't know if she knows this, kind of encourages me to break out of that straitjacket and maybe not look at her as the independent-minded and powerful woman she wants me to see her as. Take her shampoo, for instance.

Me: Shampoo?

Lewis: Yeah, it's like, how can you truly respect a woman who smells of mixed fruit?

Me: Oh, I see.

Lewis (posthaste): And it could apply to guys, too. Which kind of shows that I'm the real feminist here. I mean, how can you respect a guy who's sitting in front of you, how can you concentrate on what he's saying, when what you really want to do is bite his head off for a snack?

Me: Right.

Lewis: So that's what I mean. Sometimes, the stuff Colleen does, it goes against the image of herself that she's trying to project to everybody.

I appreciated what he said, both for its intrinsic value and for its ballpark similarity to Kendra's fetish undermining her pretense to disinterested intellectual inquisitiveness. And, as I drove us back, I realized something important about Lewis. Not only was he a good friend, but he understood me better than I had given him credit for. As with Samer, part of this had to do with his background. In Lewis's case, it was where he grew up. With so many people of Middle Eastern descent living in the Detroit metro area, he had learned about some of their nuances early on. There were plenty of Arabs, many of them Muslim, in Dearborn. But he knew that Iraqis could be Christian, as with the Chaldeans of Sterling Heights and West Bloomfield, and that there was a good chance the Lebanese he came across were also of that religion, given the immigration of so many Maronites to Grosse Pointe. It occurred to me then that a provincial upbringing, at least in a multicultural part of America, could equip you with a fair amount of general knowledge. And if you're provincial, you tend to take it for granted that everybody knows what you know. So ironically, Lewis's expectation that Kendra would be aware an Iraqi could be Christian itself stemmed from his provincialism. My Michigander friend who had never left the States wanted to travel the world in part to learn about different peoples and cultures. But when it came to some peoples and cultures, he didn't need to do that.

Following the talk with Lewis, my anger (envenomed with a modest infusion of misogyny) dissipated, and I realized that my situation wasn't so bad. For one thing, technically, I was no longer a virgin. That circumcision my parents made me undergo as an infant (and which, to my good fortune, I couldn't remember) had proven beneficial after all. If I had the admittedly-natural-but-anteater-resembling dick, I now thought, the whole issue of my not being Muslim would have come up as soon as Kendra saw me naked. And in that case, I wouldn't have gotten even the truncated sexual experience I could now lay claim to.

Of course, one might characterize the whole coitus interruptus thing as having trapped me in a zone between boyhood and manhood, a no-man's, no-boy's land in which I had never intended to sojourn. But I told myself that I'd travel beyond this wretched place in due time.

When summer rolled around a few months later, Lewis went up to Detroit. Not just for a vacation; he wanted to take a couple of written tests necessary for acquiring a Michigan state teaching certificate. If he passed the tests, the certificate would be issued as soon as he obtained his undergraduate degree from UCF. Because inner-city schools in Detroit were in desperate need of teachers, and his aunt on his mother's side (herself a teacher) had said she'd do her best to give him a leg-up once he got his paperwork in order, he figured he had a better shot at scoring a job there than anywhere else in the country. He told me that when he graduated in December, he would immediately try to secure work as a substitute teacher that academic year, which would already have begun. Over the next few years, he'd work toward becoming a full-fledged English teacher—if not in a high school, then maybe in a middle school. After that, he'd set off to conquer the world.

Meanwhile, I stayed in Orlando. In addition to taking classes, I expected to meet Richard Stetson, a guy my father had put me in touch with; he had told my dad that he'd inform me via email about when he planned to pass by Orlando on his way farther north, so that we could talk about a job. Richard had lived in Italy for a while, where he worked with my father. Shortly after we moved to Lebanon, he decided to go back to the States, turning his back on oil and natural gas in the Middle East so as to focus his energies on the citrus industry in his native Florida. Since taking a mid-level job with a company in the field, he had risen to become deputy manager of a packing plant located in Indiantown, over in the southeastern part of the state.

Richard turned out to be a friendly, voluble guy keen on extolling the virtues of the company he worked for. His exultant manner and spirited speech—delivered over a meal of Bratwurst, Weißwurst, and unexpected but welcome Wiener Schnitzel at the Old Germany restaurant in Winter Park—struck me as having a rehearsed quality, given the uninterrupted cavalcade of facts and figures his high-horsepower mouth trotted out, as well as the lauda-tory adjectives he used to describe the company (growing, dynamic, employee-friendly) and the state's overall citrus industry (solid, dependable, age-old yet future-driven). He paused every so often to violently swivel his head from one side to the other and back, facilitating a loud and ex-tended snort so reminiscent of the report of a machine-gun that the most war-hardened Lebanese would've scrambled for cover. (I myself ducked instinctively every time, but he didn't seem to notice.) The snort impressed me almost as much as his selling the company in such ardent fashion to a green graduate-to-be hoping to secure nothing more than an entry-level position. I wondered whether, hopped up on Florida oranges he'd secretly laced with acid, he might've forgotten that he'd swung by Orlando to interview a guy willing to take whatever piddling post was offered him, and instead reverted to the pitch he used when trying to poach some big shot or other from a major company.

And what *was* the job, exactly? The meager scraps of information I gleaned from Richard's expansive characterization of emotions associated with the work in question ("the thrill of receiving crate upon crate of fresh, ripe, aromatic produce; the satisfaction of shipping them off to all four corners of a hungry nation") led me to conclude that it consisted largely of data entry. Based on additional woolly descriptions ("performing the crucial task of ensuring we have backup documentation for all transactions"), I envisaged a good deal of photocopying. Which was fine by me. If anything, I was happy that it looked as though I'd have something productive to do once I graduated, and thought it great that my accommodations were taken care of; the company had an agreement with a small property management firm that allowed its employees to rent furnished one-bedroom apartments at a discount rate. And during that year in Indiantown, I'd have some time to contemplate my post-citrus future.

Richard and I shook hands after finishing our meal, which he insisted on paying for, and he told me to get in touch as soon as I obtained the one-year work permit that, as a foreigner, I was entitled to upon graduating. At that point, he would extend the actual offer to me. I thanked him and for a moment pondered how I should feel about the fact that the bar I had needed to clear in order to get the job was so very low. (Richard, willing in principle to do my dad a favor and hire his son, had quite likely just wanted to ensure that I wasn't a dunce before bringing me on.) It was cool, I decided. After all, I had succeeded in presenting myself as a responsible, studious guy, even though I didn't get the chance to say much or demonstrate any kind of specific intelligence. Maybe the opportunity for that would come later—say, in between the data entry and the photocopying.

"I'm telling you, man," I enthused, "this is going to open Islam up, so that all the liberal and free-thinking and non-conformist Muslims have their coming-out party. The ones who've been kept down or who just didn't speak out because they were afraid no one had their back—not even America, the country that's always talking about freedom and democracy and protecting the little guy. Now they're starting to make themselves heard and taking action."

Lewis: Like what?

Me: Well, with Arabs, they're not buying the argument their rulers make that they shouldn't try to change their countries' political systems because that'll create internal divisions that Israel will exploit.

Lewis: Yeah, I did see this one guy on TV, he was a Syrian dissident, and he was saying that if we go into Iraq, Syria and Iran are gonna shit their pants because they'll realize they could be next.

Me: That's right, they're terrified. Even some of America's allies, like Saudi Arabia and Egypt, are afraid they'll have to democratize or get caught in a vise, with the people rising up from within and the Americans pressuring them from the outside.

Lewis: Okay, but what does all this have to do with Islam? I mean, do you really think this stuff could help to reform the religion or at least maybe—

Me (excited): It's already happening! That's what I was trying to say before. Some Muslims aren't even waiting for the big shake-up in the Middle East; they're jumping ahead and reinterpreting or even redefining Islam right now. They're talking secularism, women leading men in prayer, even gay and lesbian rights! Check this out: In San Francisco, some of them just opened the world's first mosque for gay people.

Lewis (back to his irreverent self): Yeah, that's what I'm talkin' about! The wait is over, my friend. Time to change the call to prayer; how do you say "God is *fabulous*" in Arabic, huh?

Me: I'm serious. This is a momentous—

Lewis: So am I. Sign me up right now. Tithe me, dawg, tithe me!

Me: I'm gonna muzzle you in a minute, is what I'm gonna do. And don't call me dog.

Lewis: Hold out your rainbow-colored, camel-feathered cap, Mr. Flamboyant Imam! I got a bunch of shiny riyals with no depiction of the human or animal form on them, and they're all for you!

Me: Yeah, listen, the significant thi—

Lewis: Assalam Alaikum, I sell 'em like I take 'em, Mr. Imam!

But he was listening. Whereas polls showed that a majority of Americans would support their country invading Iraq and toppling Saddam (many because they thought he had a hand in 9/11 or because he possessed weapons of mass destruction, allegations I found dubious but prayed were not revealed as false, as that might scuttle the regime-change project), there remained plenty of folks who opposed the notion. Not Lewis. He absorbed everything I said that day, especially the part about how removing a genocidal ruler from power is always the right thing to do. Had I doubted this, what happened a couple of weeks later would have set me straight.

Lewis had called and left a message saying that he had something urgent to tell me. Breathless with excitement, he said I should call him back as soon as I got home. I did—but he wouldn't reveal anything. He wanted us to meet and talk. Only when I joined him in the breezeway on campus did I find out what was going on.

As soon as I arrived, Lewis, who was standing beside the bench facing the bookstore, blurted out, "I broke up with her." My friend looked almost defiant as we sat down.

I knew whom he meant, of course, but couldn't decide on an appropriate response. So I just said, "Why? What happened?"

"Man, you wouldn't believe what she thinks about the whole war with Iraq thing."

This made me uneasy. I had a pretty good idea of what must have happened, much better than the time I went over to Hashem's house and discovered that my assumptions were incorrect. For months, Lewis had managed to balance whatever respective influences Colleen and I exerted on him, but then I went and ruined everything by giving him a heartfelt if reckless lecture on everything that was wrong with the people who opposed liberating Iraq. And of course that included Colleen, even if I didn't mention her and wasn't even thinking of her. So they get to talking about the subject. She says something. He gets all indignant on behalf of Iraqis (thinking of me at their fore) and argues with her. She refuses to retract what she said or back down, so the argument escalates and gets nasty. And then he dumps her. Now he's without a girlfriend and telling his buddy, who also doesn't have a girlfriend, how much better off he is.

"I mean, Hunayn, it wasn't just this time. There were times before, but I didn't want to bore you with the details. Plus when we hung out, I wanted to get my mind off all that. Anyway, she'd say it was rightwing fanatics and a bunch of oil barons, that that's the only reason we were moving toward war. But this time, it was different. I did what you said."

At this, I froze.

"Yeah," he continued, "you know, asking her to put aside what the politicians say are their reasons for war, which she doesn't believe, and just answer a couple of questions, like does she know Saddam is a dictator and a mass-murderer. And guess what? She goes, 'Yes.' So then I ask her if she thinks the Iraqi people should continue to suffer under him, because nobody has the right to violate Iraqi sovereignty and take the guy out. And you know what? She says, 'Exactly.' Can you believe that shit?! So then I say she's a racist 'cause she thinks Iraqis aren't entitled to the same rights we have, and she just flips out. She starts shouting and saying *I'm* the racist, and a priv-ileged white elitist who wants to civilize people of color or some shit! So that's when I tell her, that's it, it's over: You can go back to defending the right of Arab dictators to oppress their people and commit genocide while you go to the latest nightclubs and dance the night away because

Iraqi sovereignty is more important to you than the lives of Iraqis."

I couldn't have said it better myself. That was the first thing that came to mind when he finished. But then I felt the unease again. *What had happened?*

I had inadvertently managed to get myself bound up with an upcoming military campaign, that's what. A lot was riding on this war, and not just for me as an Iraqi. For me as the guy who had stumbled into convincing his best friend in the States that he should dump his girlfriend for its sake.

A few weeks later, we had both graduated, and the time had come to say goodbye. No drama or mawkishness, though. After all, we planned to meet up again soon. And we were both about to start our professional careers, which, while not quite an exhilarating prospect—given the particular jobs awaiting us—nevertheless marked the beginning of an important and welcome phase in our lives. Thanks to his recently acquired teaching certificate (on top of his degree in English) and Detroit public schools' desperate need for qualified educators, Lewis was all set to become a substitute teacher in an inner-city district. The money de Monet wasn't bad, and he had a good chance of getting hired as a full-time middle school English teacher the following year, especially as his aunt planned to put in a good word for him with the schools she had worked for before retiring.

Meanwhile, I was gearing up for my move to Indiantown. I had received my work permit from the INS, and informed Richard of this via email. He immediately extended me an offer and asked if I could start right after

New Year's. I said yes, bought some semi-formal attire, and began making preparations for selling my furniture. A few days later, he wrote to confirm that the furnished apartment in Indiantown was ready and I could pick up the keys from him at his office when I arrived.

Jeff had known that I would soon graduate and planned to find full-time work, which would have to be off campus. When the offer from Richard came through and I gave him the details that same day at Apollo's Lyre, he listened attentively, even though his mind had of late been on the increasing competition posed by Park Ave CDs Jr., which had opened in the Student Union toward the end of the previous year and was beginning to lure some of his regular customers away. As soon as I revealed the where and what of the job, he erupted in thunderous, almost triumphant laughter. Taken aback, I looked at him in surprise.

By way of explanation, he said, "Ah, yeah, Hunayn, now you gon' see what life really all about! Better bone up on your social skills, boy. Make sure you ready to be the smilin', backslappin' nigger in the office. Ha ha ha ha ha!"

Pretending—in conformity with the culture of political correctness I'd been browbeaten with—to take offense, I replied, "Excuse me? What did you just say?"

Jeff (eyebrow raised): Oh, no, excuse *me*, good sir, have I offended you? How about I have my butler fetch you a cup of tea on a fuckin' saucer and we retire to the drawing room to discuss this matter further? Huh? Oh, hold up. Look away for a second while I adjust my wife's corset so she can join us.

Me (defensive): No, Jeff, it's just that...I don't get what you're saying.

Jeff: Man, my first job, real job that is, back in Mobile in the late '60s, I was a junior accountant at an accounting firm. And guess what? I was the only black guy in the office. You with me?

Me: Uh, yeah.

Jeff: Well, what do you think I had to do to put all my tightass, suspicious colleagues at ease? I'll tell you what. Lots of gratuitous smiling and palling-around-type bullshit.

Me: I'll keep that in mind, Jeff, even though I don't actually know whether they'll feel weird about having an Iraqi there. I mean, you can't really tell before—

Jeff: Oh, come on now, man! Look around you; it's not like the rest of the country's far behind. And listen, I never thought I'd say this to anyone, but you lucky they mostly white down there. Not the ones actually picking the oranges, of course, those guys most probably be Mexican, but the people in the office. These days, if they were brothers, ain't no tellin' what they might get up to. You heard about the surveys that say we want ethnic profiling more than white folk do, right?

Me (embarrassed, lowering my gaze): Yeah, I heard about that.

Jeff: Well, you just might be one lucky cat after all.

Me: Yeah, maybe.

Jeff (serious): But let me tell you something, all right?

Me: What?

Jeff (fierce): Don't be shuckin' and jivin' for nobody, you hear?

Me: I don't think I know what shucking and—

Jeff: Yeah, you do. You know, Hunayn, you know.

120

## 6

My colleagues had indeed learned from Richard that an Iraqi was coming aboard, which caused some commotion when I arrived. A censorious-looking matron, short and stout and ponytailed, hair pulled back so viciously that her temples throbbed, demanded to know if I'd want to perform my five daily prayers. I set her straight, and word spread that I was Christian. The only black person in the office (several others worked in the warehouse out back), a gaunt old Vietnam veteran with trembling hands whose pressed shirt always had several Star Spangled banner pins affixed to it, interrogated me about my opinion on war with Iraq. By the looks of it, he had readied himself to ask that I kindly hold still as he decorated my forehead with those pins of his. But I told him that I would support any attempt at liberating Iraq. He looked satisfied and told everybody else of my unexpected answer. After that, my colleagues collectively lost interest in me. Jeff had been overly wary on my behalf.

Thinking about this afterward, I regretted that I had squandered a couple of prime opportunities for comical confrontations. Maybe I should've pretended to be both a religious Muslim and an opponent of any war on Iraq, just to see what happened. The Vietnam vet's attempts to Americanize my forehead notwithstanding, in all likelihood I would have had to deal with nothing more fearsome than the odd antagonistic stare or lecture, to which I'd have had the pleasure of reacting with total nonchalance.

My apartment, located in a modest two-story building not far from my place of work, was cozy and clean. And I had a bit of money de Monet padding my pockets, what with the modest salary I was making, which, unlike the part-time job at Apollo's Lyre, enabled me to go off my parents' dime.

But there wasn't much to spend it on. Indiantown offered little to write home—wherever that was for a guy like me—about. Named for the Seminoles who had established it (and gotten run off long ago), the place was quiet and boring. A hotel, the Seminole Country Inn, served as a historical marker of sorts, dating to 1926, when the modern incarnation of the town took shape. That year, a big-shot railroad executive launched a venture to turn sleepy Indiantown into a regional hub for rail transportation. He brought the railroad to the town, built a station, created a wide central boulevard along with neatly ordered side streets, and prepared the groundwork for it to become a major city.

That never happened, and little remained of the early boom, though the lonely train station stayed in service for several decades. The Seminole Country Inn, commissioned by the railroad executive and built in the jumbled Mediterranean Revival style, was originally intended as his mansion. In the decades since its transformation into a hotel, it had been restored several times, and now drew tourists who wanted a taste of "Old Florida." The Inn also housed a couple of dining venues popular with locals: the elegant Windsor Room and the more laid-back Foxgrape Café, the latter a place where you could sample some down-home Florida cooking all week and enjoy a brunch on Sunday, one renowned across the county.

After my first day, I rarely saw Richard, who was always either ensconced in his office or traveling to meet with clients. My job consisted of what I had thought it would. We were a packing plant, a much smaller operation than a processing one, which had the extractors needed to turn huge amounts of citrus into juice. A packing plant simply took delivery in its warehouse of the fruit freshly picked—by Mexican migrant workers, as Jeff had indicated —at company-owned groves, packaged them for sale, and shipped them out. I was assigned the task of entering the lists of received and shipped items into the company's computerized database, as well as photocopying all manifests and invoices.

The best thing about the company was its name, Almost Ambrosia. But there was no story behind it! Had it been up to me, I would have ensured that affixed to every crate of oranges, grapefruit, tangerines, and tangelos was a note bearing a smidgen of tasty history:

The delectable citrus you hold in your hands was initially destined for the gods.

But then a beautiful Floridian dryad who would periodically descend from her favorite tree to roam our picturesque state's untamed forests and wade through its boggy swamps decided, on a whim, to sample the cornucopia we had earmarked for our maiden delivery to Mount Olympus. Its succulent fruit so seduced her palate and enraptured her being that she overcame, once and for all time, the shyness and even timidity characteristic of an arboreal nymph. Installing herself at the bottom of the stairway to heaven, she blocked us from taking the horn of plenty up to the top and placing it on the horizontal conveyor belt to Mount Olympus, and insisted that all such sumptuous stuff forever remain the preserve of the denizens of Earth, whether her fellow spirits or humans like you and us. At that historic moment, we named our saporous citrus Almost Ambrosia, for—although perfect—it would never quite become the food of the gods. And from then on, we directed it to the many mortals with impeccable taste residing in the great state of Florida, in time reaching those with similarly exquisite gustatory preferences across the length and breadth of America—which we (and doubtless you too) have always known is God's country.

The sole person of interest at Almost Ambrosia was the security guard, who could at any and all times be found sitting at his desk, and was for this reason called Always There. No one knew his real name, and he had apparently long since taken to introducing himself using the sobriquet the office workers had given him. Interestingly, he was Always There, not Always Here. The desk at which he sat was located in a narrow, longish vestibule connecting the building's entrance to the lobby. The door connecting the vestibule to the lobby was always shut—everybody knew to close it after entering or leaving—which made those in the office feel that the security guard was out there, not in here.

I made a mental note that I should find out more about the guy on my very first day of work, when I noticed that he was reading *Britain in Iraq, 1914–1932*, by Peter Sluglett.

Hearing people refer to him as Always There spurred my interest. When, a few days later, I struck up a conversation with him as I loitered in the vestibule during my lunch break, it immediately became apparent to me that this unassuming security guard was an autodidact well worth talking to.

He expressed surprise at the fact that I was Iraqi, which indicated his lack of interaction with the office workers who had awaited my arrival. Sure enough, he introduced himself to me as Always There, and I thought I detected a certain low-key pride on his part in having earned the reputation of a stolid and dependable guy who manned his post at all times. I learned from him that, as far as he was concerned, his was a plum job. A retired sheriff's deputy with a bald pate, gray walrus mustache, owl-rimmed eyeglasses, and rotund build, the avuncular Always There had come out of retirement to take this gig as a security guard because, as he put it, "I was spending all my time reading anyway, and just figured that this way I'd do the same thing but get paid for it." His coworkers appreciated having a security guard sitting in the vestibule all day, from sunup to sundown (he was the first to arrive and the last to leave), and the company compensated him financially for the extra hours. "What more could a guy want?" he said.

Always There explained to me that he was reading one book after another on the history of modern Iraq (he got through one a day) due to the current crisis, and that in order to do so, he had interrupted another project of self-edification: consuming national epics. "I was in the middle of *The Kalevala* when it looked like the whole face-off with Iraq would escalate to an all-out war, so I finished it as fast as I could and hurried on back to the county library looking for Iraq titles."

Me: And, what do you think?

Always There: Of *The Kalevala*?

Me: No, about war with Iraq, if it happens.

Always There: Piece of cake.

Me (unexpected indignation): Really?

Always There: No offense.

Me: No, yeah, that's fine. But I mean, how come? This time, it'd be all the way to Baghdad, you know.

Always There: Sure, but the Iraqi soldiers' fighting morale wouldn't have changed, right? Last time around, the army pretty much collapsed. The soldiers actually *wanted* to be taken prisoner. And whenever that happened, they were all so relieved and thankful. Made you feel sorry for 'em. You remember, doncha?

I remembered, of course. A month or so after the locker incident with Danny, the US military and its allies, having softened up the Iraqi army with unremitting airstrikes, crushed it in a lightning ground campaign. As I sat in class pretending not to notice, the other kids would make smacking noises with their lips to mimic the supposed sound of shell-shocked Iraqi soldiers kissing their victorious American counterparts' boots as they begged to be taken prisoner, scenes we had all watched on television. It wasn't just Danny and his crew, but everybody in my grade. Even the girls did it.

And then it spread. To students in the grades above us, and also to those in the ones below us—a telling development, given that normally they wouldn't dare make fun of the older kids. Sometimes I felt that Maysoon was the only in person in the whole school who didn't torment me.

The hallways were the worst. I'd approach even the most cursory verbal exchange with immense trepidation, praying it wouldn't be followed, once my back was turned, by the sound that made my heart sink and informed me, "I know what you really are, despite all your pretenses."

As always happened when I recalled that time, a feeling of shame and humiliation came over me—both because of the Iraqi soldiers' boot-kissing and because of the subsequent mockery Danny and everyone else subjected me to. But what surprised me now was that, even before these memories came flooding back, Always There's prediction that the US army would easily dispatch its Iraqi counterpart had put my back up. I hadn't known that there remained within me a lingering sense of solidarity with the Iraqi military. After all, I very much wanted the Americans to overthrow the odious Saddam and his Baath regime, and proceed with the important work of transforming Iraq into a secular liberal democracy. That desire hadn't changed. It was just that I now became aware of a parallel wish: that the Iraqi army acquit itself admirably in the war I wanted it to lose.

Before any war took place, however, I had a "voluntary" interview with the FBI to deal with. Having read news reports about the Bureau's intention to request of Iraqis and even Iraqi Americans that they submit to such a procedure, I wasn't surprised when I received a letter in the mail informing me that the US government would appreciate my cooperation in an important national security matter. The note stressed that the proposed interview, which would be conducted in person by two officers at my residence, was voluntary, and provided a phone number for me to—voluntarily—call and set it up.

The interview went smoothly. Well, sort of. I wasn't sure which evening of the week the officers would show up; the person on the phone hadn't given me an appointment, but told me that two of her colleagues would come by one evening within the next 10 working days. So I made sure to tidy up the apartment the next day, and tried to keep it that way. But I missed something lying on the coffee table in my small living room. When the two FBI officers showed up a week later, I sat on the couch while they occupied the armchairs on either side of the coffee table positioned between us.

That's when I noticed it. No, it wasn't a bong, but a… BOMB.

A manila envelope with BOMB written on it in upper-case block letters rested on the table. Now there's one envelope you'd want to push as far as you can—and never open. But as it happened, I had been the one to assemble it as well as write the panic-inducing word on its cover.

The reason for this was straightforward. I planned to mail the envelope to a literary magazine called, for reasons beyond my admittedly limited ken, BOMB. The packet included several photocopies of cutouts of my movie reviews for the *Central Florida Future*, as well as a letter I had written asking the editors to consider having me contribute book reviews and interviews with authors to their publication. I had already written several movie magazines—*Film Comment*, *Cineaste*, *Movieline*, a few Web-only outfits such as Bright Lights Film Journal and Film Threat—but then decided to also hit up other kinds of publications. I went through this second round in a rather halfhearted manner, though, and didn't rush to the post office as soon as I had assembled a packet, the way I had done with the stuff I submitted to the film mags, where I figured my chances were slim but better than elsewhere. So that's why I had a manila envelope with BOMB written on it lying on my coffee table in full view of two FBI officers trying to determine whether I posed a threat to the national security of the United States.

The jowly, double-chinned, and wattle-necked old man asking the questions (his thin-lipped, quiet, and efficacious young partner took notes) must have noticed me eyeing the envelope even as he asked me my thoughts on Saddam and listened to my heartfelt denunciations of the man and his regime. At one point, he reached out, picked it up, and handed it to me, saying "Here you go."

"Oh, thanks," I managed. It occurred to me that he might have glimpsed what was written on the envelope, so I immediately volunteered, "Yeah, I've been meaning to send that to BOMB magazine," by way of explanation.

But then I registered what I had just said and my heart sank. To make matters worse, he gave me a quizzical look. *Had he not in fact glanced at the envelope? Is that why he didn't seem to know what I was talking about?* Quickly, I added, "Not to bomb a magazine, but to BOMB magazine. Because that's what they're called, see? BOMB magazine. Yeah, go figure, right? BOMB magazine. About writers and their work. BOMB magazine. BOMB ma—"

"Tell me, something, Hunayn," he broke in. "You don't mind if I call you that, do you?"

"Oh, no, I don't mind, no, not at all," I replied.

"What do you think of…terrorism?"

Even his partner was caught off guard by the bluntness of the question. Looking up from his notepad, his thin lips parted ever so slightly.

Not me, though. Composed, having long expected to hear something of this kind and rehearsed my answer for over a week, I said, "I'm against it. When 9/11 happened, I totally condemned that. It's inexcusable, whatever grievance you might have."

Officer: Hmm. What about other kinds of terrorism?

Me: What do you mean?

Officer: Well, do you support the Palestines?

Me (my turn to be surprised): Uh...you mean the Palestinians?

Officer (irritated): Yeah, that's what I said.

Me (careful, deliberate): I support their demand for a state of their own, sure. But that doesn't mean I support everything they do...some of them, anyway...to try to reach that goal.

Officer: Like what?

Me: Like terrorism. You know, attacking civilians and all that?

Officer: Hmm.

When the Coalition Forces invaded Iraq in March, I followed the developments—via the Web at work as well as TV at home—and wrestled with a swirl of emotions: joy that the now inevitable defeat of Saddam, and the US takeover of Iraq, would free my country; relief that nearly a decade and a half of a wide-ranging sanctions regime that had devastated ordinary Iraqis, especially children, was about to end; pride that the Iraqi army took a stand in Al-Nasiriyya and fought the invaders tooth and nail; anxiety that this might portend a long conflict (despite Always There's confident prediction), and that Baghdad would suffer destruction; as well as disgust and seething fury at Saddam for his cowardice. The guy had gone into hiding while expecting Iraqi army units to stand their ground and fight, even though he had prevented battalions charged with the defense of Baghdad from having contact with one another, due to his fear they might join forces to topple him!

But when Baghdad fell (with very little bloodshed, the defending military units having melted away), and when, amid the cheers of Baghdadis all around them, the US Marines felled the huge statue of Saddam that the megalomaniacal dictator had had erected in his own honor, all I felt was elation. It was over; Iraq was free. No matter that the craven Saddam, his sons, and top officials had evaded capture; their time would soon come. Everybody knew this, most of all the Iraqis dancing on and around the toppled statue in joy. I knew it, too.

My parents, who called me from Beirut, were over the moon about the liberation, and had already made a momentous decision. "We're moving back!" my mother informed me breathlessly. "Not to Baghdad just yet, but to Erbil," she said, referring to the capital of Iraqi Kurdistan, which had retained its autonomy and seemed in no rush to get sucked back into Iraq, liberated or not. "Since your father's company is already based there, the transition will be smooth for us. And once the Americans secure central and southern Iraq, which they're in the process of doing, and a government is formed, we'll move back to Baghdad!" she continued, barely able to contain her excitement.

The idea was for my father to get a job with the oil ministry. "He wants to make sure that Iraq gets a good deal, and that the people benefit, not just the international corporations," my mom explained. "Of course, I'm also looking forward to working in Baghdad; I want to do my part to help educate the next generation, especially after what happened to the schools because of the sanctions. And you know, habibi Hunayn, you'll finally have the chance to see where you come from!"

Lewis was pretty jazzed, too. He wrote me an effusive email following the capture of Baghdad. It reminded me of how personally invested he was in the whole matter. Unlike when he had broken up with Colleen, though, I felt relieved and happy.

"It's happening, Hunayn!" began his long and rambling message. "We're seeing it right in front of us. Freedom for the Iraqi people, your people, and a whole new image for America. America the liberator, the country that helps people get rid of their oppressors."

At one point, he seemed to extemporize a poem. Wasn't half bad. Even had a few rhymes for good measure: "After I chow down on a plateful of that delicious masgouf you told me your parents thought they'd left behind forever when they left Iraq in the '80s, I think I'll go down to my favorite coffee shop on the banks of the Tigris or Euphrates. Have some spicy chai as I watch all the hot babes walk by. Bring your backgammon board if you're able, my friend, and we'll invite a couple of those girls to join us at our table."

He closed with: "Next year in Baghdad, you and me, my friend!"

Strangely enough, for me, the liberation provided only a momentary high. After the initial brief euphoria, I realized how removed I was from Iraq. For one thing, I didn't live there, and felt this more acutely now than ever before. And for another, I couldn't relocate to the country anytime soon, even if the situation continued to progress from good to better, because I had other things to do. Yes, Iraq was finally free. This was tremendous, but it also forced me to come to terms with something I had never had to confront: Iraq was my country, but I had no yearning to be there. I might want to move back sometime, but felt in no rush to do so. Faced with this reality, and the fact that the war—with its myriad and exhausting developments—had ended, I tuned out the news. Iraq was back on the right track, and I wished it the best. But I had my own life to worry about, and could now go back to giving it its due without feeling selfish or guilty.

I stumbled around my bedroom hunting for something halfway presentable to wear this sweltering summer morning. (Note to self: Stop using T-shirts—even those in the jumble set aside for the wash—as jizz rags once you finish jacking off, because you may need to wear them again before you get a chance to go to the laundromat.) Never mind, I decided, I'll just put on the crisp and ironed dress shirt I set out last night without anything underneath it to soak up the sweat. After donning the shirt, followed by pants, socks, and sneakers, I was all set. Off to work.

On my way into the office, I stopped by Always There's desk. Exchanged greetings, asked him what he was reading (*The New Iraq: Rebuilding the Country for Its People, the Middle*

*East, and the World*, by Joseph Braude), and suggested only half-jokingly that we switch places for the day; he'd do data-entry and photocopying while I'd peruse his intriguing book. Then I settled in for the day's grind, tucked my soul into a padded pants pocket so that it wouldn't get ground, and imagined being in places devoid of grinding of any kind.

Actually, from the start, this day was different. Not in the tedious tasks I had to perform, but in my anticipation of what would happen once the evening rolled around.

I had a date. Over the past couple of weeks, I had chatted online with a girl I had met virtually through a singles website. Kate was an unprepossessing brunette, at least in her profile photo: hair styled in a bowl cut, framing a pale face with a vacant stare. She had a predilection for heavy metal and liked to read violent graphic novels of the fantasy genre. In short, not somebody who would have aroused my interest back at UCF.

But I no longer attended UCF, and Orlando was a two-and-a-half-hour drive away. In Indiantown, where my colleagues were all older than I was and opportunities to socialize with anyone else were limited, Kate was a find. And, crucially, she seemed interested in me (other girls on the website weren't) and in going out sometime. We agreed on Friday. I planned to take her to the Foxgrape Café, and even called ahead to reserve a table. She said she lived near the Payson Park horse camp and would give me directions to her place on Friday before I left work.

That afternoon, as 5 p.m. approached and she still hadn't contacted me, I began to wonder if I should write her with a reminder that I needed the address and didn't have a computer at home, meaning that once I left the office I'd be unable to check my email. Maybe I should include my phone number in the message, I now thought, so that she could call me at home.

And then an email from Lewis appeared in my inbox. It took me a few minutes to figure out its subject, due to my not having kept up with the news and his not unreasonable assumption that the opposite was the case. I had been in Indiantown for about six months. The liberation had occurred some three months ago, after which I had switched off. So I went online, read about what had just happened in Iraq, and returned to the email.

Lewis had gone into shock over a mob's lynching of six British soldiers in Basra. "The guys who did this aren't the terrorists we keep hearing about," he pointed out. "They aren't a small cell of assassins and suicide bombers, the kind they always say on the news are mostly foreign jihadis who came to Iraq to screw things up. In fact, they aren't even insurgents who take on the Coalition Forces. *These are ordinary Iraqis.*"

This much was true—and it meant that, in addition to my sense of revulsion, I felt unsettled and even a bit fearful, both of events in Iraq and of Lewis's reaction. When I wrote him back half an hour later, I didn't try to analyze the mob's rage or behavior. Instead, after expressing my shock at the incident and acknowledging its horrific nature, I listed some of the positive developments underway in Iraq that I had just read about in articles that had popped up alongside those relating the gruesome Basra incident. Improved security, reconstruction drives, the formation of an Iraqi Advisory Council, the legalization of political parties. After sending Lewis the email, I noticed that Kate had written me, and clicked on her message.

Now this was some pretty cryptic shit right here. She said that, after having thought long and hard about our plan for tonight, she found it "unsuitable." What the hell did that mean?

"It's not because I don't want to go out with you, but because it's a gossipy town and you never know what people might say, and what might happen as a result."

I didn't understand her reasoning. Even after I'd reread the short message, which ended with "I'm very sorry for being so flaky, Hunayn! Best wishes, Kate," it made no sense.

At length, the possibility that she had a jealous ex-boyfriend hanging around occurred to me. Still, this was pretty cowardly. I considered writing back to tell her it was no big deal, so that she didn't think I was all torn up about it, but then decided that such a tack would be more courteous than anything else—and courtesy was the last thing she deserved. Called Foxgrape instead and canceled my reservation.

By now, it was a quarter to six. I left the office and drove around aimlessly for a while. Then I remembered having seen a video store on the outskirts of town—just off I-95—when I first came over from Orlando. Of course, I had videos at home. After loading my TV set and VCR (along with clothes and the Iraq rug) in the car when it came time to leave Orlando, I had swung by Chapters in College Park for books and Stardust Video & Coffee in Winter Park for videos. But I was in no mood to read now, and my videos weren't the kind I wanted to watch.

I grabbed the first box I came across and glanced at it on my way to the counter. "Asses Assessed: Part 4," it read in large blue letters. The pictures on the front and back showed sultry-looking milfs in various sexual positions with younger male partners. Everybody was naked, though any visible genitals were obscured by a small blue circle. Back home, I popped the video in, fast-forwarded through the initial story setup and some foreplay between a voluptuous Latina and a beefy, long-haired Viking-type sharing a patio chaise longue near an outdoor private swimming pool, and hit the play button as soon as I saw action. Should get some wood pretty soon, I figured.

Nothing doing. It was all anal—which had long put me off, in large part because the asshole, unlike the pussy, seemed ill-suited for thrusting, however game its owner was. The Latina and the Norseman changed positions every now and again, but kept things backdoor. I fast-forwarded to the next sex scene, which featured a similarly bulky black guy and a big-titted, chubby blonde in a large bathroom with shiny gold fixtures. Also anal.

The third scene involved a tattooed white dude with a ponytail pile-driving a slender Asian cougar on the carpeted floor of a swanky living room with randomly selected objets d'art—everything from Renaissance-influenced plaquettes to small Persian tapestries to a Matryoshka doll set to a Nefertiti bust—adorning the walls and coffee table. Though still all about the ass, this was serious harpooning, no doubt enabled by the woman's slim build; here, the guy didn't have to wrestle a pair of watermelon-sized cheeks out of the way. It seemed pretty painful for the delicate-looking sylph getting reamed, but at one point, as though precisely to allay my misbegotten concerns, she bellowed: "Aaaaarrrrrgh, my pussy's so jealous of my asshole right now, aaaaaaaarrrrrrrrgh! My asshole says, 'YESYESYESYESYESYESYE—' "

I switched it off. This just wasn't my thing. Took a closer look at the box the video came in. The subtitle was in much smaller lettering than the title, and in a plain black font: "Analizer Rapid-Response Team Rescues Underfucked Socialite Ladybitches from Cock-Lite Suburban Wasteland." Well, that explains it, I said to myself.

A minute later, I had started the car up again. I didn't want to spend another night—and a Friday night at that—cooped up in my apartment. Just because dinner with Kate had fallen through and the porno sucked didn't mean that all possibilities for fun were shot, right? After all, I didn't need Kate, or any woman for that matter (in the flesh or on a screen), to have an enjoyable night. All I needed was a few drinks someplace with good music.

To begin with, I just drove. I didn't have a clear idea of where I was going, except for the fact that I wanted to leave Indiantown well behind me. At any rate, the decision to get out and make the most of this night despite the set-back with Kate proved somewhat liberating, and I felt in no hurry to determine a destination for myself. All I took care to do, as I tuned in to an unfamiliar radio station and caught an intriguing program I had never come across before ("Little Steven's Underground Garage," hosted by Steven Van Zandt), was to refrain from slowing down. During the commercial breaks, I told myself how much better off I was for not having hooked up with Kate or anyone like her, and paid no attention to road signs or the passage of time. When the program ended, I realized that I was lost.

No matter. Captivated as I was by Van Zandt's glorious blending of music, history, and philosophy, and in a strangely buoyant mood, it didn't bother me in the least that I had found myself on a two-lane road out in the sticks with woods on either side of me. There was just one problem; by this time, the solitude was beginning to grate on me. I didn't quite want to interact with others, but I did think it'd be somewhat relaxing to sit in a place as people interacted with each other. Unfortunately, there was no such place in sight.

Half an hour later, the surroundings hadn't changed. This wasn't good. I became convinced that I had found the road to nowhere. It actually existed, and I was on it. When I got back, *if* I got back, to civilization, I could tell anybody who'd bother to listen that nowhere was an actual destination with a road leading to it, from which I had just returned.

Finally, following yet another half hour or so, the woods began to recede. Soon, I came upon an intersection. By the looks of it, one road would bring me even closer to nowhere. The other led to a small gas station a short distance away, across from which stood a large but dilapidated single-story wooden structure. On its walls, "Miller" and "Budweiser" signs flashed in orange and green neon lights. I drove straight over. Parked on the gravel alongside other cars, and went in.

The place, dingy and dark, was empty except for a bunch of young people gathered around a pool table at its far end. I made my way over to the very long bar and sat at the corner nearest the pool table, which stood some 30 feet away. The bartender, a short and scowling Hispanic guy, didn't seem to speak much English, but quickly understood that I wanted a Jim Beam and Coke, and brought it to me. I sipped my drink while listening to Dire Straits' "Sultans of Swing," the story of an old-school London jazz band steadfast in its refusal to go contemporary, and felt nostalgic for a time I had never experienced.

Several minutes later, I took a closer look at the pool-playing crowd. Five guys, one girl. I was momentarily struck by the fact that one of the guys was black; all the others were white. But what really caught my attention was the girl, an apple-assed, suntanned eye-magnet dressed in a cropped purple blouse that exposed her midriff, and tight, stonewash-faded blue jeans. I wanted to coat her mouth-watering light palomino muffin-top with a generous layer of vanilla icing and adorn it with bright multi-colored sprinkles. Then, crouching and turning the muffin on its own axis, I'd nibble away nonstop at its overflowing top until a 360-degree revolution had been executed and I reached the point where I had begun.

She seemed most comfortable, moving with grace and shooting with a great deal of accuracy in the ongoing game that pitted her against one of the guys. The others milled about, drinking and talking and sometimes following the action. As for her, she cast the occasional glance in my direction, smiling more than once. The third time, when I finally felt certain that the smile was meant for me, I gave her a little nod and raised my glass slightly. But, feeling shy, I quickly looked down and busied myself with examining my drink.

A few moments later, a collective cheer went up. I looked in her direction. She took to high-fiving everybody standing around, having apparently won the game. The guy who lost now came up to the bar, pulling his wallet out of his back pocket as he stopped beside me. He was wearing a black T-shirt with "Mecca" emblazoned across the chest in bright yellow letters. "Lost to my own little sister. How do you like that?" he said.

Me (looking in her direction, catching her smile again): Oh, well, that's not such a big deal. I'm sure your friends would've lost too.

Him (chuckling): Probably. At least they were smart enough not to play. They bet me I'd lose, and now that I have, I gotta get each one of 'em a drink. Not my sister, though; she didn't bet. Didn't want to leave her poor kid brother shown up *and* tapped out, I guess! Hey, by the way, I think she likes you.

Me (feigning surprise): Oh? What makes you say that?

Him: She keeps looking your way, man. For a while during the game, I thought that her being distracted like that might give me an advantage, but—"

"What're you two boys talking about, anyway?" She had joined us, grinning and winking at me. "Brad, I think it's right about time for those drinks," she said, inclining her head toward the guys still standing by the pool table.

Her brother looked at me with raised eyebrows and an expression that conveyed the message "I know when I'm not wanted and it's time for me to skedaddle" as he moved away and motioned for the bartender to come over.

His sister sat down next to me, and I almost choked on my drink. "You all right?" she asked.

I nodded while catching my breath, and turned to look at her. Sexy in a gamine sort of way, but I already knew that, having seen her play pool. Now I noticed something else; both her earlobes were full and fleshy, with one longer than the other. I wanted to stretch that one even further by having her wear heavy earrings of the kind members of a Kenyan tribe did in a documentary I watched on National Geographic. If I managed this, soon enough the day would come when I could wrap that thing around my dick and put it to good use, giving the earlobe a proper function for the first time in the history of humanity.

She asked me what I was drinking. I told her, sliding my glass over. She took a sip and remarked that it was tasty. Said her name was Cheryl and asked me mine. I duly said "Hunayn," and she looked puzzled. I informed her that it was Arabic. Now she looked mortified. So, freely adapting a joke by Arab American comedian Dean Obeidallah, I added that it meant "Unarmed, peaceful, friendly guy who condemns terrorism."

Her face unclenched and she laughed, a seraphic little chortle. My heart leapt out of my chest and into her lap, flapping about in a desperate bid for warmth, as the terrible extent of my loneliness caught up with me. I felt a strong urge to hug her. Not in an amorous way, though. Impulses both romantic and salacious seemed to drain out of my system. All that remained was a consuming, urgent desire to make her fond of me. Perhaps she might clasp the back of my neck and tell me she cared about me, or maybe just hold my hand. I wanted nothing more than for us to just sit there holding hands for a while.

"Cheryl!" The voice was sharp and imperious. It belonged to her brother. "I need to talk to you!" he added in the same tone.

Cheryl rolled her eyes at me and smiled as she got up. "Back in a minute," she chirped.

"Okay," I replied. I took a swig from my glass, finishing the drink, and turned to the array of bottles behind the bar. Finding the bourbons, I let my eyes linger on the solid selection. Not just various kinds of Jim Beam, but Maker's Mark and the excellent Old Grand-Dad, in addition to the ubiquitous Wild Turkey. I ordered two Grand-Dads when the bartender came over. If Cheryl liked Jim Beam, she'd surely go for the even smoother Grand-Dad, which I had had on a couple of occasions at Knight Lights, but resisted growing accustomed to because of its cost.

"So, Osama, that was a pretty slick move."

I turned to face Brad, who now occupied Cheryl's stool. Looking over his shoulder, I could see Cheryl back at the pool table, flanked by a couple of her brother's friends, who seemed to be teasing her. Something was wrong. Not just the Osama bit, but the derision in his voice. Tentatively, I asked, "Uh, what do you mean?"

Brad: Waiting till you meet my sister to come clean about what you really are.

Me (hurt): That's not true! My name didn't come up when you and I were talking, that's all. Yours didn't either, but I know it's Brad because I heard Cheryl say it.

Brad: Yeah, and I didn't know what *your* name was until you started talking to her and figured I couldn't hear you.

Me: Wait a second, if I really wanted to hide my name, I'd do it with everybody, including your sister. But I'm not hiding it! Like I said, the only reason I didn't mention it in the two minutes that you were here earlier is that we didn't talk about my name or country or the college I went to or my job or any of those things.

Brad: Your country?! You mean you're not even *American*? Where the hell are you from?

Me (brief hesitation): Iraq.

Brad: *Iraq*?! And you think you can fuck my sister?!

I felt a burning desire to tell him that, well before he started freaking out about me and his sister, I had ceased wanting to nibble away at her muffin-top, let alone bang her earlobe—but thought better of it. The situation called for talk that steered him away from all thoughts of his sister getting fucked by an Iraqi. *What could I say to calm this enraged all-American guy and beat back his surging tide of machismo, which was only supposed to engulf Hispanics and other hot-blooded undesirables (like me and my kind), but now threatened to submerge Brad's inherently rational and cool-headed whiteness?*

"Listen, Brad, you got me all wrong, man," I said earnestly. "I was just making a little conversation." Trying to distract him, I continued, "What I'm really here to do is drink. Man, you wouldn't believe the day I had at work. I mean—"

"Shut the fuck up!" he cut in. "Who the hell do you think you are, coming all the way over here and—"

"Fuck off!" That was Cheryl, giving it back to her brother's snickering friends, who were apparently needling her. They laughed, and one said, "Do the wives get along up in the harem, or are they totally catty with each other?"

"Hey, guys," Brad called out, irritated. He turned

around to face them as another bout of laughter erupted, drowning out Cheryl's indignant response.

I seized the opportunity to motion to the bartender—it didn't take much to catch his attention, as he was looking at me with a sort of appraising expression—for my check.

"Guys, cut it out," Brad chided them.

"Leave him be, Brad!" A fuming Cheryl now began moving toward us.

Immediately, one of the guys next to her clasped her arm. He didn't pull her back or manhandle her in any way, but he did ensure that she couldn't continue to walk forward.

The bartender brought me the check.

"Get offa me!" yelled Cheryl.

It was a torn-off piece of paper with "$100" scribbled on it. Wow, I couldn't help but marvel, this enterprising guy knows just how he's going to turn the American Dream into his reality.

"You just stay there, Cheryl, and stay out of this," Brad commanded her. "It's got nothing to do with you."

He turned to me just as I placed two folded 50-dollar bills on the fake check lying on the bar. "Where do you think *you're* going?" he demanded as the bartender snatched my money.

"Oh, I was just thinking it might be better for everybody if I left," I said, trying to sound nonchalant even though my heart was hammering my ribcage.

"Guess you just remembered your terrorist religion says you mustn't drink alcohol, right?" he said in a loud voice. His friends over at the pool table, for whom this quip was intended, hooted. He did too, as Cheryl squirmed and said a few words rendered inaudible by the commotion.

"Yeah, something like that," I said without looking at him as I rose from my seat.

Brad's hand gripped my shoulder and slammed me down onto the barstool with such force that, to keep from toppling over, I grabbed his arm for support. But instead of steadying myself, I pulled him down with me.

"Hey!" he yelled as we both tumbled to the floor.

I scrambled to my knees. Leaning toward him and extending a hand, I managed to say, "I'm really sorry, I didn't mean to—" before a kick to my chest knocked me back down again.

Brad's friends rushed to his side. They helped him up, fussing all the while, as I staggered to my feet, winded but otherwise unhurt.

Splat! Cold liquid, plus a couple of hard ice cubes, smacked my face.

"Stop that! He didn't do anything!" squawked Cheryl, no doubt still restrained.

Wiping my face with my hands and opening my eyes, I saw the black guy before me. He was holding my or Cheryl's bourbon glass, now empty, in his hand. His friends were behind him, still fretting over whether Brad was okay. A few paces behind them, near the pool table, Cheryl was trying to break free of the dutiful creep who'd held her back previously and, mindful of his responsibility, hadn't come running up with the others.

Looking again at the guy standing in front of me, I noticed his facial expression: a mix of belligerence and disdain. It resembled that of the man featured in the large color photo printed on his T-shirt. In it, a triumphant black boxer towers over an opponent, also black, whom he's apparently just knocked down—yet continues to menace him. I glanced at the caption, which read: "Muhammad Ali schools Sonny Liston...again."

"You dirty fuckin' sand nigger!" he spat at me. This was not good. I almost wished I was the Liston fellow in that picture.

"Kevin, don't even think of doing anything!" threatened Cheryl, her voice by now nearly hoarse.

He paid her no heed and shoved me with both hands, having freed up his previously engaged one by setting the glass down. I slammed into the bar, letting out a howl of pain at the impact on my spine.

"Oye, mayate!" the bartender barked.

A puzzled Kevin turned to look at him as I straightened up and Cheryl shouted something else. A notion suddenly came to mind: Perhaps while Kevin busied himself with the bartender, I should make a run for it.

"You no make problem here, understand, mayate?" the bartender said in a stern voice, glowering at Kevin.

"Shut the fuck up, wetback, and have yourself a stinky burrito, otherwise I'll call immigration on your illegal spic ass," Brad said, annoyed but dismissive. He didn't even bother to glance at the bartender.

Stepping past Kevin, he addressed me. "Now, where was I?"

"Wait, that was a mistake!" I cried out in alarm, still thinking of how I had toppled him. My fear mounting, I wanted to explain what happened.

"I'm going to make sure you never even think of American girls again," Brad said in an ominous voice so low it was almost a whisper. He grabbed my shirt collar, yanking me toward him, and I ran into his rising knee.

"Oh, shit," I groaned, doubling over in pain—but acutely aware that when your groin takes a blow, the real agony starts a few seconds later. As I sank to my knees, Kevin gripped my arms from behind and pulled me up, keeping them pinned behind me. I now stood defenseless before Brad. In a desperate attempt to break free before he smashed my testicles once again and for good, I wriggled and writhed.

A moment later, nothing had happened. Not only that, but everyone—including Cheryl—had gone quiet. I stopped squirming, the silence having distracted me somewhat from the sickening ache in the pit of my stomach caused by the knee to my groin.

"What the fuck is this?!" exclaimed Brad. He was looking at me, but not at my face.

Apparently, a couple of my buttons had come undone during the fracas, and my necklace now dangled outside my shirt. ("He may not come when you want him to, but he's always right on time," Jeff had told me of the practiced savior in whose honor I wore the crucifix.) I didn't say anything as Brad reached his hand out.

"You're a Christian?" he asked, dumbfounded. He was fingering the pendant, low-karat gold but intricately designed.

"Yes. I am," I replied with newfound equanimity.

"Fuck that, Brad!" interjected Kevin in a panicked voice, letting go of my arms and stepping around me to get closer to him.

I remained standing, and upright.

"That don't mean shit!" continued Kevin. "We not

going to fall for that, are we?"

Brad, dropping my crucifix as Kevin stood beside him, shook his head and muttered, "I shoulda known a fuckin' chameleon like you woulda converted."

"It don't mean nothin', Brad," pleaded the now importunate Kevin, "you know you can't trust these people!"

Much as I wanted to clobber the guy, I couldn't help feeling sorry for him. In fact, I almost wanted to do something to take us back to the original situation before my crucifix derailed the merry little band's ball-busting party, just so that the black Kevin could continue to enjoy some long-sought camaraderie with the white Brad.

"Relax, man," Brad told Kevin. "I'm not about to let this bitch run away before he gets what's comin' to him."

He turned to me again. "So listen, Saddam, you don't worship Satan like most of your people do. That's big of you, and don't think I don't appreciate it," he added, pinching my cheek as if he were a Sicilian mafioso—or one or another of my aunts. "I just wanna give you one little thing before I let you leave, and I know you won't mind, 'specially since, compared to what you had coming, it's totally harmless. But for being so sneaky that you went and changed your religion just to fit in here and get some girls, you deserve this."

I didn't wipe his spit from my face until I had exited the bar and the door shut behind me. Outside, I knew that I could no longer hear them laughing and hooting. But my mind was playing tricks on me; not only did their laughter trail me all the way to the car, it got inside with me and continued unabated even after I had closed the door.

Getting back home proved easy. When your priority

is to get away from somewhere, you don't worry about where you're going. You just drive and drive. Instead of becoming more anxious, as you would if you were trying to make your way to a specific destination, you grow calmer with every mile. In fact, you simply continue until, without having searched for it, a sign that points you in the right direction pops up, followed by another one, and then yet another. Pretty soon you're on a familiar route taking you home.

Which was all just as well, because the long but gradually soothing drive allowed me to drift off into contemplation—and figure out some important stuff.

A long time ago, when our early human ancestors began experimenting with communal life, men and women were assigned very different tasks. For example, when it came to dinner, the women would wash, peel, and chop the vegetables they had picked. Then they'd cook them, sometimes garnishing them with spices of various kinds. Meanwhile, the men would venture into the nearby forests and hunt wild game.

Most men, that is. Some of the men would stay behind. The same ones every time, in fact. Their job consisted of helping the women prepare the vegetables, as well as lighting and maintaining a large fire to cook the meat of the animals that the real men would kill while hunting and skin right afterward. The women would often boss their male junior partners around, telling them to hurry up and stop their daydreaming or idle gossip. "Get a move on with peeling those damned potatoes!" one would bark. Another might follow this up with, "And where are those onions? You haven't filled out your loincloths with them again to try to look like the real men, have you? You know that won't fool us!" Guffaws all around.

Of those of us aware of our descent from the vegetable-preparing men, I reflected on the drive back, some surely grappled with feelings of shame and inferiority. But I imagined that others had made peace with their lineage. Me? I'd always liked vegetables, so I told myself that my lowly origins were no big deal. Popped my Dire Straits CD into the player and turned up the volume to try to drown out the barroom laughter still tormenting me, even though it was in my head and unlikely to be affected. A melancholic Mark Knopfler sang "So Far Away," about a girlfriend he has contact with only over the phone. I gave him an enthusiastic hand from start to finish, thinking of no one in particular.

## 7

Hashem and I were sitting on the roof of his building in Winter Park, with me having just given him a brief description of what happened at the bar in the middle of nowhere the day before. This was the first time I had seen him since my outburst the previous year, though when I had left Orlando for Indiantown I wrote him a belated email apologizing for my behavior and informing him of my move. He proved gracious enough to respond—saying not to worry, wishing me luck, and adding that I should come round and see him the next time I dropped by Orlando.

Well, that's what I was doing. "The thing is, all the signs seemed to say that the situation in the country had returned to normal a long time ago," I said to him. "What'd I miss?"

Hashem: Your luck ran out, that's all. Because it lasted for so long, you got comfortable.

Me: Actually, after 9/11, I was pretty cautious. But nothing ever happened.

Hashem: That's what I'm saying. Anyway, it's subconscious. The way you assumed that because you're Americanized and sound like them, you're safe, even if they find out what you are. Otherwise, you wouldn't have revealed that your name is Arabic and then made things even worse by telling the guy that you come from Iraq.

Me: Maybe. But what about you, though? Hasn't the fact that nothing happened to you since 9/11 made you let your guard down a bit?

Hashem (flabbergasted): Nothing happened to me?! You must be joking! Dirty looks, nasty remarks, students trying to avoid working with me on projects. Other than threats and violence—you name it, it's happened.

Me (chastened): Oh, I didn't know that…I guess it's worse in your case because they can tell from your accent that you're foreign, so they immediately want to know where you're from, right?

Hashem: No, that's the good thing; I get it out of the way quickly. They might become aloof or a little cold as a result—but never worse than that, because they don't feel betrayed.

Me: Betrayed?

Hashem (patient): Yes. You see, Hunayn, with you it's different. You sound like them, so they think you're one of them. When they find out you're not, they get angry at you for having fooled them and betrayed their trust, but also at themselves for having believed that you're one of them.

Me (thinking aloud): Guess it was a good thing Richard told my colleagues at Almost Ambrosia I was Iraqi before I got there. If they had suddenly found that out during the war, they might've thought I was a spy or something.

Hashem: Yeah, probably. I mean, what do you think modern anti-Semitism is all about? In the old days, European Christians hated the Jews too. But they didn't feel threatened by them. After all, the Jews often spoke another language, dressed differently, and lived in specific areas—usually because they were forced to. And of course they didn't have equal rights, so if you were Christian you felt secure in your superiority. But then, with modernity and all that, one by one the European countries started giving Jews their rights. And when they started assimilating, you couldn't tell who was Jewish anymore. So imagine you're a bigot, right? All of a sudden you discover that your colleague or your boss or your doctor or the girl you're going out with and making a fool of yourself for is Jewish. Imagine how you'd react.

Me (impressed by his knowledge, yet uneasy): Yeah, that makes sense, but don't you think there's a big difference between Arabs and Muslims in America today and Jews in Europe back then?

Hashem: I was comparing people's attitudes toward them and us, not the levels of discrimination.

Me: Right, got it. But...I think there's another difference.

Hashem: What?

Me: You know, terrorism.

Hashem (dismissive, pitying my naïveté): Oh, please; cut me the crap!

As always when he made this remark, I imagined myself in a butcher's apron, using a cleaver to hack away at a chunk of prime-quality shit—my own, naturally—so fresh it was still steaming. "Right away, sir," I told him. "How big and walnutty and bran-fortified a piece do you want?"

"Terrorism," he continued, ignoring my question, "is what powerful countries call any opposition to their policies. Think about it. Whenever any group opposes the US or Israel, the State Department immediately adds it to the list of terrorist organizations."

I did think about it for a moment. Like much of what Hashem said, it seemed hyperbolic. But I had a nagging sense that the statement contained a kernel of truth. Presently, this

154

crystallized into a specific memory. Several years earlier, a radical leftist political faction in Turkey called Dev Sol was busy brawling with rightwing rivals in pitched street battles across Istanbul, as well as fire-bombing targets associated with the Turkish government. In the midst of all this chaos, Russell Simmons called. Said he wanted to offer Dev Sol a record contract, which would give them an opportunity to strut their exciting doo-wop harmonies, honed on street corners in the roughest of neighborhoods as they dodged beer bottles hurled by rightwing rivals and evaded arrest at the hands of the feared police. But his offer came with a stipulation: The group would first have to change its name to Def Soul.

Well, as might be expected, Dev Sol took umbrage. And a response was not long in coming. The guys promptly harmonized a harsh (yet rhyming) refusal, which they then sang into the receiver. *Guess who got added to the State Department's terror list the very next day?*

Yet something continued to niggle at me. "Okay, but what about 9/11?" I asked Hashem. "That was terrorism, right?"

Hashem (defensive): No, yeah, that definitely was. I don't deny—

Me: So the people responsible were terrorists.

Hashem: Right...but you know what? We don't really know who was behind 9/11.

Me (confused): What do you mean? The attackers left behind will and last testament things, and Bin Laden later personally boasted about—

Hashem: Yes, yes, I know all that. But how do you know it wasn't a setup?

Me: A setup?

Hashem: Yeah, a CIA setup that would make it look like the perpetrators were Muslim, so that the US would have an excuse to go to war against the Muslim world.

Me (shocked): Is that what you think this is? A war on Islam?

Hashem: Not a war on Islam, but a war on the Muslim world, to bring it to its knees and make it subservient to the West. Starting with Afghanistan and now moving on to Iraq. Stay tuned to see which country's next.

Me (unable to contain myself): But that's nuts! The US is the world's only superpower; it doesn't have to attack itself in order to come up with an excuse to attack other countries! Plus, you know as well as I do that it's not like there's any shortage of people from our part of the world who'd want to bloody America's nose 9/11-style, to punish it for its foreign policies.

Hashem: That's correct. For what it's done to the Palestinians by supporting Israel, and for the Iraqis it's killed through sanctions, and for propping up tyrannical Arab regimes that oppress their own people, America should've expected a violent reaction, a punishment.

Me: Wait a second. You said 9/11 was an inside job so that the States would have an excuse to blame the Muslim world and go to war against it. But now you're saying that it's understandable that Arabs and Muslims would attack the States because of what it's done in Palestine and Iraq. So which is it? What are you saying, exactly?

Hashem: I'm saying that I believe it was an inside job to try to justify American neo-imperialism in the Muslim world, but that if it wasn't, if it really was Islamic fundamentalist types, they had a good reason—even if what they did was terrorism, which I condemn.

Maybe I should have expected such ludicrous conspiracy-mongering (alternated with unconvincing apologetics for Islamist violence) from Hashem, I reflected as I drove back to Indiantown that night. Once the shock of 9/11 and the attendant pang of guilt had worn off, he reverted to form. This didn't just entail scrapping the deportation exercises, but sliding right back into the old and comfortable anti-American groove. Business as usual, really.

And the slights he had endured? To him, they must've come as proof of what he had always maintained about the real nature of Americans. Hashem had gone from generalizing about Americans as racists to blaming Arabs and Muslims collectively for the 9/11 attacks to generalizing about Americans as racists again, and now claiming that some of them were responsible for 9/11—though he pointedly added that if it turned out Islamic fundamentalists were in fact the culprits, then the Americans somewhat deserved what had befallen their country. At least there was a weird sort of symmetry to all this. Maybe he deserved credit for remaining true to his delusions in spite of the obvious truth, a case of "keeping it real" by shutting out reality. Hashem was no fundamentalist, and hadn't allowed post-9/11 discrimination to turn him into one. Yet neither had he allowed the attacks' mass slaughter to permanently jolt him out of his willful paranoia and fervid concocting of conspiracies, or silence his self-serving claims about perpetual Arab and Muslim victimization at the hands of the US. I no longer wanted him as a friend.

But that wasn't the half of it. It was only now, following my experience at the bar in the middle of nowhere (and, ironically, Hashem's insightful observations on the incident the following day, before he got on the subject of CIA skullduggery), that I finally concluded something important about America. *The country had indeed transmogrified into Septemberland after 9/11, and so it had remained.*

And me? I had allowed my vigilance—so acute in the immediate aftermath of the attacks—to diminish, with disastrous consequences. To be sure, Moloch, who turned out to be insatiable, had left these shores and embarked on a blood-drenched worldwide jaunt: New Delhi, Djerba, Karachi, Bali. But his earlier horrific exploits right here remained at the forefront of some Americans' minds, and continued to warp them, specifically when it came to their perceptions of people like me.

I hurtled headlong into an ever-deepening sinkhole of depression. Spent the rest of the weekend lying on my couch trying to listen to music on the radio but instead reliving the incident at the bar in the middle of nowhere, followed sometimes by the disheartening episode at Hashem's. The week beginning Monday wasn't any better, though I managed to drag myself to the office. Once there, however, I did precious little work.

Not that I spent my time surfing the Web, which was what I usually did when not industrious; I knew I'd find it impossible to concentrate on articles or even emails. So I performed the usual data-entry and photocopying, but at a glacial pace. Also, I took a lengthy break every so often to stare at the numbers on the manifest or the computer screen. It didn't matter, since no one ever checked how far along I'd gotten in entering the figures for the latest activity at the warehouse. Every so often, somebody would pass by my cubicle and dump a manifest on my desk. Though I continued to neglect work, a lingering conscientiousness prevented me from relegating the manifests to the filing cabinets, as I hadn't completed "inputting" the information they contained into the database. They started piling up. This didn't prompt me to work faster, but I did have the presence of mind to stick a few in a drawer so as not to draw attention to myself.

A week passed this way, then another. Pretty soon it was a month, and, sure enough, another.

At home, I was no less of a zombie. I tried watching TV again. Not the news, but crime shows on A&E and all kinds of documentaries on the History Channel. For a good while, nothing stirred my interest. But then I caught a documentary on seppuku, ritual suicide by disembowelment as practiced by the Japanese samurai of yore. Known to most of the world by the Japanese slang term hara-kiri, the act was intimately bound up with notions of honor and shame. This impressed me a great deal, not least because an earlier History Channel documentary on the Middle East had informed me that, as an Iraqi, I came from a society obsessed with these same notions. *How serendipitous! Pack it in Japanese-style, thereby putting an end to your infernal depression, and simultaneously remain true to your heritage.* I decided to try my hand at it.

Unfortunately, I failed to locate a single tanto or wazakishi in Indiantown or even Orlando, which I drove up to for that express purpose. However, I did manage to get hold of a katar, a dagger that originated with the Tamil people of southern India and northern Sri Lanka before spreading to the rest of South Asia. This was at a general store called "Jaffna Goods" that catered to the Tamil community in the Dr. Phillips suburb of Orlando, after I'd exhausted all other possibilities and become quite desperate. The tiger behind the counter, who had no stripes and spoke with a funny accent, offered to sell me a cyanide pill when I told him of my noble suicide mission, but I politely declined, having no idea of the honor quotient in death by self-administered poison. Bought the katar instead, even though its horizontal handle—designed so that the blade extends beyond the knuckles of a closed fist, thereby facilitating a punch-like thrust—would make it tricky for me to turn it toward myself.

Back at home, I was all set for seppuku. Despite the fact that I had a katar instead of a tanto or wazakishi, I vowed to keep everything else about the undertaking strictly Japanese. Seated cross-legged on the wall-to-wall floor carpet of my apartment's tiny living room, I opened my kimono slowly and with great ceremony. When I unsheathed the katar from its rusty scabbard, the blade caught a ray of sunlight squeezing through the blinds, and gleamed in resplendent glory. After devising a grip that would allow me to thrust the dagger in the opposite direction of that intended, I shut my eyes to better savor the sweetness of the occasion. *Ah, this is beautiful*, I purred; at long last, the time has come to plunge the katar into one end of my almost flat belly and slice all the way across for the prize of momentarily messy though ultimately sempiternal honor.

Yet, opening my eyes and about to impale myself, I remembered that I hadn't written a jisei! Such negligence was inexcusable. (What would my sensei think?) Scrambling, I unearthed a note pad and a pen. Then I settled back down to compose a glorious death poem, as any honorable samurai wishing to off himself and release his spirit into the afterlife must do.

That's when it hit me. *I had no idea whether Japanese was written left to right or top to bottom.* For all I knew, it could be a scandalous combination of bottom to top and right to left! Well, this ruined everything, I lamented by way of a whimper. Hope of deliverance, so high a moment ago, now plummeted. All honor was lost. Shit, even the thrill was gone. And nothing could be done. Absolutely nothing. So that was that; instead of committing seppuku, I kept on living.

My coming to terms with continued living meant that I finally emerged from my depressive state. Now, however, a new problem presented itself. I hadn't so much made a conscious decision regarding my future as allowed time and circumstance to make it for me. Leaving the States once my work permit expired at the end of the year had by this point become the only thing I could do if I didn't want to run the risk of legal trouble.

To begin with, during my months-long mope following the incident at the bar in the middle of nowhere, I didn't take the GREs and fulfill the other admissions requirements set by those colleges—including UCF—that I had considered applying to. Deadlines for the 2004 Spring Semester applications had passed. That closed off one of two options for remaining in the country legally.

My departure became inevitable when, shortly after my failed attempt at seppuku, Richard indicated that he was blocking the second option: Almost Ambrosia sponsoring me for employment-based permanent residence. He sent me an email requesting that I provide him with a list of my duties and responsibilities, "so that we know how to prepare your successor for the job going forward." My slacking off at work had finally caught up with me.

I didn't mind, truth be told; I could no longer stand the drudgery. So I wrote Samer. In our previous exchange of emails shortly after my graduation from UCF, he said that he had just taken a job as a content editor at *The Daily Star*, Lebanon's English-language newspaper. He'd also moved out of his parents' place in Hamra and was sharing a three-bedroom apartment in adjacent Zarif with two guys he knew from AUB. That got me thinking; I now told him about my situation and inquired about job opportunities at the *Star*.

None of this meant that, had I managed to avoid slipping into that lengthy funk following the incident at the bar in the middle of nowhere, I would've wanted to enroll in college again and stay in the States. When, despite my presumed familiarity with American culture, I was made aware that nearly two years after 9/11, America was still Septemberland, I felt like some dopey kid at school thrilled to think he has friends, only to discover—after an eternity— that his "friends" view him as a gullible fool whose company they tolerate just to see how long he takes to realize they're mocking him. Even if my shock, dismay, and humiliation hadn't coalesced into depression and defeatism, I might still have decided that the time had come for me to give up on the States. After all, long after I concluded that everything had gone back to normal, and as a result lulled myself into a sense of security, danger came careening around the edge of a bar and headed straight for me.

For two years, I had watched Arab and Muslim Americans on TV whine about how, after 9/11, they were made to feel that America was no longer their home. Only now did I understand what they meant. In my case, though, the problem was precisely the opposite; Septemberland had come to resemble my most recent home, and reminded me of it.

And if that was the case, I figured I might as well go back to Lebanon. At the end of the day, whether Americans were going to discriminate against you or give you dibs on some booty (in either case due solely to your name or origins), they'd need some practice before standardizing their approach and attaining predictability. For the time being, a guy like me couldn't know where he stood, as evidenced by my inability to ascertain the nature of Kendra's attraction to me before disaster struck, my obliviousness to Kate's veiled message about my unsuitability as a date in Indiantown (along with the possibility that the reason the other girls on the dating site had shunned me was because they'd looked up my Arabic name), and my waltzing into public humiliation—and a painful knee to the groin—at the bar in the middle of nowhere.

Lebanon was way ahead of the States in this regard. There, after an initial unpleasant social baptism—such as what Samer and I experienced that night in the Saint Joseph's University area—you'd know what to expect when inserting yourself into similar situations in the future. As a result, if things turned ugly, you had only yourself to blame. That's exactly what happened my senior year of high school.

The first day of class, during an assembly held in the auditorium, we received some odd and disconcerting news. In order to help Lebanon in its continued quest to recover from the recent civil war and simultaneously foster greater interaction with our social environment, ACS had decided to mandate community service for all high school students. If, by the time graduation rolled around, you hadn't put in the required hours (30 for those of us who were already seniors, as opposed to 120 for freshmen), you'd receive a general diploma instead of the full high school one. Naturally, this infuriated us all. Community service?! Wasn't that for people who'd committed misdemeanors?

I put off doing anything until the spring, when I began to worry that time was running out. So I volunteered with Habitat for Humanity, which was building modest homes for poor people in areas of the Bekaa Valley near the town of Zahle. Working with them suited me for a couple of reasons. To begin with, I endorsed the Christian ethic animating the organization and wanted to help put it into practice. The undertaking in question was also one I associated with masculinity. As I told Samer, who had volunteered with Beirut's fledgling public library system, "I've never done this before. We're talking about work that real men do—like with a toolbox and shit. Just you wait, chicks are gonna line up to run their dainty fingers along my calloused palms."

Plus, I got to spend every Saturday night at our vacant little cottage in Zahle, rather than catch the bus back to Beirut. My parents had rented the two-bedroom house on the southern outskirts of the quaint Christian town several months earlier, thinking they'd take a break from the hustle and bustle of Beirut every weekend. But after following this regimen for a while, they tired of it, finding little to do in an area where they had no friends. As they had signed a one-year lease, however, the place would remain theirs for some time yet, so they were happy for me to make use of it. I rode my bicycle to and from the nearby village where Habitat's current project was underway, and loved the whole arrangement. Moreover, after a while, having a house to myself every Saturday night didn't just imbue me with a sense of independence; it provided me with a venue for what Rasha and I had in mind.

Because she wore a headscarf and came from a family she told me was quite conservative, I initially assumed that, whatever rebellion Rasha engaged in, she would ensure that it didn't go too far—in deference to her parents but also out of personal conviction. So when she and I were painting the interior of a living room one Saturday afternoon (to my dismay, they never had young volunteers perform heavy manual labor) and she told me that the previous night she and some of her classmates at a nearby college had had a "wild time" out on the town in Beirut, I pictured her flanked by a bunch of faceless hijab-clad girls as she gorged herself on non-halal cheeseburgers till the sun came up.

Yet very soon, I discovered that I had gotten her all wrong. To my surprise, her own hijab, which was often loosely tied and always a bright color (never dour black or bland white), didn't represent religious fervor or even any sort of conservative sensibility on her part; it was simply a concession—perhaps the only one—to her parents. And although she spoke almost no English, I found several things about her quite attractive: a peculiar facial expression (one that often took shape when I tried to make a clever remark) in which her eyes narrowed and her lower lip poked out to the side for something that was half tickled delight, half predatory molly grin; a manner at once demure and flirtatious; and curvy, child-bearing hips that filled out her jeans, which never needed a belt to hold them in place. Wessex-in-Lebanon's sly yet sassy village lass both enchanted and excited me.

Every so often, as the two of us were painting this or that room together, she'd announce that the time had come for a break. These breaks, which she forced me to observe, involved much kissing—again, at her instigation. Soon enough, we had progressed to necking (she had to loosen the part of the hijab around her throat so that I didn't get a mouthful of fine, perfume-scented Egyptian cotton). Then it was groping each other. Because the last thing I needed was a boner—someone could have walked in on us at any moment—I didn't let Rasha rub my crotch or turn around and grind her backed-up bubble butt against it, despite her rather strenuous efforts to do both. Meanwhile, I restricted my hand caresses to her boobs as well as that bouncy be-hind of hers. So it was pretty tame, overall. But when she told me it was too bad we didn't have a real place of our own, I couldn't help myself and informed her, in a burst of spittle, about the cottage in nearby Zahle.

"Well, that would solve our little problem, wouldn't it?" she said with a wink.

Of course, I felt a mite fearful, what with my awareness that getting involved with a Muslim girl from a religious family in quasi-rural Lebanon could portend trouble. Plus, there was the not inconsiderable matter of experience. Rasha, who was only a year older than I was but attended college and had her sights set on parlaying her volunteer work with Habitat into a job with another NGO, possessed a far better grip than I did on making out (my only prior experience with a girl consisted of some kissing with occasional tongue) and had probably already lost her virginity —or, knowing her, ordered it in no uncertain terms to get lost. Still, my desire for her, and my pride that she wanted to take things further, propelled me forward.

I knew that I'd forever remember the day. And not just because of the little tryst, now planned and confirmed, that the fast-approaching night promised, but thanks to something that happened before the appointed time. Following some torrid petting in between incompetent painting that afternoon, I provided Rasha with directions to my place so that she could drive over in the evening. Then I cycled back to the house to get ready for the big occasion. Showered and put on some nice clothes. Got myself a bite to eat—though all I had in the kitchen was oat bran and milk—after which I turned on the TV to see what was happening in the world.

The news anchor informed me that the UN General Assembly had just passed a resolution condemning Israel's decision to build thousands of housing units exclusively for Israeli Jews in the Palestinian neighborhood of Jabal Abu Ghnaim, which lay in Occupied East Jerusalem. This resolution censuring Israel was endorsed by 131 countries. Though some abstained, only three voted against it, with Israel and the US (the usual suspects) joined by the Federated States of Micronesia.

Which was another one of those uncanny coincidences, because I had swallowed whole an unsweetened Micronesian during my dinner right before the news came on. Not on purpose, of course; I simply failed to notice the pesky little bitchass as he splashed about in my cereal bowl. He was, after all, a Micronesian.

A couple of hours later, Rasha and I were in my bedroom. The smell of her body as my eager lips skittered over her neck and breasts in between our undressing disoriented me. Not that it was unpleasant—a bit like honey sprinkled with salt. It just wasn't something I ever got from the women in the handful of grainy and muffled-sounding (pirated) copies of pornographic films I watched over and over again, which the owner of a small video and CD store in Hamra had sold out of a back room before the cops busted him. Of course, legally available (non-porno) VHS originals, despite their vivid picture and crisp audio, similarly lacked the capacity to stimulate my olfactory senses, as they never came with the kind of "scratch and sniff" stickers I had read were distributed in US movie theaters screening John Waters's *Polyester* back in 1981.

Rasha, by this time hijabless (which left with me with an inexplicable sense of loss) and almost naked (which thrilled me), bent down and slipped off her cherry-red panties as her flattened raven hair slowly came to life and tried to throw itself all over her face. Then she clambered onto the bed. Lying supine, legs splayed, she instructed me to continue stripping, which I had stopped doing in order to better stare at something conspicuous attached to her body.

*Chick had bush.* Now this was unexpected. I trimmed my pubes regularly, and couldn't remember the last time I had seen real bush on a woman (or a man, for that matter) in those pornos I watched; when not shaven clean, the women sported the faintest, thinnest, and most expertly trimmed strip of fuzz. This copiously hirsute and vaguely triangular thing was different.

As a matter of fact, I wasn't certain that what I saw before me was pubic hair at all. It appeared as though a coal-black mink had curled up between Rasha's legs and fallen into a deep, imperturbable slumber. Hibernating, perhaps. Its shaggy pelt enveloped the entirety of her pussy, as if safeguarding it from me. Even a spelunker with the requisite flashlight strapped to his hard hat would find it difficult to locate the mouth of her love tunnel, I found myself thinking. Anyone else looking to go digit-dipping or clit-flitting would have to slice through hillocks of clumpy fur with a blind breaststroke, preferably aided by a basic knowledge of pussy radius.

Not that I was trying. In addition to the mink between Rasha's legs, another unfamiliar spectacle presented itself to me as I stood there, now completely naked but not yet hard, unopened condom wrapper within reach on the nightstand. Though lying on the bed, the girl was far from inactive. Rasha had unselfconsciously taken to pleasuring herself, rubbing her (invisible) clit with the fingers of her right hand while her left one roamed over her breasts and stomach and back again, sometimes squeezing an erect nipple. She had shut her eyes, though their lids fluttered every now and again, thanks to some pretty feverish clit-flitting. I stood there, naked but still limp, concerned that the mink would wake up and snap off her nimble little extremities—even more so when she began shoving them down its throat.

Then, eyes still closed as she continued to play with her clit one second and choke the mink the next, Rasha said, "Come on, Hunayn. Put your cock in my pussy."

Normally, just fantasizing about a woman prompting me to put my cock in her pussy sufficed to get me rock-hard—and well on my way to an orgasm. Now, I had a real woman telling me just that, after having led up to it by stripping, lying naked on my bed, and readying herself for me. So much the better.

Well, in theory. I had never fantasized about, let alone heard, a woman utter such words in Arabic. It seemed almost shameful, even as I found the forcefulness of Rasha's tone daunting. My mind reeled.

"Stick it in, Hunayn. Come on, fuck me," she moaned, her eyes still shut.

I stroked my dick, but it held firm—or rather, soft. Even my banishing thoughts of imaginary minks from my mind in favor of focusing on the real minx sprawled out before me made no difference.

Because I had failed to obey her increasingly urgent exhortations, I was expecting the imminent mutual awkwardness of Rasha having to come to terms with the fact that I couldn't fuck her. She would feel disappointed. That was natural. Maybe angry. Also understandable.

What I didn't expect was what happened. Although, looking back every so often in the years following the incident, I convinced myself that a few aspects of the sight I presented while standing there were mildly amusing, I still couldn't account for her body-convulsing reaction when she stopped twiddling her twat, opened her eyes, frowned, sat up, and beheld me.

"Ack-ack-ack-ack-ack-ack!" A concatenation of cackles. "Ack-ack-ack-ack-ack-ack!"

I wanted to crawl under the bed without her noticing, and stay there until it was safe to come out. Too late. Instead, I remained glued to the spot. Terrified of making eye contact with her, I fixed my gaze on my flaccid member, which I was tugging at with fury to no effect. Rasha interrupted her hysterical quacking to shriek in what appeared to be a gasp for air, snorted, and then nearly choked in a fit of giggles. I could feel her pointing in my direction, pointing at my body's unmistakable expression of its inadequacy.

Hours later, when they came for me, I was awake and fully dressed. Not because I expected them, but because after Rasha had gotten dressed and left, smirking even as she said "Don't worry, Hunayn, it happens," I finally stopped trying to get myself hard. Instead, I put my clothes back on and sat on the living room floor, quiet and diminished, my mind replaying what had just happened, my body cringing in the dark. At some point, I heard the doorbell ring. As I walked to the foyer, I realized that it was early morning; sunlight had crept into the room.

Getting grabbed and bundled into a car, which then sped southward down deserted streets toward Haush al-Umara, Rasha's village, stirred nothing in me but a sense of resignation. So they had found out. Punishment was now inevitable, and imminent. Not a big deal. After all, it couldn't be as bad as what had happened a few hours earlier. In fact, nothing could. Sandwiched between two young men in the backseat and looking out the front windshield, I remained as dazed as ever by the night before, and not particularly concerned with what awaited me that morning.

A short while later, I found myself seated in a straight-backed chair in the middle of a dingy little room, devoid of other furniture except for a scuzzy and sunken old couch a few feet away that was occupied by two of the three guys who had brought me there. The third one, who had driven the car, was standing in front of me and leaning forward, so that as he yelled in my face, just inches away from his, the pungent odor of garlic sauce—which the Lebanese insisted on slathering all over their chicken, beef, and lamb, as though intent on making distinct dishes indistinguishable from one another—assailed my nostrils and made me want to retch. I couldn't make out what he was saying, so involved was I in trying to protect my olfactory senses from the all-out assault of his acrid breath, and keeping the bile shooting up my stomach from flooding my throat. In fact, I could barely see the guy; my eyes had welled with tears, the way they did whenever we drove by landfills with heaps of burning trash.

Thwack! A slap across my face.

This restored my focus somewhat; tears shot forth from my eyes like water spurting out of a double-barreled Super Soaker, and I could see clearly again. The guy in front of me, clean shaven and with a mound of straw-colored hair atop his head, looked to be in his early 20s. He had chapped lips and a little blob of snot dangling from one nostril.

"You Nazarene dog! Who do you think you are?" he shouted.

Thwack!

"Our girls are a red line! Understand? Stick to your own filthy kind!"

Thwack!

By now my eyes had welled up again, but this time from the slaps, as opposed to the rancid smell of my tormentor's breath. Though my cheeks smarted, I felt no fear or humiliation. My even keel and distant countenance didn't go unnoticed.

"Are you listening to me, you son of a whore? She was supposed to have gone for a sleepover at a girlfriend's house, but we saw her parents' car at your house."

Thwack!

"Consider yourself lucky you're just a kid. If you were older, know what we'd do? Here's a taste…"

Thump! This last was a roundhouse. I saw it coming but did nothing. The punch knocked me to the floor.

Once the garlicky brute and his crew had driven me back out of their village and deposited me on the southern outskirts of Zahle, I started walking home. Soon, panic set in. What did these guys, who were probably related to Rasha, have in store for *her*? All kinds of lurid scenarios invaded my mind—including an honor killing. So I ran instead of walked.

It still took me half an hour to get home. As soon as I did, I called her—hoping it wasn't already too late.

She seemed surprised to hear my voice, in all likelihood having decided that our encounter the previous night was our last, and asked, "Why are you out of breath?"

Me: Listen, Rasha, these guys, I don't know if they're your brothers, but they might come after you. They know you were here!

Rasha: I don't have any brothers. You mean Omar? He's my second cousin. He has a couple of guys who follow him around.

Me: Well, get out now! Take the car and leave! He's going to kill you!

Rasha (chuckling): Omar? You've got to be kidding! He saw me at the supermarket just now and started shouting that I was a whore, so I sprayed him with the can of mace I keep in my handbag and he couldn't see anymore and fell down. Everybody clapped and cheered. Ha, ha, ha! After that, he said he was going to tell my father I was at some guy's house last night, a Christian guy, and that I have loose morals. So I told him, "Go ahead; I won't deny it if he asks me. But I'll also tell him that I had sex with *you*, Omar, and he'll be furious with you!" Ha ha ha ha!

Me: Okay.

Rasha: Hey, wait a second. How did you know about him? He didn't bother you too, did he?

Me: Uh, no. No, nothing like that. I just heard that... some guys from your village saw your car here last night... and got really pissed.

So that's how the situation got sorted out. Just as well, really. The last thing I needed after my experience the night before was to wrestle with the guilt I would have felt had Rasha ended up brutalized or worse for what we had done. Even if such guilt would have displaced the guilt of my failure to perform.

And Garlic Breath roughing me up a little? Predictable, given what he had discovered about me and Rasha. Neither when I was a captive-of-sorts in his hands nor when I looked back at his actions—as I did now, lying on the couch in my Indiantown apartment and contemplating a return to Lebanon—did his behavior surprise me. I had known that if any of her male relatives found out about us, there would be a price to pay. They did, and there was. We were in Lebanon, after all. If anything, I considered myself lucky to have received a relatively light punishment, and was thankful that Rasha faced no repercussions.

What I did feel whenever I recalled the whole mishap was mortification at my sexual inadequacy. Ever since the fiasco with Kendra, I would also sometimes wonder about the nature of my attraction to Rasha. Had there been a bit of Kendra in my lusting after a headscarf-wearing Muslim girl? And what about Rasha? *Did I even need to ask myself whether she was really drawn to my scrawny body and lackluster personality, or to something else about me?*

Fittingly, during this period marked by recollections of Lebanon, Samer replied to my email. He told me that *The Daily Star* had promoted him to online editor, and was casting about for native speakers of English to fill a couple of vacant content editor positions. The paper was willing to sponsor foreigners, thereby allowing them to reside and work in the country legally. He was confident he could help me get hired, but needed my résumé and some writing samples.

This was heartening. I wrote him back, thanking him and including everything he had asked for, and informed my parents of my intention to return to Lebanon.

Another email from another friend wasn't heartening in the least. Lewis, who had never responded after I'd written him back following his message about the Basra lynching, now sent me a new message. Thanks to the subject line—"What the fuck?"—I knew straight away that something bad had again happened in Iraq. My dread at opening the message was twofold; I feared learning of some horrific incident as well as feeling the sting of Lewis's somewhat accusatory tone. But, of course, I had to open it.

It was worse than I thought. This time, the victims weren't even military personnel. A suicide bomber had blown up the hotel serving as headquarters for the UN Iraq Mission, killing 22 people, most of them UN personnel. Among the victims, who included foreigners and Iraqis, was Sergio Vieira de Mello, the Brazilian head of the Iraq Mission. He and several others bled to death in the rubble for lack of an organized and competent rescue operation.

Hey Hunayn,

What the fuck just happened? I've been watching the footage on TV and it just doesn't make sense. I mean, the UN is there to help the Iraqis. Why did this terrorist and the group he's part of want to kill UN people? How do you explain this massacre? Can you even explain it?

Lewis

I had no explanation. After racking my brain for one over a period of several hours at work and then at home that day, I came up with the notion that the bombers might have derived their motivation from the UN's now all-but-scrapped sanctions regime, which impoverished and killed so many Iraqis for over a decade. If so, perhaps this was a one-off incident; now that the group that sent out the suicide bomber had exacted its revenge, no further action was needed. I told Lewis as much in my response. I also told him about my plan to move back to Lebanon in a couple of months, saying that we should meet up before that happened.

With a sense of duty but a heavy heart, I began following developments in Iraq again. The situation in the north, to which my parents had just moved, remained stable. In the rest of the country, it was a different story; in addition to terrorist attacks like the one Lewis had brought to my attention, armed groups were trying to fill the security vacuum. Yet I noted with some relief that ordinary Iraqis quoted in the Western media reports I was reading remained cautiously optimistic about their country's future, and tended to ascribe the sporadic violence, even when directed against their kith and kin, to criminal elements capitalizing on the chaos and anarchy, rather than ideologically minded people. It also came to my attention that the decent folk were pushing back against the criminals and the more dangerous Islamic extremists. At one point, 200 Muslim intellectuals and politicians signed an open letter urging religious authorities, the Iraqi Governing Council, leaders of political parties, and the Coalition Provisional Authority—in other words, everyone wielding official power—to take action against Shiite militias harassing Christians in the southern city of Basra and elsewhere.

Christians themselves, at least the ones interviewed by the news outlets whose reports I read, weighed the harassment they were experiencing against a lifetime of friendship and professional association with Muslims, and downplayed the phenomenon. One guy, a construction worker, said, "I am from a village near Mosul. I have lived and worked across the length and breadth of this great country: Mosul, Falluja, Baghdad, Hilla, Basra. Everywhere I went, I informed everyone that I was a Christian. No one told me, 'You are not one of us, you don't belong here.' No one treated me any differently; they all respected me and my religion."

On a particularly lonely Sunday just over a week after my email exchange with Lewis, by which time it had become clear to me that he wasn't going to reply, I felt in need of some company. So I popped by the office. Had a hunch I might find someone at his usual post.

Good call; Always There was there, as he always was. I feigned surprise at seeing him and said that even though I had been almost certain that the office would be closed, I wanted to make sure. Said I had some work to catch up on, and asked him what accounted for his presence. Apparently, the higher-ups wanted a security guard around on the weekend. He was happy to oblige. Did some extra reading. Got paid extra, too.

I went inside and headed for my cubicle. Passed some time by staring at the blank computer screen. Then I walked over to the vending machine and got myself a Coke. Figured that when I stepped back out into the vestibule and tried to engage Always There in conversation, he'd think I was taking a well-deserved break from work.

I found him still hunched over, engrossed in his book. After a minute of loitering and sipping my drink, I asked him, "So, whatcha reading?"

He looked up in surprise, having failed to notice that I had rejoined him. Then he lifted his book, which had lain flat on the desk, toward him, enabling me to see its cover and back. The title was *Embracing Defeat: Japan in the Wake of World War II*, the author one John W. Dower. This was interesting, I thought, recalling my failed attempt at seppuku. I asked what had prompted him to change tack all of a sudden and explore such a subject.

"Iraq," he answered.

"Really?" I asked. "You think the Coalition should use the US occupation of Japan as a blueprint?"

Always There (putting the book down): Probably. More so than post-war West Germany, if you ask me.

Me: How do you mean?

Always There: Well, in Japan back then, you had a country that had even less experience with democracy than Germany—which had very little. That makes me think of Iraq. Plus, you had a culture that, for several decades, had been based on martial values and warfare. But look at Japan today; it's almost the opposite. And democracy, which the US established with the help of some of the local elites, is going pretty damn strong.

Me: Right. You know, I keep hearing leftists say that you can't bring democracy in on the back of a tank, it's gotta come up organically or whatever. But that's not really true, is it? You can transform a society from the top down.

Always There: Sure, in theory. But in practice, the last time anyone did this sort of thing was a while back. Japan and West Germany, that was in the late '40s and early '50s, you know.

Me (a bit frustrated): What difference does it make? You can do it again, anybody can do it again. You just have to gear yourself up for the challenge. Why is it any different now?

Always There: The difference is the era we live in. This sort of project...whatever its objectives are...

Me: Wait a second. Are you saying that any and all reasons for occupying Iraq are equally bad?!

Always There: No, just that they're equally...tragic. Don't matter whether you want to do something good, like install democracy, or something bad, like set up another dictatorship but this time one that follows your orders. Either way, chances are you'll upset most everybody in the world. After all, regime change in Iraq is an imperialist project in an anti-imperialist age. And going against the spirit of your time is just asking for trouble.

*Well, let's hope that doesn't apply to this situation.* The same thought came to mind several times over the next couple of weeks, as I followed developments in Iraq. I could see that there was cause for concern. The Americans' disbandment of the Iraqi army increasingly appeared to have been a grave mistake, as it left hundreds of thousands of young men without jobs. The Shiites were provided for by Iran-backed political parties and their militias, but the Sunnis were left high and dry. Some teamed up with the radical Sunni Islamists Saddam had released from jail on the eve of the invasion. (He had correctly calculated that they would cause mayhem when the country inevitably fell to the Coalition forces.) Their numbers were augmented by arrivals from an assortment of neighboring countries, especially Saudi Arabia, certain of whose princes financed these groups' operations. And then, of course, American soldiers' heavy-handed and even violent treatment of civilians, especially in majority-Sunni areas, offered a further incentive to take up arms.

As the date of my departure approached, I wrote Lewis with the details. Was also sure to say that I very much wanted to see him. I held on to the hope that he'd respond for as long as I could. With each passing day, I'd tell myself that he might write or call at any moment with the surprise announcement that he was back in Orlando, having flown down for the express purpose of seeing me off.

No such luck. My last full day in Septemberland drew to a close and I still hadn't heard from him. I knew now that it was too late; he wasn't going to write me. Tomorrow I would drop off the keys to my apartment at the office. Next, I'd drive to Orlando, stopping at Carmax to finalize the sale of my car (for a song), which I had discussed with them when in town a week earlier. Then I'd order a cab and go to the airport.

Taking stock of my situation, there was no escape from admitting that I was leaving this place without having accomplished either of my missions. At least I got halfway to the finish line with the one I had set before 9/11. But following that aborted sexual encounter with Kendra, I hadn't come close to either hooking a girl as my companion or simply fucking one to completion. Of course, my attempts to reach the other goal, which I set for myself following 9/11 and forthwith assigned priority, proved a dismal failure. Navigating my way through the protean muck in which Septemberland was awash clearly fell beyond my abilities. *The time had come for me to move to a place I understood.*

In my dream that final night in Septemberland, I had a friend. His name was Jihad, and he was traveling with me. At some point, making our way through the bustling throngs at the Orlando airport, we got separated. I looked and looked, including in every nook and cranny of our gate, but couldn't find him anywhere. The final call for us to board the plane came over the public address system. I began to panic. I had to find my friend before it became too late and we missed our flight! Cupping my hands around my mouth and standing in the middle of the long concourse, gates on either side of me and travelers everywhere, I shouted at the top of my voice, "Jihad! Jihad! Jihad!"

People began to scurry away from me, but I paid them no heed. Instead, I continued hollering while rotating in the same spot, the better to make myself heard to everyone. This also served to give me a panoramic view of my surroundings. Now I saw swarms of uniformed men and women, guns drawn, sprinting toward me from all directions. Judging by the movement of their lips, they were calling out to me. But I couldn't hear them. And for some reason, I also couldn't stop shouting "Jihad!"—even when they pulled up a few feet away and trained their weapons on me. As the bullets simultaneously pierced all my vital organs, I woke with a start.

# PART II
# SEPTEMBERWORLD

8

From the Mayflower Hotel (where my parents had put me up, taking a room for themselves on the same floor for six days before returning to Erbil), I walked over to Hamra Street and caught a cab to Gemmayzeh for my job interview with *The Daily Star*. Samer, who had picked me up from the airport a week earlier and insisted on playing Mark Morrison's "Return of the Mack" over and over again on his car's CD player during the drive to the Mayflower—until it seemed that Morrison himself tired of singing it—had paved the way for my meeting with the new editor-in-chief of the paper, a guy named Nabil Tartousi, by vouching for my skills and competence.

Tartousi, who had a lanky body out of which grew a brontosaurus neck topped by a teeny noggin, ushered me into his oversized yet otherwise featureless office. As soon as we sat down, he proceeded to speak expansively, in heavily Lebanese-accented and faintly embarrassing English—made all the worse by its clichés, mixed metaphors, and outright mistakes—about his plans. He wanted to transform "TDS," as he called the paper (doubtless uncomfortable with its tabloid-redolent name), into a region-wide publication, and its website into the Middle East's most popular news portal. "We are taking the region by storm and grabbing the bull by its horns so that we make TDS the biggest name in the business that is rolling off everybody's tongue if they are somebody. And this is why we need a 1,000 percent effort from our team, so that we higher our chances of success in the new dynamic and accelerating and booming market that is our target which we have put our eye on."

I wasn't sure it helped that, hearing me converse in English, Tartousi could probably tell I was a native speaker. Nor did it make any obvious impression when I mentioned my knowledge of Arabic, which would prove handy if I wanted to consult Arabic-language sources of articles I was assigned to edit. When I spoke, he seemed bored. His wee head soared upward, swooped down, or lunged this way and that in desperate search of something to peer at in the oppressively bare office. Or else he just looked at me with an absent expression and nodded mechanically. Meanwhile, I couldn't take my eyes off the stubbly isthmus of prematurely slackening flesh connecting that bobbing head with his torso—and did some nodding myself as my gaze locked on to his oscillating Adam's apple.

But he did ask me if I was willing to start work in a week, and I said sure.

My next appointment was a social one—with Nadia, a former high school classmate whom I hadn't seen since my first visit back to Lebanon during my freshman year at UCF. Most of the handful of classmates I had been friendly with and now considered looking up had left the country. But Samer told me that Nadia, by this time separated from her husband and the mother of a little girl, was still around, and that when he mentioned to her that I was back in town she said to say hi and ask me to please call her.

I wasn't surprised that she had separated from her husband. I'd never met him, but had long known from

Samer that she didn't love the guy. She agreed to marry him only because he was the most physically attractive of the small crop of suitors her parents had approved, and also because—she confided to Samer—she was aching to have sex. Unlike many women of our generation and socioeconomic class, Nadia had decided to remain a virgin until marriage. Not for ideological reasons, but due to the shock, embarrassment, and anger her conservative Druze family would experience should they discover that she had had sex before marriage. She was probably also aware that those young men her parents considered eligible prospects would themselves be somewhat traditional and want a virginal wife. So she chose the man, a distant cousin, who most appealed to her out of the few who had emerged successful from her parents' stringent vetting process.

My sophomore year at UCF, when I was in Lebanon on vacation, I asked Samer why newly married Nadia hadn't rebelled against her parents and found someone she loved, even if he wasn't Druze like her and her family.

"Because they'd have disowned her," he replied.

"Did they own her in the first place?" I asked.

"Well, that's the expression, Hunayn."

Following her marriage, Nadia voluntarily dropped out of college without having earned a degree in order to become a housewife and later a mother. Things went smoothly enough for a couple of years, but eventually the relationship foundered. She was too passionate and headstrong to accept an arrangement of convenience for the rest of her life. Now she lived with her daughter and a nanny in an exclusive apartment building—complete with a uniformed doorman, a concierge seated behind a massive marble desk, and an in-house maintenance team—at the end of Hamra, in an otherwise run-down neighborhood some distance from the main street. Her husband, with whom she was still on good terms, supported them financially and visited a few times a year (from Doha, Qatar, where he worked as an assistant hotel manager). Samer said her parents probably also supported her, as they came from old money and could afford to.

Nadia greeted me with an affectionate hug and kisses on both cheeks. She hadn't changed much. Never pretty in the classical sense, what with a chunky figure (plus point: thick and bulging everywhere it counts, as good old Jeff would say) as well as a large gap between her two front teeth, her signature personality trait had always been a spiritedness that nothing could extinguish—not even a life-changing decision to defer to her parents' conservatism and sectarian hang-ups—and a disarmingly chummy attitude with the guys. Indeed, my second instinct upon meeting her was to give her shoulder a little jab and suggest she join me and Samer for a couple of drinks. (My first instinct was to wrestle her to the floor and immediately have sex with her.) She sat me on the couch in the capacious and well-appointed living room, got us a couple of bottles of beer from the kitchen, and asked me what I had been up to all this time. We talked about some of the stuff we had done over the past few years, and I pretended to know only the outlines of her story, which she related to me—so far as I could tell—in almost as much detail as she had done with Samer. One thing she told me that I hadn't known, however, and which impressed me a great deal, was that she was back at AUB, studying to finish her undergraduate degree in business administration.

Then we began to revisit some of our experiences in high school, with Nadia waxing nostalgic. "Ah, those were the days, weren't they, Hunayn? You know, I look back on that period as so great, even though at the time I was in such a hurry for it to end," she said wistfully, applying moisturizing cream to one hand and then the other. "What? My palms are dry. What are you grinning at?"

Me: Still with the hand cream, huh? I was just remembering how some of the guys in our class freshman year would say the reason you did that was because you gave all the seniors handjobs, and we had to figure out how to get in on that game now rather than wait three years.

Nadia: They used to say that?!

Me: Yeah, and then our senior year finally rolled around and nothing happened.

Nadia: Ha, well, serves you right!

Just then, the Filipina nanny came in and told "Madame" that her daughter Maha was ready for bed. Nadia excused herself and left the living room, telling me she'd be back shortly. As I sat there waiting for her to put her kid to bed, Bruce Springsteen's "Glory Days" came to mind; I couldn't quite determine how I felt about that. I wasn't old—I knew that much. And that meant I had time to come into my own and live my life. But girls like Nadia went and brought a new life into this world before fulfilling their own. And maybe that meant they never would. Could the joys of parenthood (and, in cases other than Nadia's, marriage too) compensate for the stunting of one's self-realization?

She returned a few minutes later and said, "So listen, Hunayn, you wanna watch a movie?"

Me: Actually, I was wondering if you'd like to come out with me and Samer for a bit. We were thinking of going to Gemmayzeh for drinks.

Nadia: Oh, come on, you know I can't do that. I've got Maha.

Me: But she's asleep.

Nadia: Yeah, but she could wake up. Duh!

Me: Well, the nanny can take care of her, right?

Nadia: No, she wakes up, she wants Mama.

Me: I see.

Nadia: You know, Hunayn, having a kid changes everything. Especially if you're a woman. My priority in life is to provide my daughter with a loving and nurturing home environment, so that she grows up feeling safe and secure.

Me: Your maternal instincts move me deeply.

Nadia: I'm serious!

Me: So am I. In fact, I can't help but notice that your figure has that fecund, child-bearing quality that—

Nadia: Oh, shut up, Hunayn. Anyway, we could watch a DVD if you want.

Me: What do you have in mind?

Nadia: I just got a copy of *Monster*, pirated but supposed to be very good quality. You know, the one where Charlize Theron plays a serial killer? Based on a true story. Filmed in Florida, by the way, where all the murders took place.

Me: Actually, I'm not a big fan of movies about serial killers.

Nadia: Really?

Me: Yeah, 'fraid so. To tell you the truth, I don't even like serial killers themselves that much.

Nadia (laughing): Okay, you win, Hunayn.

We decided to call it an evening. She hugged and kissed me goodbye, making me promise to come see her again soon. By this time, it was night. With each step I took away from the building's plush lobby, outside of which stood the sole functioning lamppost for at least a block in any direction, the blackness came closer to enveloping me. The receding light made for a curious gloaming. Not the kind that serves as muse for a maudlin poet, one desperate to fling back the darkling canopy a merciless firmament unfurls over the land every time the poor sod sits down to another insipid TV dinner without female company, but the sort that gives an egalitarian-minded nighttime pedestrian a fit of pique. The farther I got from Nadia's building, the more I kept my squinting eyes trained on the ground to avoid tripping over anything as I wended my way back to Hamra Street.

In one sense, the fact that Tartousi did virtually no work was a blessing; with his spotty English, he'd almost certainly have ruined any articles he tried to edit. But you'd think he'd write the paper's short daily editorial and pass it on to one or another of the senior editors to correct and polish, rather than saddle them with the job of composing the pieces, especially as we were a small operation, not a major publication with a large staff. No such luck. He farmed out the task to those already burdened editors, contenting himself with specifying the topic they should address and the position they should take. The rest of the time, he sat in his ridiculously roomy office surfing Middle Eastern news websites and comparing their coverage to that of the *Star*. When he stumbled upon an item the guys who pulled articles from the wire services had yet to upload onto our site, he would remain seated at his desk, but his elongated neck, now undulating furiously, would snake its way out of his office, through the short but winding hallway, and into the newsroom, where he would berate the poor souls at length.

Because Tartousi had assigned me to the print edition, I wouldn't get the chance to work with, or even at the same time as, Samer. The team he headed up as online editor was tasked with contributing news stories and features to the website throughout the day. Samer and his crew would start at eight in the morning and break off at 5 p.m., which is when the members of the larger print edition team would file in, remaining in the office until 1 a.m. I would have the misfortune of interacting on a frequent basis with one Harry Effendi, my immediate superior, who oversaw both the Lebanon and Middle East desks, across which I edited news articles and longer feature stories.

Between a portly gentleman and a fat slob lies a very fine line. Effendi, who was in his late 20s, stood on the wrong side of that line every day, thanks in large part to his slovenly eating habits, which included speaking with his cavernous mouth stuffed full of food and dribbling a mixture of ketchup and mayonnaise down his chin and onto an unlaundered shirt half tucked into pants he'd never button up at the top. Almost as repulsive was his cadaverous pallor, the likes of which would put the northernmost European vampire to shame, a filthy, matted mass of hair the ochroid hue of a desiccated plant, and a rumbling, phlegmy cough doubtless exacerbated by his periodic smoking, which he'd tromp off and do by the elevator every hour without fail.

Effendi's chief personality trait, smarminess toward the editor-in-chief, was just as disagreeable. He laughed at all of Tartousi's lame jokes, adopted his views on Lebanese and regional affairs, and otherwise brownnosed him constantly. Yet I sometimes suspected this wasn't so much a calculated ploy to ingratiate himself with his boss as the manifestation of a psychological need to revere a figure of authority, whether in the workplace or at home. Effendi idolized his father—with whom he still lived—the way a child might, and often tried to convince his colleagues of the man's supposed myriad and extraordinary abilities.

It didn't work with most of us, but he did (ostensibly) succeed with one of our feature writers, Brigitte, a gawky, spindly-legged San Francisco transplant with a daddy longlegs-style gait that made you think her wobbly knees would buckle at any moment, a succession of high-pitched yelps for a laugh, and an opportunistic inclination to curry favor with Effendi at every turn. For one of her articles, Brigitte wrote a sycophantic profile of a Beirut doctor who treated patients with sleep disorders. Par for the course insofar as her lazy modus operandi was concerned (most of her articles were puff pieces), except that the doctor was Effendi's father. Even worse, Effendi edited the piece. I was on probation at the time, a period Tartousi had told me would last one month, and thought it prudent to bite my tongue and refrain from saying anything that could jeopardize my quest for contractual employment—especially as permission to reside in Lebanon beyond two months depended on it—so this textbook case of unethical journalism went unremarked upon.

In general, things in Lebanon were much the same as when I had left the country some five years earlier (except for greater opportunities for shopping, a more varied night-life, and many non-Mercedes taxis). So long as you didn't agitate against Syria, and provided you steered clear of crossing people with connections to the security services or organized crime (sometimes one and the same), life was not unpleasant. The country had its problems, but they were chronic and thus familiar to me. Moloch's ongoing carnivorous exploits in Lebanon, though morally unconscionable, remained small-scale in scope, as he spent most of his time and energy in other parts of the world these days.

Meanwhile, Septemberland, mired in a global war on terrorism as murky and hazardous as it was costly, with large sectors of its populace still—if not more—paranoid and bigoted, was behind me. (I had no urge to look back to that place, except when it came to my friendship with Lewis, who I desperately hoped would write me at some point.) And whereas Iraq was sliding ever deeper into war, Lebanon had already experienced that crucible. It came out of it—back in 1990, when I was in Rome—battered and bruised, to be sure, but still breathing. And in 2000, when I was in Orlando, the Israeli army withdrew from the southern region it had occupied for a couple of decades, save for a sliver of disputed land that the UN maintained belonged to Syria, not Lebanon.

On a personal level, however, something saddened me that Christmas season, my first in the country since 2000. Yes, the custard apple trees on Hamra Street's sidewalks had wire lights with tiny flashing bulbs of various colors wound about their short and slender trunks for the festive season. But no carols filled the air with joy. I looked up at the lampposts; not a loudspeaker in sight. Walking up or down Hamra Street was no longer the same. I asked one of the receptionists at the hotel when the municipality had stopped putting up the loudspeakers and playing the carols in December, and he said two years ago. I couldn't bring myself to ask him or anyone else about the reason, knowing that if it emerged that conservative Muslims had called for scrapping the custom and gotten their way, this would shatter one of my most cherished assumptions about where I lived.

One month after I'd started with the *Star*, and upon receiving my first paycheck, Tartousi told me that I had passed my probation and offered me a contract. I took it, and the newspaper applied for a residence permit for me from the General Security arm of the Lebanese state. I moved out of the Mayflower and rented a furnished studio in a Hamra apartment building which consisted exclusively of such units, signing a one-year renewable lease that didn't oblige me to pay more than a month's rent in advance at any given time. A place of my own again, and a new spot for the Iraq rug. My parents told me they were proud of me and sent along more money de Monet; thanks to my father's job in Iraqi Kurdistan's booming oil market, they were doing well in Erbil (Kurdish name: Hewler, pronounced "how-lair") and didn't want me cash-strapped in increasingly expensive Beirut. I decided against buying a (used) car— despite the fact that mere possession of one could increase my chances for amatory adventures—as I didn't want to blow a good chunk of my monthly salary on installment payments. Instead, I made use of shared taxis. Before long, a residence permit indicating that I was gainfully employed arrived at the *Star*'s offices. I began to grow confident that coming to Lebanon had been a good idea.

She sat reading Waguih Ghali's *Beer in the Snooker Club* the next table over from me at Café Younes in Hamra. I had taken note of her—a bountifully bodied babe who could most likely polish off a crateful of Almost Ambrosia oranges in a single sitting—as well as the book, so when she asked me if she could have one of the sugar sachets on my table, as the waiter had forgotten to bring any with her coffee, I was quick to answer in the affirmative and then immediately tried to strike up a conversation about the novel, which she agreed was thus far both funny and wise. She asked me whether I was American, to which I replied, "No, I'm Iraqi, but English is my first language."

She said, "Oh, cool." Her name was Joelle. She seemed a bit shy—though not with her mirthful, toothy smile, which she flashed more than a few times as we spoke—but invited me to join her at her table, which I did. We got to talking about the nearby Lebanese American University, or LAU, where she was studying economics, and then moved on to all kinds of other topics. A couple of hours later, by which time the sun had set and she said it was time for her to go home and do some work for a class she had the next day, it was raining again. She agreed to let me walk her back, as I had brought an umbrella and she hadn't. Her home, as I knew by then, was an apartment in a building just off the LAU campus, not far from where I lived.

Standing outside the building's entrance, holding the umbrella up as she rooted around in her handbag for the keys, I resolved on the spot to do something. Of course, even if I had the courage to, I couldn't grab her and lock her in an embrace, thanks to the infernal umbrella. Maybe I could achieve the same effect verbally? Then she held up the keys in triumph, smiled through the strands of long, chestnut brown hair dangling down her face, and said, "I'm sorry I can't ask you in; I just have so much work to do!"

Me (quick attempt at humor): That's probably for the best. You never know what kind of guys hang out at Younes.

Joelle (giggling): Is that right? So what about the one I met today?

Me: Well, he's a gentleman, make no mistake about that, but he's also definitely attracted to you, so maybe you shouldn't trust him.

Joelle (coy): Really? But what could he do?

Me: Are you kidding? He could kidnap you and take you to his home village in Iraq. You would *never* escape.

Joelle (laughing): Wow, he'd go to all that trouble? I'm impressed!

So was I, truth be told, if not simply because I didn't have a village in Iraq; I was from Baghdad. I then asked her if she might want to hang out some night. She hesitated, which surprised me, and then said she didn't know. I hid my dismay and gave her my phone number, telling her to get in touch if she wanted to have a drink or another coffee "or whatever." She entered it into her cellphone and thanked me. Then she said goodnight and went inside.

*What was that all about? Why did she go cold all of a sudden?* Weird. I re-examined our exchange several times over the next few days. Yet I couldn't figure out why, after her friendly and even flirtatious behavior, she balked at the notion of hanging out with me. I hadn't even made it sound like a date!

I tried to take my mind off the incident by pondering the situation in Iraq. Of course, I was already following developments there, but now I did this in a more sustained manner, to try to connect the dots from this bombing to that militia clash to all those neighborhood expulsions. Conditions for ordinary Iraqis were worsening. Sunni and Shiite militias launched ghastly sectarian cleansing operations reminiscent of the Lebanese civil war. The Shiite majority, now in the ascendant, wanted revenge against the Sunnis for the oppression its community had suffered under Saddam, and took to exacting it with zeal. At the same time, Sunni extremists, some of them foreign, hated Shiites more than they did Americans, and couldn't countenance such people attaining their fair share of power. So they took to launching indiscriminate attacks on Shiite civilians. In Baghdad and beyond, Shiite and Sunni militias expelled thousands of members of the "opposing side" from their homes and neighborhoods, with the US army failing to do much about it (and American soldiers at Abu Ghraib busy torturing prisoners). Most of these people took refuge across town, where their sect and its militias predominated.

But Christians, who fielded no militias, had precious few places to go. Many were forced into exile. (The same applied to other minorities; the small Mandaean community of Baghdad and southern Iraq fell prey to Shiite militias and emigrated en masse, while the larger Yazidi population of the north was targeted by Sunni extremists but—for the time being anyway—remained largely beyond their reach.) As a result, a disproportionately high number of Iraqi refugees in Syria and Jordan were Christian. In the news reports I was reading, many said that they had fled because of the "general security situation," meaning war followed by anarchy, but increasing numbers cited specific cases of harassment and expulsion at the hands of Shiite or Sunni armed groups.

Sunni–Shiite violence, deplorable as it was, struck me as by and large the result of a political power struggle exacerbated by intolerant interpretations of Islam. But with violence directed against Christians and other small minorities, the reverse seemed to hold true; the attacks were for the most part expressions of religious intolerance, compounded by additional reasons. After all, Christians were not even trying to contend for power, which meant that killing or expelling them brought no strategic gain.

I was in the middle of an extended contemplation of worsening developments in Iraq a week or so after I'd met Joelle when the phone rang. It was her! I perked up at once. She said she'd like to speak to me in person. I couldn't help but rejoice, despite her even voice, which she seemed to have deliberately calibrated. We agreed to meet at Younes.

And that's where I learned why she had acted so strangely. With the two of us sitting across from each other, Joelle looking rather grave with elbows on the table and hands clasped, she said that she couldn't get involved with me "in that kind of way," and apologized if she had initially given me cause to think otherwise. "I'm a serious girl," she added, which failed to shed light on her thinking.

Then, finally, the long-awaited explanation: She wouldn't enter into a romantic relationship unless she could envisage it becoming serious and leading to marriage. Unfortunately, she could foresee no such outcome with me for the simple reason that I was a foreigner.

Upon hearing this, I immediately suspected that the real reason had to do with religion. Judging by her Western first name and the fact that she hailed from the seaside town of Batroun in the north (her parents rented the apartment in Hamra so that she wouldn't have to commute every day), she was Christian. What with the overwhelming majority of Iraqis being Muslim, she had probably assumed that that's what I was. *What should I do?* Play up my association with Christians by revealing my Chaldean affiliation, and thereby make myself more attractive in her eyes? I had resolved to never do such a thing.

But now I faced the possibility of a potential girlfriend slipping away due to a mistaken assumption on her part. And if I didn't correct that assumption, who knew how long I'd have to wait for another shot at a romantic relationship? True, if you can't hold fast to your principles in times of pressure, you're not really a principled person. But what if the principle in question is that, whether you're loved or reviled, make sure it's for who you are, as opposed to whom you're associated with? Wasn't Christianity part of who I was?

"I'm Christian, you know," I told her suddenly.

She seemed confused for a moment. Then a look of slight annoyance crossed her face.

"Yeah, I'm Chaldean," I continued, undeterred. "The Chaldeans are Catholic—like the Maronites, for example."

This was the community I suspected she belonged to, given her hometown of Batroun as well as the odds; the majority of Lebanese Christians were Maronite.

In a gentle voice, the expression on her face having softened, a hint of sympathy detectable in the beginnings of a compassionate smile and a head tilted to one side, she said, "I don't care about such things."

Me (defensive): No, I know. I just thought that, maybe, you know...

Joelle: No, I understand.

Me: It's part of the culture. Caring about what sect someone is. So sometimes you're not sure...

Joelle (glad to agree): A *big* part of the culture. My God, the Lebanese are so sectarian!

Me (not wanting to be patronized): Right, but it's even worse in the other Arab countries, especially when it comes to, you know, relationships. I mean, like, marriage between a Christian man and a Muslim woman, that's something—

Joelle: Unacceptable.

Me: Unacceptable, yeah, but not just that. It's—

Joelle: On both sides. The fanatics, I mean.

Me: Both sides, that's true. But it's also often illegal, and even when it's not, the security services act like it is, harassing and jailing the couple. So even if they get married abroad, where there's civil marriage, and then come back, they still won't be safe. The only way out is for the guy to convert to Islam. When it's the other way around, though, a Muslim man marrying a Christian woman, that's acceptable according to Islamic law.

Joelle: Well, I guess it's a good thing that in Lebanon, the problem is mostly just cultural, the police don't do what you said—the harassment. I mean, it's true we don't have civil marriage, but if you go to Cyprus and do it there and then come back, the Lebanese state recognizes it. I even talked about that with my ex. He was Muslim.

Me: Oh.

Joelle: Yeah, like I said, I don't care about that stuff. What matters to me is that my kids are Lebanese. And, I'm sorry, you're a great guy, really, but as you know, foreign men aren't eligible for Lebanese citizenship. And kids can only get it from their father.

Me: Right.

Joelle: So if I married a non-Lebanese guy—and I told you I only get involved with someone if I see a potential for marriage—Lebanon would consider my kids foreigners. They'd need residence permits just to live here!

As I had no social life, and because my efforts with Joelle had fallen flat, during my free time I once again found myself with little to do. Solution? More Iraq news—naturally. Which by now chronicled a situation that seemed to deteriorate by the day.

Throughout the next few months, as I kept abreast of reports on sectarian violence in Iraq and the increasing danger to small and defenseless minorities, my thoughts often drifted to Dietrich Bonhoeffer, the German Protestant pastor who stood up to the Nazis over their persecution of Jews. I had learned about him in a UCF history class on Germany's home front during the Second World War.

What I admired most about the man was that, taking his cue from Jesus Christ, he defied his sociopolitical context. Bonhoeffer knew he'd better step well out of that whole framework, because the more he thought about context and the many possible consequences of intervening to help those in need, the more reasons he'd come up with for inertia, especially in a place such as Nazi Germany, which murdered its dissidents. Perhaps true heroism doesn't consist of superhuman deeds only a handful of people can perform, but rather actions that fall within the ability of all those who know right from wrong. Once you determine what the right thing is, Bonhoeffer seemed to say, do it immediately and in a mulish manner, without regard for anything else. If enough of you manage this, you can reverse evil's advance and change the course of what seems inevitable.

Khaled, a history major, was also in that class, and he too felt drawn to the remarkable pastor and activist, particularly as the man had practiced what he preached, rushing to help the oppressed without regard for what might befall him. (The Nazis arrested Bonhoeffer in 1943 and threw him in jail. Two years later, still unrepentant, he was executed.) In a rare demonstration of tact, Khaled chose to wait until the professor had concluded that day's lecture on German domestic resistance to Nazism before telling me privately that he considered Bonhoeffer "the Jim Dandy of his times."

I didn't understand the reference, so I asked him to explain. He told me that long ago, this Jim Dandy fellow was in a submarine, not doing much of anything, when suddenly he got an SOS from a mermaid queen. Apparently, someone had hooked her with a fishing line and was about to reel her in.

"What'd he do?" I asked Khaled.

"What did he do?" he replied. "I'll tell you what he did. Jim Dandy to the rescue, my friend. Not: Jim Dandy sat back and thought about all the repercussions of getting involved, and how he might get hurt trying to save the mermaid queen. No! Jim Dandy to the *rescue*."

And then the church bombings happened in Iraq. On August 1st, 2004, bombs exploded nearly simultaneously outside several churches belonging to various denominations as parishioners emerged following Sunday services. Five explosions took place in total (four in Baghdad, the fifth in Mosul), while a sixth bomb failed to detonate. One of them was set off by a suicide bomber. Casualties included 12 killed and dozens wounded. A lightly injured priest with a bloodied arm sat outside one church crying, and asked, "What do the Muslims want? Why do they hate us?"

No one claimed responsibility for the attack, which many analysts attributed to Sunni Islamists affiliated with, or inspired by, Al-Qaida. As I mourned the victims, I wondered about the survivors. If they found out that I had supported the war, would they hate me? Or did they still hold out hope, like I did, that things would turn out for the better? I also couldn't help but wonder what Lewis, who had clearly soured on the war, would think of the irony of his Iraqi Christian friend having supported it, only for this to happen. Was he imagining my sorrow and experiencing a bit of Schadenfreude?

I decided to find out. For months, I had waited in vain for him to write me. Maybe he wanted *me* to—once more— reach out to *him*, I now thought. Might as well do it sooner rather than later. I'd tell him just how horrible I felt about what had just happened in Iraq, and give him a chance to respond. If he did, I could put up with that unsettling accusatory tone I had detected in the earlier emails back in Indiantown, and could even tolerate any cruel "Serves you right" sort of remark he might fire off. All that would be a small price to pay for getting our friendship back on track.

So I wrote him an email. I didn't attempt to balance the bad news with an account—however brief—of some of the more encouraging developments in Iraq, as I had done previously. I just told him that the bombings broke my heart, and I didn't know what to make of them. "It never occurred to me that this sort of thing might happen in the new Iraq," I wrote. "As you probably recall, I dismissed the notion that minorities would be discriminated against, or that Sunnis and Shiites would fight each other."

Staying on the subject, I confided to him that I had come to feel a certain resentment toward my parents (something I hadn't communicated even to them) for having led me to believe that virtually all Iraqis shared our family's patriotism, secularism, and religious moderation. However, so that he didn't think I was trying to escape blame, I hastened to add that I should have known better. Assuming that everything wrong with Iraq was concentrated in the person of Saddam Hussein and consequently that removing him from power would be the panacea was just plain stupid.

He wrote back! Right away, too. I was sitting at my desk at the office and had begun editing an astonishingly frivolous article on the joys of eating a zaatar or cheese manqousheh for breakfast when my account notified me that I had received an email. At once thrilled and apprehensive, I ceased work on the article and clicked on the message. A few minutes later, one of our writers asked me, "Are you all right, Hunayn? You look...I don't know...sick."

I tried to mumble something as I turned away and buried my face in a dictionary. My hopes notwithstanding, what I had long suspected turned out to be true.

Hunayn—

You're right; you should have known better. After all, Iraq is your country. You could have said you didn't know what was going to happen, or just kept your mouth shut. But instead you went around talking like you knew everything. Although I'm not the kind of guy who passes the buck, I can't help but think that when it comes to my support for this disastrous war, you're the one to blame. While even you yourself admit that you should have known better, you can't say that about me. Sure, I could've hit the library and read up on Iraq's history—and in the process learned that there's no such thing as an Iraqi people—but that's not something you'd expect the average person with a life to do. All the more so if he has an Iraqi friend he trusts to tell him the truth about that shitty country. I believed what you told me. And I went to bat for you. Why do you think I broke up with Colleen? You say you feel "resentment" toward your parents, even though you admit you should have known more about Iraq. Well, how do you think I feel toward you? You know what? I'm not going to tell you. Instead, I'll just say one final thing. This is the last email you send me that I will bother to read. Save yourself the trouble and don't write me anymore. I am not your friend.

Lewis

⑨

Dressed in a black wool sweater stylishly speckled with dandruff he'd frequently shake out of his skein of tangled and knotted hair, Effendi was leaning back in his recliner —the only one in the office, and which he had paid for out of his own pocket—as he shoved a gigantic, lardy monstrosity of a hamburger into a mouth he'd opened so wide that his beady eyes disappeared completely. Worse, he insisted on holding forth even as he ate, admonishing the writer seated in an adjoining cubicle to order the same artery-clogging concoction from a nearby fast food joint, rather than leave the office for lunch. This proved too much for me to look at.

Even with my gaze averted as I waited for him to conclude his harangue (which I wished he'd screw up the courage to try on me sometime, so that I'd have the pleasure of rebuffing him), I still couldn't escape all the revolting aspects of his eating habits. I heard the wet smacking sound of his lips in addition to his gurgling voice as— mouth obviously stuffed with food—he explained: "The news never stops, even when you want to have lunch." To my dismay, the young woman he was addressing didn't retort that the news did seem to stop whenever he wanted to go off for a smoke.

At some point, he must have noticed me standing there, because he cut short his lecture abruptly and said, "Yes?"

I turned to him. His face was purplish and puffy from the exertion of eating and talking at the same time, lips slightly parted, tongue working assiduously to pry loose a morsel of meat trapped between two ketchup-smeared teeth. A few inches down, two clumps of coleslaw—often added to hamburgers in Lebanon—had caught on his sweater. I steeled myself and began. "So, listen, you know how we change 'Jerusalem' to 'Occupied Jerusalem' in the wire reports we use?"

Scooping up a clump of coleslaw—now seasoned with dandruff—from his chest and sticking it in his mouth, he replied, "Yeah?"

Me (gagging): Well…I was…thinking…

Effendi (mild concern): What's wrong?

Me (composing myself): Nothing. I was thinking that we shouldn't do that when the report is filed from West Jerusalem, which is part of Israel proper.

Effendi (puzzled): West Jerusalem?

Me (prepared to enlighten): Yeah, you know, like stories filed from the Knesset. Now, I know much of what became Israel in 1948 was supposed to be part of Palestine according to the UN Partition Plan of 1947, and Jerusalem was supposed to be an international zone or something, but the situation's obviously changed since then. I mean, even the Arab countries don't consider West Jerusalem and Haifa and Jaffa occupied. They use the term only for the areas occupied in 1967—like East Jerusalem.

Effendi: But we've always used "Occupied" for Jerusalem.

Me: Right, that's what I've noticed. But I'm saying it should depend on whether we're talking about East or West Jerusalem. The Arab and international position is that only

East Jerusalem is occupied and that Israel should withdraw from it.

Effendi: Well, I don't care about them. We've always done it this way.

Me: But the "them" includes Lebanon. And we're a Lebanese newspaper, so I don't see why it'd be a problem—

Effendi: We have our own standards. And anyway, imagine if we stopped doing it and someone noticed. They might start saying we're legitimizing the occupation.

Me: That's the thing, though; we wouldn't do it for stories coming out of East Jerusalem, so how could anyone accuse us of that?

Effendi: They just would. And we'd have got ourselves in a mess for no reason. Really, Hunayn, it's just not worth it.

It wasn't long before something happened that caused this and similar *Star*-related annoyances, which I had fixated on to keep from wallowing in self-pity over getting spurned by Lewis, to recede into those storage spaces of my mind stacked with unaddressed but minor concerns.

On Valentine's Day, 2005, a massive explosion rocked the Saint George's Bay area of coastal Beirut. We soon learned that one of the many fatalities, and apparently the target of the bombing, was Rafic Hariri. The Sunni former prime minister, who had resigned his post a few months earlier in opposition to Syria's continued meddling in Lebanon's governmental affairs, was rumored to have been on the verge of crossing over to the largely Christian movement agitating for the restoration of Lebanese sovereignty. Had he done so, the bulk of the Sunni community, among which he was immensely popular and which had begun to chafe under Syrian occupation, would have almost certainly gone with him.

Though they didn't skimp on coverage of the assassination itself, local media outlets (including the *Star*) proved noticeably slow in reporting on the groundswell of anti-Syrian sentiment among ordinary people, much of which was manifested in spontaneous protest rallies. This stemmed from their shared fear of the punishment the Lebanese state, beholden to Syria, might mete out to those who covered the phenomenon, and was heightened by the suspicion that the Syrians and their Lebanese cohorts had assassinated Hariri. If the "Seerians" could kill a former prime minister, I overheard an apprehensive Tartousi whisper to a senior editor, imagine what they'd do to us. The Lebanese government's shuttering of a television station a few years back following its criticism of Lebanon's president—Syria's still-sitting sycophantic scullion—would look positively restrained by comparison.

Yet very quickly, beginning with Hariri's funeral procession, the protests grew too big and stormy to ignore. Clamorous, too, with specific demands; in what observers and participants dubbed the "Independence Intifada" and the "Cedar Revolution" (after the tree emblazoned on Lebanon's national flag), the young people flocking to Martyrs' Square every day called on Syria to withdraw its army and omnipresent intelligence operatives from Lebanon. Some of them erected tents and vowed to camp out in the Square until the Syrians left and their Lebanese puppet government resigned. Pressure on the Syrian regime by the Lebanese protesters as well as Western and Arab capitals mounted, and local media, the *Star* included, began to report on the full extent of the popular uprising and corresponding political realignment taking place.

Every so often during this period, the feeling of nausea I got following 9/11, when I worried that the violence we had just seen might spiral into a tsunami of blood that would engulf the country, bubbled up in my stomach and seeped into my mouth. At such times, I wondered if restricting his diet to the victims of small-scale carnage he wreaked every now and again might no longer sate the increasingly gluttonous Moloch, in which case he'd follow up the slaughter of Hariri and 21 other people with a good deal more butchery. But then I'd remind myself that what Lebanon was passing through now didn't resemble in the least that apocalyptic September day, when thousands perished in inconceivable ways, and we were jolted by the realization that the most powerful country in the world was no longer safe.

Plus, I could see a silver lining here; many Lebanese considered the assassination the last straw, and had taken to the streets demanding their country's freedom. Those who felt otherwise, such as the mainly Shiite supporters of Hezbollah, also made their voices heard, but failed to stem the pro-sovereignty tide. Meanwhile, Syria didn't want to risk becoming a pariah state. The Syrian president had reacted to the initial wave of pro-sovereignty demonstrations by promising an umpteenth "redeployment" of his troops (which consisted of shuffling them around rather than pulling them out of Lebanon) and a few other cosmetic changes. But now he buckled under Lebanese popular and international diplomatic pressure, going before his rubber-stamp parliament to announce the withdrawal of all Syrian troops and intelligence operatives from Lebanon.

This was momentous. I felt that Lebanon would now finally come into its own again. The country was sovereign for the first time in decades. I took to walking to work every afternoon, buoyed by the almost ubiquitous sense of new-found freedom, and wanting to experience its most concentrated form in Martyrs' Square, which I'd saunter through on the way to Gemmayzeh. With its brand spankin' new banks, restaurants, and boutiques, its restored parliament building, and its renovated (and cordoned-off) Roman-era public baths, the district was unrecognizable from the time Samer and I had wound our way home along its edges following that unpleasant incident in the Saint Joseph's University area some years back. Now thronged by people of all socioeconomic classes and ages, including children scampering about happily, with loudspeakers affixed to lampposts and hooked up to a public address system blaring a mix of patriotic songs and the latest bubblegum pop, and hawkers peddling everything from scarves with a Lebanese flag print to various kinds of food and refreshments, it radiated a carnivalesque ambience.

After Hariri was assassinated, his closed coffin was placed on display near the huge, yet-to-be-inaugurated mosque whose construction he had funded. (The coffins of his bodyguards were given a separate spot a few feet away.) Springing up shortly thereafter was a montage of blown-up pictures depicting the stocky, silver-mustachioed politician variously smiling, praying, and looking stately. This make-shift mausoleum, covered with a large awning, attracted visitors every day, many of whom recited prayers for the deceased, took photos of the somewhat lurid scene, or scrawled pro-Hariri and pro-sovereignty graffiti on a nearby wall.

In the center of Martyrs' Square, facing the four statues commemorating the Ottoman Turkish authorities' public execution of separatists on this very spot during the First World War, there now stood a stage on which a bulletproof glass booth was wheeled out every time pro-sovereignty speakers were to address the crowd, so that they could do so without fear of assassination. Overlooking the stage was the huge screen on which the demonstrators had watched Syria's president tell his parliament that he had decided to withdraw his army from Lebanon—the point at which the crowd, and much of the nation along with it, realized it had triumphed and erupted in jubilation.

I failed to register that the male voice I had heard was addressing me until I felt a punch on my shoulder. It wasn't painful, but neither was it playful. Although I had heard the question "Where are you from?" in Arabic amid the festive din, I didn't think it directed at me as I waited for the grilled corn on the cob I had ordered from a street vendor trundling about a large and unwieldy cart that served as a poor man's deli-on-wheels.

I turned to the side. Before me stood a skinny, pimple-faced teen in a T-shirt advertising "IndepenDANCE 2005," apparently some sort of rave at an open-air venue taking the country's political regeneration as its theme. Even though I was now facing him, he barked, "Hey, you!"

Me (contemptuous): What?

Him (exaggerated pronunciation): Where…are…you …from?

Me (harsh): What's it to you?

Him (stepping closer, smirking): You're Syrian, aren't you?

Mystery solved. He had heard me order the corn cob and mistook my Iraqi-Lebanese accent for a Syrian one. And, of course, he disliked Syrians. Still, I considered it strange that such a little dipshit should act tough with an older, stronger guy he must've known he'd fail to overpower in any sort of physical confrontation. "Look, kid," I told him, "I don't know what your problem is, but I suggest you—"

"Syrian?! Syrian?!" shrieked a guy who grabbed my collar and swung me around so that we stood face-to-face. He scrunched up his nose repeatedly and in quick succession, like a rabbit. Together with his furiously trembling lips, this made his goatee morph into a different shape every second.

"Who's Syrian? Where's the Syrian?!" bellowed someone else nearby.

I pushed away the manic, goateed guy who had manhandled me. He tried to charge back but was unceremoniously shoved aside by two other young men jostling for position as a crowd began to form. I noticed that the street vendor, exemplifying the storied Lebanese mercantile spirit, had seized the sterling opportunity to make money afforded by this outbreak of xenophobia. He was bringing out the Lebanese flag scarves he sold and arraying them over his cobs of corn, in the not unreasonable expectation that the mob of rabid nationalists assembling around me would make for good customers.

"Hey there, nice clothes you've got on; your day off?" someone snickered as he tugged at my shirt.

"Yeah, that's why he finally showered!" said a man I couldn't see. Riotous laughter all around.

Standing before me, having emerged victorious from the jostling session, was a chubby fellow in his 20s whose patchy beard failed to conceal his face's babyish ruddiness. "Do you know what we do to Syrians?" he yelled, as much to the excitable mob as to me. A chorus of hoots sounded, and the men started to shove me more violently, one of them kicking my behind.

Just as I was fixing to open up a can of Iraqi-flavored whupass on the cretins, the can opener I kept on me at all times since moving back to Lebanon caught on my pants pocket. The chubby guy standing before me didn't know what I was reaching for, but wanted to find out, so he lunged at my waistline. I tried to spin away, but because I was surrounded, succeeded only in executing a little half circle. This meant that my other front pocket, the right one, was now turned toward him. He tore it easily—I was wearing gossamer-like summer slacks—and snatched my wallet, which he held up in triumph for all to behold. This set off a collective cheer, followed by another round of shoving. In a video of the incident with everybody but me airbrushed out, I'd look as though I were performing some kind of frenzied dance with a whole lot of jerky movements.

Someone slapped me, stinging my cheek and inflaming my already wounded sense of manhood. Still I did nothing. Then the guy rummaging through my wallet pulled out the flimsy-yet-spiffily-laminated residence permit indicating—in the barely legible handwriting of one of Lebanon's countless trusted and meticulous civil servants—my Iraqi nationality. As it turned out, this proved just as effective in averting a lynching as my thwarted plan to whup some ass.

"Iraqi?!" the guy cried, scrutinizing the card.

"Yes," I replied in as self-possessed a manner as I could. "May I have my wallet back?"

He didn't answer, his gaze still fixed on the document he held in one hand, with my wallet in the other. The crowd began to reorient itself, people craning their necks toward him instead of me, stepping closer to the guy, and jockeying for position. I took the opportunity to slip my wallet out of his hand as the crowd engulfed him; he didn't even notice. My residence permit was now passed around from one person to the next. The same look, incredulity shading into disappointment, etched itself on the face of every guy who examined it.

One person at a time, the mob melted away, their asses unwhupped but in a collective sling fashioned out of a very large Lebanese flag. The last guy to inspect my residence permit flung it back at me disconsolately and walked off in a huff. I stooped, picked it up, and put it back in my wallet, which I secured in the intact front left pocket of my pants, the one my assailant hadn't ripped. The lemming of a street vendor now slunk up to me. Looking sheepish—having just demonstrated his moral puniness compared to both Dietrich Bonhoeffer and Jim Dandy—he made to give me my cob of corn with a theatrical bow, holding up his free hand with the palm facing outward, indicating a refusal of payment.

*Should've worn eyeglasses instead of contact lenses*, I muttered to myself as I flounced off without the cob. That might've set me apart from the Syrian laborers in the minds of the Lebanese. Or in the minds of anybody, for that matter, irrespective of their biases. Didn't the communist-inspired Khmer Rouge kill all Cambodians who wore glasses, precisely because they deemed them less likely to be members of the much-vaunted working class in a poor and underdeveloped country? Had these Lebanese thought me Syrian, but of a higher socioeconomic station than that of the many Syrian menial workers in Lebanon, perhaps they wouldn't have set upon me.

At any rate, I avoided the downtown area, and Martyrs' Square in particular, after that (even on days when I wore my glasses). Yet despite the nasty experience, as well as my growing awareness of the disturbing spate of violent attacks on Syrian laborers across the country, I remained optimistic about Lebanon's prospects now that it had regained its sovereignty. Almost everybody I knew felt the same way, including my parents, who came for a visit and stayed at the Mayflower for a week, bringing me a pair of shirwal— traditional Kurdish baggy pants—as a humorous gift, and looking happy and relaxed.

The only exception was Nadia, who believed that we should brace ourselves for more bombings and assassinations, which she maintained were inevitable. She elaborated on her bleak outlook one night as the two of us sat chatting in her living room, her daughter and the nanny having gone to bed. "Oh, I'm sure the Syrians are going to accept getting kicked out of Lebanon!" she said, trying to sound scornful despite a faltering voice.

When I replied that it was obvious they were fuming about what happened, but that, precisely because they were now gone, they couldn't do much about it, Nadia looked at me in astonishment. "How can you be so naïve, Hunayn? Don't you know they have a small army of Lebanese agents? Just wait. You'll see; they'll have their revenge."

My roving gaze settled on a svelte and fetching short-haired brunette seated at the bar and looking somewhat officious in a gray business suit. Normally, this would intimidate me somewhat; surely a woman decked out in such no-nonsense attire was out of my league. But this one? She was shod in preposterously high-heeled pumps in an attempt to compensate for her short stature, and struggled to conceal her distaste every time she took a dainty sip from a drink that looked as though it were a cocktail—and therefore light on the alcohol to begin with. I saw a girl, fresh-faced and guileless despite her pretensions. A young professional just starting out in her career, going out of her way to don a newly laundered suit (I considered it unlikely she was still wearing that day's work clothes) in order to signal to all and sundry her entry into the adult world, and doing her best to drink a beverage she associated with it. Of course, I too was a young professional having only just landed a job of any consequence, but I felt emboldened by my apparent ability to read her.

This was at Pacifico on Monot Street, near Saint Joseph's University. What a difference a few years could make! The area where Samer and I had come up against those self-styled defenders of Christian women's virtue back when we were in high school had by this time established itself as a trendy hangout spot.

As it happened, she was there with another woman, also young but older than she was, dolled up and dressed in a low-cut black silk blouse, the exposed parts of her fake cannonball breasts and deep-valley cleavage shimmering with glitter she had sprinkled liberally here and there. Relaxed, confident, and in her element, the vamp looked as if she wanted to stimulate the erotic inclinations of any guy who could convincingly rhapsodize about his extensive real estate holdings and the fleet of fancy cars in his garage. This in fact seemed to be underway; she was flirting with a sleazeball behind sunglasses around whose finger twirled a car key noticeably ring-twinned with a silver replica of a leaping feline, and whose shirt was unbuttoned almost all the way to his navel, the crucifix (also silver) hanging from his necklace entwined in an overgrown forest of coiling black chest hair. Meanwhile, her friend, the demurely dressed and endearingly callow young woman who had caught my eye and to whom my gaze continued to revert, toyed with her cellphone and took the occasional sip from her drink, following which she would always wince. She had no one to entertain her.

A few minutes later, I had initiated a conversation with Zaina, as she was called. Before trying, however, I made it a point to act bored and unimpressed by everything around me—even once I'd stealthily made my way to the barstool beside hers, my interest eventually piqued not by her, but by her drink. In response to my question, she told me it was a margarita. I said she didn't look like she was enjoying her margarita, and she conceded with a chuckle. "Where are you from?" she asked me. I told her. Next, I got us a couple of Moscow mules, a drink for which Pacifico was well-known. To both her and my delight, she liked it, and this further facilitated our getting acquainted with each other.

She told me she was 25, had earned an MBA in finance from a university in London (as soon as I heard this, I switched to English), and was employed by the Central Bank of Lebanon—located at the beginning of Hamra Street—as part of a team set up to combat money laundering. Pretty impressive. Her friend, busy working the splay-shirted douchebag, ignored us.

Before long, Zaina grew tipsy; she started giggling and asking me about my love life. I told her it was non-existent and she giggled some more. When I turned the question around, she informed me, looking serious, that she had recently broken up with her boyfriend because he was a pervert. Curious, but careful lest she misinterpret my curiosity as titillation, I said, "Hmm, that's too bad. But, uh…what kinds of things was he into?"

Zaina (faint look of disgust): A threesome.

Me (caught off guard): Shit. Well, yeah, I know what you mean. It's almost like…like he's saying you're not enough for him, that he needs both you and another woman to satisfy him.

Zaina: No, he wanted us to do it with another guy.

Me (simultaneous surprise, relief, and disappointment): Oh. Well, that's just…you know…like…

Zaina: Not something I wanted to do.

Me: No, absolutely, with good reason.

Zaina: So, what about you?

Me: Me?!

Zaina: Yeah, you like perverted stuff? What are your sexual tastes like?

Me: Oh. Well, uh, they're rather pedestrian, to tell you the truth.

The smirk that flitted across her face didn't escape my notice—though I couldn't tell whether it was caused by the word I had used or an expectation on her part that a real man, while not necessarily kinky, would never prove quite so bland and unexciting. "Pedestrian, huh?" she said, a clear gibe.

"Yeah, like, you know," I stammered, "maybe me and a woman, on a bed, with, you know, love...between us."

Zaina didn't mind that I was Iraqi or Christian, even though she was Lebanese and Muslim. This had much to do with her ideological orientation; she belonged to the Syrian Social Nationalist Party. I knew a thing or two about the SSNP, which had first come to my attention years earlier in high school, when I happened to see some of its younger members prancing down Hamra Street in would-be military formation as part of a larger demonstration held by the party in support of the Syrian regime and against Israel.

What I knew wasn't encouraging. The SSNP was founded in the 1930s by Antun Saadeh ("The Leader" to his acolytes), a Lebanese who wanted to unite Lebanon, Syria, Palestine, and Jordan, later adding Iraq, Kuwait, and even Cyprus, into a single powerful state called Syria. According to Saadeh, "science"—no less—proved that the people of these countries were in reality all Syrian. There was, however, one alien element in the countries that made up the Syria of Saadeh's imagination: the Jews. His party was blatantly anti-Semitic, making no attempt to distinguish between Zionist Jews who maintained that Palestine rightfully belonged to them, and non-Zionists who believed otherwise and didn't support the State of Israel that arose on its ruins. The struggle between the Syrians and the Jews was old (one of the SSNP's heroes was my ancient homeboy, nasty Nebuchadnezzar) and eternal.

Tellingly, the SSNP sought to agglomerate all the region's diverse communities (except the Jews) into an undifferentiated mass with a single ethno-racial identity, the supersized Syrian one, and even a single religious

221

identity, a fusion of Islam and Christianity. But the party's totalitarianism was perhaps best exemplified by Saadeh's assertion that "the individual is a mere potentiality." Syrian individuals would remain mere potentialities until made to dissolve in the Syrian nation in a great orgy of coerced self-abnegation. This would create a brainless monolith free of internal fissures and answerable only to its Führer.

I decided then and there to probe Zaina about one of the party's myriad objectionable traits—its anti-Semitism. After all, I liked this girl and got a definite vibe that she liked me, but I didn't want to hook up with a meretricious, Jew-hating incarnation of my bête noire, the predatory Moloch always lurking in the shadows. "Tell me something, though, Zaina," I said to her, "you guys hate Jews regardless of whether they're Zionist, right? Well, isn't that anti-Semitic?"

Zaina: No—we're Semites ourselves; how can we even *be* anti-Semitic?

Me: Indiscriminate Jew-haters. How's that? Your belief is that the Jews live to destroy the unity of the Syrians and steal their land and all that, right? Well, that's your specific anti-Semitism—or, if you prefer, blanket anti-Jewish hatred. The Syrian Social Nationalist kind.

Zaina: But we oppose the Jews because of something they've done, a big crime. The Jews stole Palestine and are killing our people—that's why we're against them.

Me: But listen, you can oppose Zionism, and even fight those Jews who oppress the Palestinians, without going in for the idea that all Jews for all time are chomping at the bit to do that, right? I mean, the problem is that your ideology says almost all Jews have always been a nasty bunch, especially toward Syrians, and always will be.

She didn't say anything, which made me feel vindicated. In subsequent conversations over the next weeks and months, as the connection we made that day deepened into a romantic relationship and I finally achieved the long-desired goal I had nurtured since my time in pre-Septemberland America, Saadeh's quasi-fascist doctrine rarely surfaced. And, truth be told, I felt reluctant to press her on certain points—including the guy's anti-Semitism—for fear of alienating her. Zaina had become my first girlfriend, and this was due in part to her adherence to a secular party with a regional outlook that opposed both religious sectarianism and country-based parochialism between "Syrians." It seemed as though no part of my identity could count against me; *this woman took me as I was.* I felt tremendous relief, along with the sense that my already deep affection for her, born of an immediate emotional bond, could in time blossom into love.

Plus, she had a snug little pussy, this one. It gripped my cock as tightly as an apprehensive child might clutch its mother's pinky for protection in a strange and dangerous world. Now, my dick was bigger than an average woman's pinky, but admittedly couldn't provide Zaina with much protection. Nevertheless, I figured it might yet secure her salvation (an altogether sweeter deal for Zaina, whom I was looking out for), provided I gradually fucked the Saadeh-worship clean out of her. In the meantime, the sex was frequent and vigorous. I marveled at my resulting serenity. It's as though you can't fool your body by masturbating; it knows that you're not giving it the real thing, and you remain unfulfilled irrespective of how often you try to please yourself, and how creative you get. Also, she agreed to go on the pill, meaning we could dispense with condoms. The result—for me, at any rate—was a distinctly more pleasurable physical sensation.

So I decided that only if Zaina spouted odious aspects of Saadeh's ideology would I confront her. Otherwise, I wouldn't go looking for trouble.

Meanwhile, Nadia's gloomy premonition came true. Bombs exploded, usually at night, in both residential areas and industrial zones, causing extensive damage. Casualties were limited—few people died—but the frequency of the explosions and their random nature put everyone on edge.

And then it got worse. Pro-sovereignty politicians, journalists, and intellectuals got picked off in professional-looking assassinations, usually via explosive devices stealthily attached to their automobiles or in roadside bombings as they drove by unawares. The victims were mostly Christian, as were the areas targeted in the nighttime bombings, making me wonder whether the perpetrators were motivated in part by sectarian considerations.

There is no such thing as a six-month anniversary. The term "anniversary" is derived from the world "annual," meaning yearly, so "six-month anniversary" is a contradiction in terms. And an evident one, at that.

"My God, Hunayn, that's the very thing you shouldn't have said!" Nadia informed me after I finished telling her of a recent argument I'd had with Zaina. She laughed.

I explained to Nadia that I had discovered the hard way that she was right, but protested that it had long been my habit to point out the misuse of words when I came across any such instances. Then, probably making myself look even more foolish, I pedantically provided her with an example: "At one point at the *Star*, we were about to run a story on Hariri's second son, who as you know is trying to fill his father's shoes and become a political leader. Well, in the article, the writer mentioned that Hariri seems to like to have the honorific 'Sheikh' added to his name. I wasn't assigned to edit the piece, but had a look at it anyway. And I noticed something. The article said he liked it *appended* to his name. I told everybody that that's incorrect, because the honorific comes before, not after, the name, meaning that it's *prepended* to it. But no one listened, and they ran the article with the mistake."

She laughed her throaty laugh again, and I felt a pang of melancholy at the knowledge that she was leaving Lebanon. For Nadia, the bombings and assassinations, and the attendant feeling that security was unraveling, had grown too much to bear. I understood this, but as we sat side-by-side on her sofa that night, I realized how dearly I would miss her. True, we hung out only occasionally, and I had seen very little of her since I got together with Zaina, but I enjoyed our talks and admired her feistiness a great deal. Separating from her husband, enrolling in college again, raising a child. And now? Going back to square one—dropping out of college yet again and moving with Maha to Qatar in order to live with her husband.

"Technically, we're still married," she reminded me, "so I won't have any difficulty getting a residence permit there, even without a job. And he's okay with the idea, especially 'cause he'll get to see Maha more. We're going to try to make the marriage work and be a family."

"Yeah, okay, but you separated for a reason, right?" I asked. "I mean, what happened to earning your degree, getting a job, and maybe finding a man you love to share your life with?"

Her eyes downcast as if she were ashamed, she said quietly, "Those things will have to wait."

Then, looking up at me, she said in that same quiet voice, but with an ominous mien and newfound determination, "This is no country to raise a child in. And things will only get worse."

A couple of months later, as 2005 drew to a close, I tried to take the tumultuous year's measure. The assassination of Hariri had catalyzed a popular but peaceful uprising that shook off Syrian rule in Lebanon. This naturally enraged the Syrians, but also struck fear into the hearts of those Lebanese—Hezbollah and even Shiites in general—who viewed Syria as their protector. Further assassinations of figures who had agitated for the country's sovereignty widened the rift between the pro- and anti-Syrian camps, as did the UN's stated intention—at Lebanon's request—to establish a Special Tribunal charged with investigating who killed Hariri and other pro-sovereignty figures after him, and prosecuting the suspects. (The pro-Syria crowd, including Hezbollah, immediately called the Tribunal a Western-Zionist conspiracy targeting Syria and its allies in Lebanon.) This rift became the defining feature of political life, paralyzing the Lebanese state and exercising the minds of people from all walks of life.

Nevertheless, some Lebanese managed to take time out from their country's domestic troubles to show the world their fanatic side. In response to a Danish newspaper's publication of a cartoon mocking the Prophet Muhammad,

Hezbollah's leader claimed that had a single Muslim successfully carried out Khomeini's fatwa demanding the murder of Salman Rushdie for his novel *The Satanic Verses*, this wouldn't have happened. Reacting to the same incident, Sunni Islamists didn't content themselves with storming the building housing the Danish consulate in Ashrafieh and setting part of it ablaze, but proceeded to hurl rocks at an adjacent church. (Why not? There's no difference between the Danes and Lebanese Christians, right?) A few months earlier, the London subway and bus bombings had been carried out in the name of Islam by British Al-Qaida terrorists, but Sunni Islamists in Lebanon were not moved to demonstrate against the attacks, let alone burn and destroy property.

Meanwhile, violence in Iraq had spiraled to a horrifying level. (As a result, my parents had indefinitely postponed their planned move south to Baghdad.) Sometimes, the scale of the carnage reminded me of what Lewis had said about the 9/11 attacks, and I would find myself thinking that, if you put morality aside, the number of Iraqis that other Iraqis killed on a daily basis was nothing short of spectacular. All this seemed to delight anti-Americans the world over, including leftists in the West and the US itself, who crowed about the fiasco-in-the-making.

Apparently, the blame—all of it—lay with the Americans. The invasion rendered the paroxysm of violence "inevitable." But what if post-war Iraq had emerged a peaceful country? I wondered whether the people who had believed in the inevitability of Iraqi savagery would have come forth and said, "This civility is very impressive; we admit that we thought the Iraqis were barbarians who would butcher each other as soon as we removed the totalitarian regime governing them. It turns out we were wrong."

When contemplating the matter, my thoughts sometimes drifted to a scenario in which Lebanon, already precarious in the wake of the withdrawal of its longtime Syrian overlord, suffered a further destabilizing event. Say, a full-blown domestic conflict between the country's two squabbling political camps, or a foreign invasion. Would that make it understandable, perhaps *inevitable*, were some Lebanese Muslims to expel me from majority-Muslim Hamra, and maybe even kill me? Or would reasonable people give free will its due and hold such criminals responsible for their actions?

Unsettling questions all, but not the kind to keep me up at night. Not yet, at least. I made a mental list of the good things about my personal situation—and Lebanon's, too. The country had regained its sovereignty, even if it now faced an ongoing terrorist campaign targeting individuals who had helped accomplish this long-sought goal. Ordinary Lebanese, even when finding themselves on opposite sides of the political divide, largely refrained from committing acts of violence against each other. Meanwhile, my job was exasperating, but it paid the bills and kept me from having to move to Iraq, the prospect of which scared me even though I knew that the autonomous Kurdish-administered north was stable. For the first time in my life, I had a girlfriend, albeit one who was ideologically fanatic and politically blinkered. And although I'd long given up on the idea of Lewis forgiving me and restoring our friendship, and despite the fact that Nadia had recently left the country, Samer, my closest friend, was still here.

I felt I needed to achieve one more thing to make my life complete. This thing made itself known to me the moment Zaina and I became a couple; ever since, I had tried to muster the courage requisite for the challenge.

When Rasha arrived at Barometre, just around the corner from the AUB campus, I almost didn't recognize her. Where was the hijab fighting a losing battle to devour all her hair, a shameless lock of which always managed to repose provocatively on her forehead? The smile—lower lip poking out to the side and all—was hers, but her ruby-tinged cheeks didn't have to push back against that bothersome garment intent on making her moonfaced. She embraced me warmly (I had thought that we'd probably do the somewhat formal three kisses on the cheek thing), and we sat down. Immediately, she began scolding me for having emailed her. "I mean, really, Hunayn," she said in English, rolling her eyes as though dealing with a recalcitrant but endearing child, "you should have just called me!" Given a choice between looking sheepish and pointing out that she hadn't given Samer her phone number, I picked the former option.

I hadn't located her myself, of course, and wouldn't have known how to. Samer, utilizing his general resourcefulness, his intimate familiarity with the intricacies of Lebanese culture, and his car, extracted a portion of the needed information from this grocery storeowner and that mechanic on a day trip out to Haush al-Umara that he graciously undertook for the sole purpose of helping me achieve my mission. Armed with several leads, he then drove into Zahle proper, where she now lived, and found her. He told me that when he asked her if she might be interested in reconnecting with me, she laughed and said of course. So he took down her email address, just as I had asked him to. And now here we sat at Barometre. Rasha was radiant, poised, smiling, solicitous—in short, the quintessence of self-possessed young womanhood.

Her speaking in English relieved me somewhat, as we had no shared history in that language—specifically, no failure on my part to achieve an erection as she urged, "Put your cock in my pussy." But relief isn't ease or comfort, both of which continued to elude me. Part of the reason was that when, with studied nonchalance, I worked "my girlfriend" into a sentence, she clapped her hands and effused, "You have a girlfriend, that's so wonderful!" The distinctly maternal nature of the statement unnerved me to such a degree that I forgot to add that Zaina and I had been together for just over six months, which I had figured would prove to Rasha that I could have sex, something I had wanted her to know for several years now.

The other reason for my discomfort and diminishing confidence was the discovery that it remained the case that her life experience far exceeded mine. As we sat there, the mouthwatering scent of grilled kafta we had ordered wafting toward us from the kitchen, she told me about getting her BA, which she had been working toward when I met her, and a subsequent MA (in public administration). Also her becoming deputy director of an NGO campaigning for a law to protect women from domestic abuse and a separate law to grant them a quota in parliament, even as the organization provided shelter and counseling to battered women—including foreign housekeepers—with funds donated from Western human rights groups.

And then there was her marriage. With great relish, she recounted defying her parents and extended family on the matter. "He was Christian," she said, leaning forward and winking.

I looked away instinctively and blushed as I thought of how poorly I must've stacked up against him in her mind.

"He even told me he'd convert, if I wanted him to—but I forbade it," she added, laughing heartily. "We were going to do the civil marriage thing in Cyprus, but then I decided it would be a lot more fun for me to piss my whole family off by converting to Christianity, so that's what I did!"

After obtaining their undergraduate degrees and securing jobs, they tied the knot in a Greek Catholic church and rented themselves a nice little apartment in Zahle, where he was from and where that particular Christian community predominated. "But not too close to his parents," she said with another laugh, "because neither of us wanted them dropping in all the time!"

Eventually, her parents reconciled with her and even came to accept her husband, Pierre. But recently, after a couple of years of marriage, she and her beau had called it quits. (I wondered if this was because she had tired of the young man—which would have partially assuaged my unreasonable resentment of him—but I didn't want to pry.) How to go about obtaining a divorce had since become an issue, she grumbled. The Greek Catholic Church, in full communion with the Holy See, didn't permit it, and Lebanese citizens who had had a Greek Catholic marriage in Lebanon, rather than a civil one in another country, were under their Church's jurisdiction when it came to this and related personal status matters. I told her that, as a Chaldean, I too was a Catholic, and knew something about how such matters affected the various Catholic communities in Lebanon and Iraq.

"It's ridiculous, isn't it?" she said angrily. "I mean, here we are in the 21st century, and this is still going on!"

Me: You know, if the two of you converted to a non-Catholic branch of Christianity with a different interpretation of—

Rasha: I know, we heard about a Maronite couple who became Syriac Orthodox just so they could divorce.

Me: Yeah, that's what I mean. So, is that what you're gonna do?

Rasha: I don't think so. Changing your sect…the paperwork that goes with that is a hassle. And remember, I already did that once. I don't want to do it again.

Me: Okay, so that means what?

Rasha: It means we have to get special permission from the Vatican. I think they call it an annulment, so it's not actually a divorce, but it's basically the same, at least as far as we're concerned.

Me: I think I've heard about that, but isn't it risky? What if they turn down your petition or request or whatever?

Rasha (broad smile): That's always possible, but I know a way to make sure the priest we talk to here in Lebanon will recommend that annulment when he sends our file to the Vatican for the higher-ups to make the decision. You see, Hunayn, there are certain things, sexual things, that the Catholic Church doesn't approve of.

This caused me to tense up. *How had I managed the dubious feat of bringing the conversation around to the very subject I had sought to avoid from the start—her intimidating sexuality?* "Ah, right, ehe, ehe, ehe," I managed feebly.

Rasha wasn't finished. "But I told Pierre that *he* has to be the one to complain to the priest about *my* deviant tastes, not the other way around," she continued, voice rising. "And me? I'll agree with everything he says and admit to the priest that I only married the poor, innocent guy so that I could force him to do all these kinky things to satisfy my cravings. Ha ha ha ha ha!"

## 10

Sitting at home listening to the sound of explosions in the city's southern suburbs, an area subjected to incessant bombing by Israeli warplanes, I grew restless and frustrated. It was July 2006. Which shouldn't have been any different from June 2006. But it was. One month you're celebrating the wonderful news that a team of intrepid explorers has located Noah's Ark atop the Alborz mountains in Iran (to the chagrin of those still holding out hope for Ararat in Turkey) and busy musing: *Now that humanity has solved that enduring mystery, perhaps we can finally focus our energies on finding the Giant Beanstalk, which we've ignored for far too long.* And the next month you're twiddling your thumbs in your pitch-black studio apartment with nothing to do but shudder at the thunderous sound of bombs detonating across town.

It all started with Hezbollah launching an unprovoked attack on Israel, killing several soldiers and snatching two. The Party of God claimed it wanted to force our southern neighbor to release its handful of remaining Lebanese prisoners—including a notorious terrorist who had sneaked into Israel decades earlier, where he murdered an infant and caused the death of a second, among other crimes—and also punish it for continuing to occupy that sliver of disputed land we kept hearing about on Hezbollah's television channel. The Jewish state responded to the attack (which took place in Israel proper, not the tiny disputed territory) with a massive aerial assault on Lebanon accompanied by both land-based and naval artillery fire.

As the Israelis rained down all manner of ordnance on targets in the south of the country and the populous southern suburbs of Beirut, both majority-Shiite regions, Hezbollah showered northern Israel with rockets. In Lebanon, residents of the affected areas fled in droves to safer parts of the country; many even went as far afield as Syria. Meanwhile, Israelis—Jews and Arabs—living in the northern part of their country made a dash for central and southern Israel. Trusty old Moloch was back with a vengeance; this time we had a real war on our hands.

The *Star*'s management decided to suspend the night shift and have us print-edition people work alongside the online team during the day. This was deemed necessary because several of the print writers and editors, particularly those who faced a longish commute to and from work, had stopped staying as late as they were expected to at the office. Additionally, some of the Westerners on staff had begun gearing up for a hoped-for but still unannounced organized evacuation of foreign nationals. Various countries' plans for such a move were complicated by the airport's closure in the wake of an Israeli airstrike, and the perceived risks of chartering buses to drive people to Syria, what with Israel trying to disrupt the transportation routes of Hezbollah and even the Lebanese army, which it distrusted. Increasingly, it appeared that any mass evacuation would have to take place by sea.

The paper shrank to a pitiful four pages, almost every article providing news about the war, such as casualties or information on which roads were still serviceable. Meanwhile, rolling blackouts became the norm; the Israelis had flattened a couple of power plants, and those that remained functional couldn't supply the entire country at the same time. For businesses housed in buildings that had their own diesel generators to supply them with electricity—as was the case where the *Star* rented office space—this wasn't a big deal. But at home, for hours on end, you couldn't follow the local TV stations' continuous coverage of the mounting destruction. Yet neither could you take your mind off the situation by watching a DVD, playing some music, or surfing the Web.

That is, unless you paid one of a number of resourceful independent generator operators in your neighborhood to supply you with electricity. I was reluctant to do this, both because of the expense involved and because of the possibility that it would turn out not to have been worth it, should the Israelis suddenly end their campaign and the stingy generator guy refuse to reimburse me for the required advance payment I would have had to extend him at the start. I almost regretted not having bought a laptop, expensive as such a thing was. When the power got cut, the batteries would have kept it running, and me sane.

Despite my growing alarm at the death and destruction, I tried to keep things in perspective. While the Israelis pummeled Shiite areas of the country, such as the south and Beirut's southern suburbs, they spared the other regions. For example, though both neighborhoods were tense, Gemmayzeh and Hamra sustained no attacks. When my worried parents called from Erbil to ask about me, I said I was fine, and assured them that the Israelis were not bombing, rocketing, shelling, or strafing either the area where I lived or the one where I worked.

I'd talk to Zaina on the phone most evenings. All she wanted to do was slam Israel. This, coupled with the weblinks to news stories on the victims of Israeli bombing she'd send me daily, began to grate on my nerves. (I reminded her on several occasions that I worked in a newsroom, but to no avail.) In the evenings, I began to wish that the power cuts would disable the phone lines. At least I still had no cellphone—couldn't stand the things—which would have made me reachable day or night, at home and everywhere else.

Of course, I too was angry, but I found Zaina's shock at Israel's behavior inexplicable, and at times a touch disingenuous. After all, Israel's critics in the Arab world often denounced its oppression and collective punishment of the Palestinians in the Occupied Territories, and recalled the Jewish state's similar misdeeds against the Lebanese during its two-decade occupation of south Lebanon. If we believed our rhetoric about Israel's ruthlessness—and I, for one, largely did—why would we acquiesce in Hezbollah's manufacturing of a situation in which Israel enjoyed an excuse to once again demonstrate this trait at our expense?

Because subjecting myself to anti-Israeli diatribes from Zaina over the phone was not much of an improvement on sitting around in my dark apartment and doing nothing when the power got cut after sundown, I took to going back to Gemmayzeh at night and hanging out at a bar or two. I did this alone; Zaina wasn't going out at night—partly because she was wiser than I was, but also so as not to worry her parents, with whom she lived in the seafront area of Raushe.

In Gemmayzeh, many bars had long paid a monthly sum of money to neighborhood operators of electricity generators as a backup for the occasional power outage, while those that hadn't taken this precaution made sure to do it now. So they continued to do business. The crowds might not have been reaching their usual levels, but plenty of people came out every night nonetheless. Although Gemmayzeh was where the *Star*'s offices were located, meaning that I could pop into the bars for happy hour as soon as I finished work in the afternoon, I chose to go home instead and relax for a while. Later, having eaten and showered, I'd watch TV until the power got cut, which usually happened at 9 p.m. (though the energy ministry didn't issue a schedule for the blackouts or inform us how it was going about rationing electricity). At that point, I'd go out and catch a cab to Gemmayzeh for drinks. A couple of hours later, I'd head back home for the night.

But on July 19th, a week into the war, something happened that impinged on my new routine. That morning, while we were at work, an Israeli fighter jet rocketed four trucks in Ashrafieh, adjacent to Gemmayzeh. Rumor had it that the trucks were carrying missile launchers.

By day's end, it had become clear that the trucks in Ashrafieh were carrying drilling equipment for water wells, which the Israelis must have mistaken for missile launchers. That night, after replying to an email from my parents and again telling them not to worry, I set off for Gemmayzeh. The bars, however, were closed. Tried nearby Monot, but it was the same deal. Whereas I had observed the day's developments with alarm but concluded that there wasn't much I could do about the situation, apparently the bars' proprietors had adopted a more prudent tack: minimizing the risk to themselves and their patrons by not opening. So I went back home.

At the office toward the end of the next day, word was that the bars were set to reopen. While talking to Samer, I gingerly broached the idea of the two of us going out for a drink, as we both had tomorrow off—a rarity. Of course, I hadn't allowed the prospect of work the following day to deter me from staying up almost every night the past week, but I didn't want to give him the impression I was partying away while people were getting killed. I also figured that even if he was aghast at the destruction Israel was raining down on Shiite areas, he might well need something to take his mind off the subject.

"Yeah, let's do it!" His response was immediate, almost defiant. Now I began to wonder whether the conflict had put him in an anti-Hezbollah mood, so that he wanted to thumb his nose at the militants by living it up all night long.

Over the phone later that evening, he told me he was gearing up for a grand time, and that we needed to make sure to hit some hopping, oblivious-to-the-war spots. I realized Gemmayzeh and Monot were unlikely to fit the bill. When he picked me up in his car, I suggested we try Brummana, a low-lying Christian mountain village only 10 miles (as the crow flies) east of Beirut. He agreed. During the civil war, when Beirut often saw heavy fighting, a ring of villages around the capital developed a vibrant nightlife. These areas slipped into an inevitable decline once the war ended and Beirut regained a measure of security, but I suspected things had reverted to their older state with this latest conflagration, even more so following the Ashrafieh strike.

Thinking we'd listen to music, I had set aside The Cat Empire's album *Two Shoes*, which had only recently arrived in Lebanon on CD. But as we headed out, driving through east Beirut and then up Mount Lebanon (thereby sticking to Christian areas and avoiding the highway), it became clear that Samer wanted to vent his rage instead. At Hezbollah, not Israel. To him, the party's reckless attack was designed to divert the Lebanese people's attention from their internal disputes, especially that concerning whether Hezbollah should surrender its arms to the state, as many were urging it to do.

Separately, he bristled at many Israel critics' implication, when lambasting the Jewish state's "disproportionate" response, that it should voluntarily restrict its retaliation to the scale of Hezbollah's attack. "I mean, don't they realize that promising a proportionate response means doing away with your deterrent power?" he asked, a tone of incredulity in his voice. "If I don't like you and I know that punching you in the face would mean you'd come back at me with the same, I might do it. But if I have even the slightest fear that you might pull a knife or a gun on me, let me tell you, I wouldn't dream of chancing it."

Me: Okay, but the Israelis never made it clear they would respond so disproportionately to such an attack, so it's not like Hezbollah knew Israel would come at them in such a massive way. It looks like they miscalculated.

Samer: Then they're idiots.

Me: Right, but maybe the Israelis knew that and were waiting for them to make a stupid move like the one they just made. That way, they could seize the chance to have their air force destroy both Hezbollah and Lebanon.

Samer (incredulous again): Destroy Lebanon?! You think Lebanon is being destroyed?!

Me : Well, yeah, I mean, what do you call all this? Pinprick strikes?

Samer: No, of course it's more than that, but my God, man, this is not the destruction of a country! My neighborhood is fine, so is yours, and we're driving—at night, no less—to a village untouched by the air raids, so that we can have a good time. Trust me, this is not destruction. Yes, they're bombing roads leading to the south as well as bridges all over the place, but you can see that other than that, they're concentrating on the Shiite areas, especially the Hezbollah strongholds.

Me: Okay, so they're destroying those areas.

Samer: Yeah, that's the disproportionate response everybody's complaining about. And now Hezbollah knows that if it ever does anything like this again, Israel will retaliate even more disproportionately. That's when you'll see real and total destruction. And for that to never happen, what's happening now has to happen. It's the only thing that'll convince the Hezbollah crowd and their leader that they should stop themselves from attacking Israel.

As we approached that section of Brummana's main street where most of the bars were located, we ran into severe traffic. Just as I had suspected, lots of folks had decided to bypass the Beirut nightspots and make their way to this dependable old mountain village. It took us a while to nab a parking spot, and after we got out of the car we had to elbow our way through swarms of people milling about outside each establishment, only to discover that it was filled to the brim inside. Even finding space to sit outside, which we eventually managed at one place, proved difficult, and many people stood for want of seating. Nobody seemed

241

to mind, though; the mood was bright and breezy. Samer and I would have preferred to sit at the bar inside, but this arrangement, which consisted of sharing an oblong wooden table with a bunch of other people, would suffice.

Because we failed to win the attention of the sole (and harried) waiter, I went inside to get us our drinks, a Jim Beam and Coke for me and a gin and tonic for Samer. By the time I returned, some 10 minutes later, he and a few of the guys at our table had struck up a conversation. I took my seat at the end of one of the two wooden benches on either side of the table, with Samer seated across from me. After passing him his drink and taking a tentative sip from mine, I tuned in. They were talking, predictably enough, about the war.

Samer didn't seem to notice that I had placed his drink in front of him, so involved was he in telling his listeners a variation on what he had told me in the car. "You know something," he was saying, "we see all these people streaming out of the south seeking refuge, and we...of course...it's natural that we should feel for them. And yes, Israel tells them to leave their villages because it's going to bomb them, so they know for sure they'd better get out fast. But so many of us, the Lebanese, we just get stuck on that, what Israel's doing, and don't go beyond it. And that's what Hezbollah wants—for us to forget that it provoked the Israelis. So these displaced people, let's help them, but without allowing ourselves—"

"Actually, I don't think we should help them," interjected the guy on Samer's right. "If it was up to me, we'd go out with our weapons and force them to go back where they came from. We might not be strong enough to fight

Hezbollah, but we don't have to take their people in. And what could Hezbollah do about it, while they're busy fighting Israel?"

I assumed that by "we," the guy meant Christians, as he wore a cross around his neck. The Christians were split over Hezbollah, including its most recent action, with this division apparent in the divergent political positions adopted by the two major Christian political parties. I threw a sidelong glance at Samer, who looked stunned. He had always made a distinction between Hezbollah and Shiite civilians, even if most of the latter supported the party. In his naiveté, he expected others to do the same.

"I agree," the guy on my left chimed in. "But I would go even further. I'm from Beirut, and I have cousins in the Future Movement," he said in reference to the country's main Sunni political party. "The other day, we were talking about whether the Israelis will manage to crush Hezbollah, and I was saying that if they do, that's our chance. We must move against the Shiites once they're down—especially in Beirut, which is not even their city—and take advantage of the situation to put them back in their place."

If the first guy's statements had floored Samer, I hardly imagined he was in a better state now. Looking at him, though, one couldn't tell; this time, he had quickly absorbed the shock and put on his familiar inscrutable face. But I was pretty sure I saw it darken a bit.

And with good reason. Here's a man who shuns the ideological ghetto of Shiite power and takes on its gatekeeper, Hezbollah, which he views as a theocratic menace to Shiites' historical secularism and to Lebanon's relatively liberal culture. He expects to find like-minded people from other communities, only to collide with the disturbing reality that some of those who share his hostility to Hezbollah also hate Shiites; in fact, they oppose Hezbollah in part because it's helped raise up the Shiites. Meeting Samer, who criticizes Hezbollah openly without revealing that he's Shiite, they imagine they've found an ally. And they behave accordingly, spouting anti-Shiite vitriol and fantasizing aloud about violently suppressing the community in its entirety.

Whatever Samer was thinking, he went pretty quiet after that, exchanging only brief remarks about strictly military aspects of the conflict with the guys. I contributed a few comments as well, given my familiarity with that dimension of the situation, which the *Star* was attempting to cover in detail. When the conversation drifted to cars and real estate, Samer went completely silent, and I followed suit in short order. Because he was so pensive, twirling his glass slowly at its base and peering into it, taking only the occasional sip, I decided not to bother him with idle chatter of my own.

As the war intensified over the next couple of weeks, the Israelis continuing to bomb the country almost around the clock and even speaking of a ground invasion, countries with foreign nationals in Lebanon scrambled to organize their evacuation. They would have to do this by sea, because the airport had not reopened following the airstrike targeting its runways, while driving to Syria was not only dangerous but exorbitant, given that the opportunistic tour bus and taxi companies had jacked up their prices. The ships' trajectories en route to and from Lebanon's territorial waters had to be coordinated with the Israelis, who had imposed a naval blockade on the country.

My parents called again, having heard about the decamping foreigners. Convinced that this portended the destruction of Lebanon, because soon the Israelis would feel they could unleash just about everything in their arsenal with impunity (all fears of accidentally killing precious Westerners and sparking a diplomatic crisis about to dissipate), they begged me to leave. Again I reassured them as best I could that I was safe, but also took the opportunity to explain that Iraq was not among the countries organizing or participating in the sea-borne evacuation, meaning that I couldn't join the exodus even if I wanted to.

A sense of abandonment took hold of the delicate Lebanese psyche. Excepting the minority that wanted Israel to crush Hezbollah even if it destroyed Lebanon in the process, the Lebanese resented the fact that while Western countries acted in concert to evacuate foreign nationals, they conspicuously refrained from making an effort to pressure Israel to end its offensive. Indeed, many people grew outraged when the US opposed the idea of a ceasefire between Israel and Hezbollah, all the more so because Uncle Sam supplied the bulk of the Israeli army's weapons and munitions. The Americans seemed to have yielded to demands by hawkish Israeli politicians and generals that their army be given more time to degrade Hezbollah's capabilities and simultaneously punish Lebanon for not having clamped down on the party—which was not only impossible, as evidenced by its steadfastness in the face of the Israeli military onslaught, but would have provoked civil war. And all the while, the Israeli air force went about its grim business.

The Israelis' cavalier attitude to civilian casualties on the Lebanese side, together with their tendency to congratulate themselves for alleged displays of restraint, proved galling even to those of us who disapproved of Hezbollah. Israeli politicians of all stripes adopted their military's smug claim that it was a moral army. (Some even declared it the most moral army in the world.) It didn't seem to occur to them that perhaps the people on the receiving end of the army's exploits, rather than the military institution itself, might be better placed to judge the veracity of this claim. Meanwhile, whenever anyone reproached the Israelis for causing so many civilian casualties, they'd trot out their glib talking point about Hezbollah using human shields, of which there were plenty of suspicions but precious little evidence. Or they'd reply that they could have killed many more people, but had done them the immense (and presumably unwarranted) favor of warning them beforehand to flee their homes.

The war changed Hamra. Schools and even public spaces swelled with people, as these were the venues where the displaced from the south and the southern suburbs sought refuge. Those camped out in parks, exposed to the elements, would have fared much worse had the war occurred in winter. As it was, many of them stood in dire need of supplies, having had little chance to secure all the necessary provisions for the ongoing dismal scenario before fleeing their homes. Indeed, when the Israeli army issued warnings to people in specific areas to leave, most did just that—without tarrying. Hezbollah's social welfare arm tried to tend to their needs, but found itself overwhelmed.

Even this didn't make the displaced sour on the party; many used their appearances on TV—courtesy of gaggles of reporters asking them how they felt—to express their unstinting devotion to Hezbollah's leader.

By the time August rolled around, the Israeli ground invasion had become a reality, though it was restricted to the south, where battles pitting the Israeli army against Hezbollah fighters raged. In between grappling with war-related news reports and trying to take my mind off them by drinking in Gemmayzeh bars (which had filled up again), I was blindsided my Samer's revelation that he had received a job offer from an English-language newspaper in Saudi Arabia, and planned to set off for the wealthy but obscurantist Islamic desert monarchy as soon as the war ended and Beirut's airport reopened. He told me this at the office one afternoon when he walked over to my cubicle. "I'll explain everything later," he added. "Let's meet tonight at the Cabin and talk."

Captain's Cabin was the oldest bar in Hamra, dating to 1964. For some time following my return to Lebanon from Septemberland, rumors swirled that entrepreneurs would turn Hamra's Makdessi Street into another Gemmayzeh, but we stopped hearing anything of the sort after Hariri's assassination. So Hamra remained pretty much the same, offering little in the way of nightlife. Still, the area's few bars enjoyed a certain disarming charm, boasted an intriguing history, and attracted a distinctive and loyal clientele.

When Captain's Cabin first flung open its doors back in '64, the bar's patrons came to include the flight crews of Middle East Airlines, Lebanon's national carrier. In fact, the Cabin's founder and first proprietor was a former

MEA pilot—hence the name—though he curiously chose to endow the place with a nautical theme, hanging up a couple of helm wheels on the walls.

Now, a little over four decades later, by which time Adnan, the nephew-by-marriage of the original proprietor, had become the Captain of the Cabin, the regulars included local and foreign journalists, as well as teachers at the nearby high schools—especially ACS and IC—who needed a watering hole where they wouldn't run into their students. (Adnan was almost unique in that he carded younger potential customers.) The place was a dive—mismatched barstools, decrepit tables and chairs, wood paneling in various stages of decay, bumpy pool table, something between an unkempt garden and an ill-maintained patio out back—but a spacious and homey one. The prices were the best in Beirut. Samer and I generally disliked going there only because we didn't fancy running into colleagues, but otherwise it was the ideal spot for a couple of guys who wanted to have a serious talk, as Adnan refrained from turning up the sound system's volume so high that the music drowned out all conversation, which was the norm in Gemmayzeh and Monot bars. Since Samer had already decided to leave not just the paper but the country, the prospect of a *Star* staffer eavesdropping on our talk must have not fazed him.

As it happened, there weren't any *Star* people—or anyone else—about; the place was empty when I arrived. I took a seat at the end of the bar, where the stocky and square-skulled (but thankfully not blockheaded) Adnan was watching a local TV channel featuring a roundtable discussion on the ongoing developments by some of the same gassy pundits I had seen on other channels earlier that day at the office. Usually in good spirits, today he seemed morose, the conflict having by the looks of it ground him down into resigned helplessness. He muted the volume so that we could speak. "Everybody's gone," he said glumly, and proceeded to explain that many of the foreigners and Lebanese dual nationals who hung out at the Cabin had left the country.

Business had been increasing steadily since spring of the previous year, when the Syrian army withdrew from Lebanon, taking with it the intelligence unit housed in a building just a few yards up the street. I hadn't known about the existence of the Cabin before the Syrian withdrawal, so unfrequented was it in those days. I discovered it a while later, after seeing people milling about outside one night, and began to pop in on occasion. I'd talk to Adnan, who'd tell me about his recently concluded travails. Precisely because of the nearby presence of the Syrian intelligence guys, he explained (lowering his voice, as though they were still hovering about), people had avoided the place. From 1997—when Adnan returned to Lebanon following a couple of years abroad in order to care for his ailing father and take over the by then floundering business—until 2005, he stuck it out despite the dearth of patrons.

When the Syrians withdrew in the spring of that year, his fortunes began to change. Whereas talk of transforming this particular area of Hamra into another Gemmayzeh ended once Hariri was killed, due to understandable jitters on the part of prospective investors, places already up and running began to benefit from the breath of freedom the longtime occupiers had left in their wake. Over the next year, the Cabin earned a reputation as a hangout for journalists and high school teachers, while carousers loath to live it up within earshot of Syrian spies also began to drop by quite often. All this came to a screeching halt with the war, and a doleful Adnan was left to wonder if his establishment's latter-day rejuvenation had ended for good.

When Samer arrived, he took a seat beside me and immediately began bringing me up to speed on his surprising news. He told me that as soon as it became clear that Lebanon was at war, "or, more accurately, had been plunged into war by Hezbollah," he began thinking of relocating to another country. As the destruction mounted and Hezbollah refused to back down, he started emailing job applications to newspapers and magazines in all six countries of the Persian Gulf.

"With each passing day, Hunayn, I realized that what the Israelis were doing might not be enough to deter Hezbollah in the future, which would mean that it's only a matter of time before the next explosion," my friend explained. "And let me tell you, I sure as hell don't want to be around for that one," he added in grim, somewhat melodramatic fashion.

I couldn't help but wonder about this explanation, particularly in light of our encounter with those guys in Brummana. The discussion we'd had that night gave Samer a taste of what Shiites could expect were Hezbollah neutralized. Not exactly encouraging, and not something he'd want to experience. Fear of people exacting vengeance on any and all Shiites had probably played a role in his decision to leave. But another factor was quite likely just as critical; even if those dogpiling the Party of God and its support base decided to spare anti-Hezbollah Shiites, Samer and many other decent people in this group wouldn't want to be remotely associated with, let alone get lassoed into participating in, the collective punishment of the majority of their community.

I didn't mention any of this, as I didn't want to make him uncomfortable. Instead, after he urged me to also try to find work in the Gulf and leave Lebanon to its current and future woes, I asked him how he'd handle Saudi Arabia's enforcement of gender segregation, and the country's strict ban on pre-marital romantic relationships of even the most innocuous kind.

He shrugged and said, "I guess I'll just be celibate."

"Celibate?!" I exclaimed. "What, like Jesus?!"

"Actually, I was thinking more like Morrissey, to tell you the truth," he replied. "But Jesus is okay. In fact, Jesus is just alright, so that'd certainly work."

His determination to leave Lebanon, coupled with his equanimity about swearing off women, irked me. After all, not counting Zaina, he was the only real friend I had left. Khaled had removed himself from my life by committing a crime years ago, I had dropped Hashem, Lewis had cut me off, and Nadia, already a mother, had gone back to being a wife—in another country, no less. If Samer moved abroad, we'd have to revert to being pen pals, much like when I lived in Orlando and he in Beirut. We'd probably see each other only once or twice a year.

"But listen," I pressed, "what about the whole Islamic thing? If you and your coworkers are out on the street one day when it's time for prayer, those guys from the religious police, the ones running around and brandishing those wooden canes, could come over and tell you to hustle to the mosque. You can't say you're not Muslim, because work permits for foreigners over there list their religious affiliation; you know that, right? Do you even know how to pray?"

Samer: No, I don't, and I never have. But if I do end up forced to go to the mosque with my coworkers, I'll just say that I haven't prayed in so long I've forgotten how, and they can show me.

Me (frustrated): Man, I just don't think you realize how religious they are. Islam governs every aspect of their lives. And it makes them all the same. In fact, I think everyone's called Muhammad over there.

Samer (rare chuckle): Actually, that's more the case in Egypt, except for the Copts, of course. Like Muhammad Hosni Mubarak and Muhammad Anwar Sadat. Egyptian Muslims—

Me: Yeah, it's like if it's not part of your name, you stick out and everyone wants a piece of you. Really, man, think of a Jew among non-Jews out in the Eastern European countryside or something—a painted bird, like in that novel.

Samer (alarmed): Wait, isn't that anti-Semitic?

Me (excited): That's exactly what I'm saying; in the story, they all persecute him! Just like if you catch a bird and paint it all kinds of colors and then set it free, when it rejoins its flock the other birds consider it an intruder, so they attack the poor thing and pluck its feathers out until they kill it!

Samer: No, I mean you said "Jew."

Me: What?

Samer: That could be construed as anti-Semitic. Perhaps, to be safe, you should say "Jewish." You know, like, "a Jewish person among non-Jewish—"

Me: Oh, for goodness' sake, man!

Samer: I'm just saying, you know?

Me: Well, shut up, okay?

Samer: Okay, sorry to interrupt.

I didn't take Samer's advice and try to land a job in the Gulf. This was partly because I had a low opinion of their English-language newspapers, the standard of which couldn't even match that of the *Star*—itself hardly a paragon of quality. But I also wanted to get out of journalism altogether, which had long taken to grating on me. Where to go?

Iraq, of course, wasn't an option. The country had descended into open conflict between Sunnis and Shiites earlier in the year, when Sunni extremists blew up a Shiite shrine. Meanwhile, the plight of Christians had worsened. And nobody, least of all the newly empowered Shiite-dominated government in Iraq or the Americans who had empowered it, was doing anything about it.

Some of the Sunni Islamist groups rampaging through Iraq were giving Christians an ultimatum: convert to Islam and attain equality with us; pay the jizya protection tax and accept second-class status in return for the right to remain Christian; or face the sword. Centuries earlier, the first Muslims, in compliance with the injunctions of the Quran, had imposed this draconian set of conditions on the ever-increasing number of non-Muslims whose lands they conquered, and expected gratitude on the part of Christians for not simply being killed. Now, the nightmare had returned.

As a result, more and more of my coreligionists were migrating to the relative safety of rural northern Iraq. I read articles about some of them settling in the Nineveh Plain, the birthplace of Assyrian civilization. Though now a somewhat desolate area, it nonetheless remained home to a string of Christian villages. And while the Nineveh Plain fell outside autonomous and well-protected Iraqi Kurdistan, the people moving there apparently considered it remote enough to afford them safety and security.

Other Christians were taking no chances and moving to the Kurdish region itself. My parents, who lived in Ankawa, a Christian suburb of Erbil, told me that a good number had begun to make their way there after being allowed entry by the Kurdish peshmerga who patrolled the boundary line between Kurdistan and the rest of Iraq. Reports filtered back to my parents about the scene at the checkpoints through which the Christians streamed in. The women sobbing as they clutched portraits of their murdered loved ones (some killed for not paying the protection tax, some killed despite paying it, some killed just for their faith), the men grim and determined to convince the peshmerga to allow them passage, which they generally succeeded in doing.

I could join them. But why? It had begun to seem that any part of my country, even the secure Kurdish north, just wasn't for me—at least for the foreseeable future.

Now, it wasn't as if I wanted to stay in Lebanon. For one thing, I had come to realize that, contrary to the assumption I made when coming to terms with my having to leave the States, I didn't in fact understand how things worked here. Worse, a drooling Moloch had decided to squat right smack in the middle of the country, and who knew which of us he'd scoop up next and pop into his masticating maw? Nevertheless, I hadn't applied for work elsewhere, meaning no alternatives were available to me. Also, it was in Lebanon that I saw an opportunity to land a job that had nothing to do with journalism.

Ironically, the country's recently changed circumstances —courtesy of Moloch—had made this possible. Surely the war, which prompted foreign residents to abscond irrespective of longstanding professional and personal ties to Lebanon, had deprived high schools such as ACS, my alma mater, of many of their teachers. Although a large number of the American and Canadian teachers of English and history were probably not in the country to begin with, given the summer vacation, they weren't all about to return. For one thing, the airport was still closed.

But even if the war suddenly ended and the airport fixed its runways in short order, many of these teachers wouldn't hurry back to a country that might again erupt in conflict at the drop of a hat. And the beginning of the school year was less than a month away. This was my chance to segue from editing to teaching English (the gig Lewis had by now most likely secured in Detroit), bypassing the acquisition of credentials such as certificates and experience. The way I saw it, my UCF bachelor's degree in English literature together with the fact that I was an ACS graduate should stand me in good stead for the job.

## 11

Zaina and I were strolling through the René Mouawad Garden, a small public park on the edge of Hamra that bore no trace of the crowded sanctuary for the displaced it had been just a couple of months ago. The war was over. It had ended in early August, shortly after an incident in which Israeli airstrikes killed nearly 30 civilians, most of them children, sheltering in a building in a southern village. The incident galvanized the international community into pressing Israel to accept a ceasefire. Embarrassed at the casualty toll, chary of mounting criticism, and aware that the US now also wanted the conflict to end, Israel acceded a few days later, as did Hezbollah. The ceasefire held, and was soon recognized as having ended hostilities. The war had lasted 34 days and killed some 1,200 Lebanese (approximately half of whom were civilians) and 160 Israelis (mostly soldiers), injured many more and temporarily displaced hundreds of thousands on both sides, as well as caused extensive damage to Lebanon's infrastructure. In a remarkable admission during a televised speech following the war, Hezbollah's leader revealed that had he had an inkling of the consequences, he wouldn't have green-lighted his party's opening attack on Israel. And then he blithely proclaimed that those consequences amounted to a divine victory for Hezbollah.

Now empty save for a few mothers pushing strollers, the park was ideal for a young couple seeking a spot of sylvan splendor. Zaina and I held hands and walked along its perimeter. We had been together for a year and a half now. My teensy-weensy yet super-spunky squeeze. If, as a lark, I wanted to wear the shirwal my parents had brought me from Erbil and walk around outside, I could slip her into one of the two little side pouches and amble down Hamra Street without people noticing anything unusual other than the pants themselves. Was that a *princess* in my pocket, though? Not quite. Pretty and bitchy enough, to be sure, and the sort of girl who preferred an electric toothbrush to save herself the effort of moving the regular kind up and down, but one in thrall to a quasi-fascist political party as opposed to bling and fashion accessories.

Still, I was touched by the support and encouragement Zaina gave me when ACS had hired me as an English teacher a couple of months earlier. Because of the school's severe faculty shortage in the English and history departments, the administration was promoting some people early and abolishing all teaching assistant posts for the year. And, of course, they were hiring to fill the gaps. I learned as much in my interview with Ms. Wilson, head of the English department for both the high school and the middle school. A New Englander in her 60s with a refined but somewhat dry demeanor, Ms. Wilson informed me (with the not-so-subtle insinuation that I should feel grateful) that the exceptional circumstances meant they were willing to hire "someone who is neither a North American nor a Lebanese national" for a full teaching position.

I was assigned to the middle school; at ACS, this consisted of seventh and eighth grade. I would teach three seventh-grade classes and one eighth-grade one every day. This was less daunting than taking on high school with no prior teaching experience, but I still had my concerns. Could I control a classroom of rowdy adolescents? Would my teaching style capture their attention, or fall flat and convince the school administrators that they had erred in hiring me?

Zaina sat me down, placed her hand over mine, squeezed it firmly, and said, "Hunayn, you're just right for this job. I know you'll do brilliantly. And it's a good career move too, especially at this time. Now you'll be able to say that within just a few years of graduating college, you managed to become a content editor at Lebanon's English-language newspaper, and then a teacher of English language and literature at one of its most prestigious schools. I'm proud to have you as a boyfriend."

As luck would have it, Issa Sabra, whom Ms. Wilson appointed as my mentor, wasn't haughty or bossy or patronizing in the least. Five years older than I was, with a wife and infant daughter, he proved too self-involved to bother himself with peering over my shoulder and telling me what to do, or even dispensing useful advice. When it came to the specifics of teaching the mediocre material I was saddled with, he let me do as I pleased.

That's not to say he left me alone, though. Issa liked to run his mouth about whatever was on his mind, and jumped at the chance to address an audience, even one that consisted of a single person, and an obviously uninterested one at that.

Also, Issa often felt like a whore. I knew this because he told me as much. Constantly. It was a manifestation of his tendency to articulate his emotions in sexualized terms. Several reasons accounted for Issa's feeling like a whore. All had to do with the supposed ordeal of living in Lebanon, where he had been born and raised. (He had gone to IC for high school, graduating the year before my family moved to Lebanon from Italy.) Issa complained about everything from rampant sectarianism to Lebanese motorists' disregard for traffic laws.

Perhaps the biggest factor in putting him off Lebanon was his treatment at the hands of the school's administration, which, though local in membership, had long had in place a policy of favoring North Americans over Lebanese (irrespective of their relative merits) for the subjects of English and history, paying them a higher salary, and throwing in a housing allowance. "You see, Hunayn, because they don't realize that a Lebanese like them can be a native speaker of English, they kept me as an assistant to foreign teachers—many of them with little or no experience—for the past four years, like I was their little whore."

"Whose little whore?" I asked. "The administration's or the foreign teachers'?"

"Both! This is the first year I get a shot at teaching my own classes, and that's only because of the war and all the foreigners running away."

I sympathized with him. Figured it must have been tough—these past four years—to play second fiddle to people accorded preferential treatment largely because of their ethnicity. (And it did seem that ethnic origins counted for more than anything else; those Lebanese who had US or Canadian nationality were viewed as not quite "real" Americans or Canadians, and for this reason they too had to toil away for years as low-paid assistants before becoming

English or history teachers.) But Issa had caught a break, and was now teaching high schoolers, which was what he wanted to do, so I couldn't help but think that maybe he ought to ease up on the whining. Also, although I agreed with many of the criticisms he leveled against Lebanon, it nevertheless unsettled me when he insisted that all Lebanese (except himself, of course), and even all Arabs, were extremists of one sort or another. "And I don't just mean the usual religious or sectarian or ethnic nationalist kind," he said. "Look at the school administration; they're fanatic the other way, so that they kiss Westerners' asses, just like all those companies in Dubai."

Dubai—like my childhood home of Abu Dhabi, a city in the United Arab Emirates—was where Issa had lived and worked for a few years after graduating from AUB with a BA in English. He wrote English-language copy for an advertising agency, and learned just how hierarchically arranged humanity was in the UAE. Emiratis stood at the top, by mere virtue of being locals. Just below them were North Americans and Western Europeans. The Lebanese held a slot somewhere in the middle of the totem pole, above other Arabs as well as South Asians such as Indians and Pakistanis.

Oddly enough, Issa's sole fond memory of Dubai had to do with whores—real ones, whom he spoke of with unexpected tenderness. "They were everywhere, Hunayn," he said wide-eyed, as that delicious reality re-boggled his mind. "I swear, at night, when the weather cooled a little bit, you couldn't walk outside for more than five minutes without one of them propositioning you. And the bars, most of which by law have to be in hotels, were overflowing with the more high-class ones, the kind I went for."

Me (a mite uncomfortable): Hey man, you weren't married back then, were you?

Issa (wistful): No, no, I was single. And let me tell you, the Russians were the best.

Me: Russians, huh?

Issa: Absolutely—and not the young and girlish ones that all the stupid Lebanese and Arabs wanted so they could pretend they were with virgins. No, I'm talking about the older, experienced ones. They were more worldly and independent-minded. Knew how to behave in elegant restaurants, spoke better English thanks to their clients over the years, and didn't live to do whatever you told them to do. Sure, they were chubbier and had more cellulite, but I still found them beautiful and sexy. And yeah, their boobs might've been a bit puckered and sagged a little, but they were soft and yielding. Not like implants, which all the younger women had. What matters is how they feel, not how they look, you know?

Me: Right.

Issa: And they're supposed to feel like water balloons, not air-inflated ones.

Me: I imagine the master balloonist up above will forever appreciate that observation. He's probably sick and tired of watching his handiwork ruined through those atrocious boob jobs so many women are having.

To my moderate surprise, I proved a competent—if unremarkable—teacher. Being back at ACS in a role other than that of student didn't throw me, and I got into the groove of my job in pretty short order. Although I had no hand in devising the curriculum and found myself stuck with vapid yet overrated material, such as John Steinbeck's *The Pearl*, J. D. Salinger's *The Catcher in the Rye*, and Ernest Hemingway's *The Old Man and the Sea*, I always took great care to craft variegated lesson plans, leaven my lectures with anecdotes, and involve the students in discussions. And it turned out that I had what it took—a lot of vigilance, a touch of gravitas, a certain rapport with my charges—to manage a classroom.

A good thing, too; had it been otherwise, I might have failed to put a stop to Hadi's heckling of Jacob in my eighth-grade class. The loud-mouthed and unruly Hadi would exclaim "Yaakov! Yaakov!" whenever Jacob spoke—until, at the end of that first week of school, I said, "Shut up, Hadi," and shot daggers at him.

Jacob was American. He was also Jewish. His Lebanese antagonizer apparently hadn't given him grief about this—or anything else, for that matter—the previous year, when he had come to Lebanon from the States. Jacob's homeroom advisor, Nariman Khuwairi, told me as much when I asked her. She taught social studies, and this was the second year she had both kids in her class. (The previous year, she had served as assistant to their social studies teacher, a Canadian woman who hadn't returned.) Nariman explained that it had all started the first week of school, when Hadi asked Jacob, point-blank and in front of everyone, whether he approved of what Israel had just done to Lebanon.

Jacob was somewhat taken aback, as nobody had previously singled him out for questioning on Israel—which he didn't seem to have any affinity for. But he answered in a clear and straightforward manner that he thought the Israelis had overreacted. Nariman told me that most of the kids looked satisfied with this reply.

Not Hadi, though, who believed or was pretending to believe (Nariman couldn't say for sure) that Israel had no right to respond militarily to Hezbollah's attack, given its continued imprisonment of Lebanese militants and its occupation of that infamous sliver of disputed land. He announced all this in strident fashion, adding that it was "totally obvious," but Jacob refused to budge. As a result, Hadi launched a relentless campaign to associate him not just with Jewish identity but with Israel, and to devalue both, even though it was never clear that Jacob's position on the recent conflict was animated by his Jewishness or some measure of Zionism. Nariman complained to me that Hadi had become quite disruptive in her class, and that his antics and insults were only making him more popular.

I found all this curious. *Did the summer war change Hadi, or merely present him with a golden opportunity to come into his own as a bully?* Had it really begun to rankle him that Jacob was Jewish, or did he suddenly realize that this aspect of the kid's identity now rendered him more vulnerable than anyone else, meaning that the choice of whom to bully became obvious, and a latent desire on Hadi's part could finally manifest itself?

It was difficult, if not impossible, to say. Whatever the case, the abrasive Hadi had taken to hectoring the quiet and self-possessed Jacob in Nariman's class—and probably all others they shared. And, ever desirous of constancy in his newfound role as bane of the sole Jewish kid's life, he was trying to find ways to taunt him in my class, too. Once, during a spontaneous discussion between the students about which of them faced the most difficult commute, what with Israeli air raids having rendered bridges or tunnels or stretches of highway on their usual routes impassable, Hadi turned to Jacob, seated just a few feet away, and sneered, "Of course, some of us are totally cool with what happened, 'cause of who our father is."

I interpreted this snide remark as a dig at Jacob's Jewishness—and immediately slapped Hadi with an after-school detention. "One more ethnic slur like that," I warned him, "and I'll ask the principal to suspend you."

"But sir," Hadi protested (using the unctuous form of address that some of my classmates had employed back in my days as an ACS student, and one that still had currency), "it's not something ethnic! His father's job was to fix Beirut's streets and solve the traffic problems, so I was just thinking that because of the war he now has more work to do and is gonna make a ton of money."

Clever comeback, I thought, while also inferring that Jacob's father must be some kind of urban planner or civil engineer. "Well, you know what, Hadi?" I replied, quick on my feet. "Implying that a classmate's parent is a money-grubbing opportunist is no better, and I won't allow it."

So I succeeded in shutting down Hadi's in-class attempts to bully Jacob. The kid remained an obstreperous and attention-seeking nuisance, though, especially when not in disingenuously respectful mode. Often, he seemed intent on asserting himself in the face of my (mild) exercise of authority. When he tried to do this, I would deal with the situation in a manner that, while not quite harsh, did include a measure of spite. Once, he sauntered into class quite late—deliberately, by the looks of that unhurried gait. Everyone was seated and I had already begun my lecture.

The perfect way, really, for him to be seen thumbing his nose at me. Indeed, he lingered beside the door, anticipating a censorious remark he could respond to by rolling his eyes or some such, thereby showing everybody he didn't care. But because I ignored him, he found himself in a bit of a pickle. Rather than give in and take his seat quietly, he decided to raise my hackles. In a defiant tone, he said, "Hey sir, guess what?"

I turned around. Those of his classmates not already watching to see what he was getting up to now also shifted their attention to him. A smirk disfigured his face.

"I didn't do my homework," he announced. "It looked really boring, so I just watched TV instead."

Lots of chortles, some laughs.

"I'm not going to spank you," I replied gravely. "Don't even think about it."

The class went quiet. Hadi, sounding uncertain, said, "What?"

Me: You heard me. If you like that sort of naughty stuff, that's your business, but don't come around here expecting me to play along.

Hadi (flustered): Oh, no, I wasn't…

Me: Don't worry; it's okay. If I were a kid like you and had a hot babysitter taking care of me while my parents were out, I might be like, "Hey, guess what? I peed my pants!" so that she gives me a solid paddling. Know what I mean?

Hadi (anxious): … … …

Me: But listen, I'm *not* your hot babysitter. And you know what? I'm not going to spank you!

Hadi (placatory): All right, all right!

Me: Now go sit down.

Hadi (relieved): Yes, okay.

Me (muttering): *Not* gonna spank you.

Even normally restrained students snickered as Hadi, momentarily diminished, scuttled past them on his way to his seat at the very back of the classroom.

While Hadi grew more subdued in my class, and Jacob seemed well-adjusted, I knew that this didn't necessarily reflect the situation when they were elsewhere. Nariman, of course, had told me that she was experiencing difficulty keeping the disorderly Hadi in line, particularly when it came to his picking on Jacob. That was bad enough. But students' encounters with one another at school were not restricted to class. This meant that "incidents" could occur out of teachers' sight, as I knew from my own experience with Danny and company. And when I took to watching Jacob during the lunch break and the shorter recess we had earlier in the day, it became clear that he had to contend with a good deal of unpleasantness.

No high drama of the bullying variety, but more than a few instances of cold-shouldering. At one point, some of the eighth-grade boys squared off against their ninth-grade counterparts for an impromptu soccer match. Jacob was on the eighth-grade side. But so was Hadi. And he not only refrained from passing the ball to Jacob when the latter was open and in a position to score, but, by the looks of it, prevailed on most of his teammates to do the same. It struck me that Hadi, unlike Danny, didn't inspire dread in his peers, and might not even have harbored a wish to, but nevertheless got his way with them.

Sometimes, I witnessed sly mockery, as of the kind perpetrated by Layal, a pretty Syrian American girl with a cheery disposition, loquacious tendency, and seemingly endless waves of dyed blond hair cascading down her back. One day, she approached Jacob as he loitered about. I was standing some distance away, and edged closer to eavesdrop on their conversation. From what I could gather, he had lent her some money the previous day, Thursday, so that she could buy a sandwich from the school "cafeteria" (in reality, a kitchenette with a counter for takeout orders). Now she was expressing her gratitude, and presumably about to pay him back. Both of them were smiling, Layal in her fixed and rather inane way, and Jacob somewhat shyly out of the corner of his mouth, sweaty forehead plastered with wilting tendrils of inky hair, hands thrust in pockets as he hunched his shoulders in an obvious attempt to compensate for his height. Having duly thanked him, Layal pulled a bill out of her purse. Smirking, she said, "I thought I'd better get it to you before your Sabbath or whatever, so that you don't charge me any interest." She didn't even bother to wait for him to take the money, but instead slipped it into his tennis shirt's breast pocket.

Jacob averted his gaze in humiliation. Then, still looking away, he removed the bill from his pocket while forcing a tinny chuckle. When he turned back to face Layal again, it seemed as if he wanted to give it back to her and say something. Probably that the matter was no big deal and he didn't need to be reimbursed. But she had walked away, so all he could do was stand there stupidly with the money in his hand.

I should have known better than to talk to Zaina about Jacob. I had decided to tell her about his plight to see whether I might arouse any compassion on her part. But when I explained the overall situation to her, she seemed unmoved. So I took to recounting some of the ugly incidents he had endured, and then asked, "What do you think of all that?"

Zaina: I don't understand what the big deal is. You look around and see what the Jews just did to Lebanon, you follow the news about what they do to the Palestinians every day, you know all about the Nakba, and this is what concerns you? This Jewish student and his feelings?

Me: I'm very concerned about those other things, but also about this student. It's not an "either/or" deal, is it?

Zaina: Actually, it is. Especially if he refuses to criticize Israel, like you said.

Me: That's not what I said. I said that he refuses to criticize Israel on cue. Some of the students think it's his duty to bash Israel every time they tell him to. But he's criticized Israel in the past, including over this latest war on Lebanon.

Zaina: So why did he stop?

Me: I just explained that. He didn't want to be their little terrier and sit or roll over or do anything else just because they told him to.

Zaina: How convenient. He puts his own comfort before the lives of people Israel kills. He's against what Israel does—some of it, anyway—but if he comes under pressure to say that, he won't do it.

Things got worse from there. I told her she was being deliberately obtuse, and that Jacob's insistence on his personal autonomy was brave and commendable. She retorted that I didn't know what bravery was, and if I wanted to learn I should take a look at the Palestinian kids who confronted Israeli tanks with stones. I ventured that bravery took different forms. She replied that Jews were cowards, and if it weren't for Israel's air force, we would have defeated the country long ago. I said that with folks like the SSNP around, I was glad that that hadn't happened, as it would've resulted in a reverse Nakba. She told me to shut the fuck up and run on back to my new Jewish friend at school because he was sad and needed me to give him a nice little pep talk.

If Samer were here, I'd talk to him about Jacob, it occurred to me more than once in the aftermath of that rather colorful tiff. But I didn't even know whether he was coming to Lebanon for Christmas. Of course, the main thing was that I missed the guy. Wanted to hang out with him and hit a bar or two. But while doing that, I could always tell him Jacob's story and seek his advice. Figured he might have an idea or two as to how I might help the kid without embarrassing him.

And he could give me all his news, too. That was the problem with long-distance written communication like ours; it wasn't detailed. Sure, from time to time, we sent each other brief messages. But these consisted of an inquiry about how things were going over there and a general update as to the situation here. Not much more than that.

I decided to write him. And on this occasion, I had something to say in addition to the usual stuff. Not about Jacob—that rather heady subject would have to wait until his next visit, when we could have a real talk. For now, I wanted to find out when that visit would take place, but also offer some advice of my own as to how he might in the meantime play a pivotal role in changing at least one aspect of Saudi Arabian culture for the better.

I had long known of the scrupulously observed Saudi custom of using one's right hand for eating and greeting somebody, and one's left for wiping one's ass and the like. This neat separation of tasks was set by the Prophet Muhammad himself, apparently to improve the hygienic standard of a people who lived in an arid desert land and might go for long stretches of time without access to water.

I proposed to Samer that he invert the rule and use only his left hand for eating and handshakes. "When people take offense, as they inevitably will," I continued, "tell them that you agree wholeheartedly with the principle behind the injunction, but that you've wiped your ass so many times with your right hand that you'd feel awful extending it to them. And then, to get the point across, sniff that right hand and feign queasiness."

"You know what we're gonna do, me and the wife and kid?" said Issa. It was lunch break, and we were standing out in the courtyard, our backs against a couple of lockers as we chatted. "We're gonna leave, that's what."

Me: Where to?

Issa: Not to another shitty Arab country where the people are even worse than the Lebanese, that's for sure. I'm talking about emigrating, leaving permanently.

Me: Why don't you move to Israel? You're already a Sabra.

Issa: What did you say to me?!

Me: Ooh, prickly, just like the Birthright brochure warns!

Issa: What?!

270

Me: Just don't tell them that you're Muslim, or that your first name is Jesus. But hey, speaking of *not* moving to Israel, there's this American kid named Jacob in one of my classes. Know 'im?

Issa (slightly disoriented): Um...yeah...I had him last year. Smart kid.

Me: So you know him well?

Issa: Not really...Remember, I was a teaching assistant. I mostly helped the students who fell behind on assignments and stuff.

Me: Okay, but you know he's Jewish, right?

Issa: Uh...yeah, actually, I do. He was open about that. And it was never an issue. Yeah, it's coming back to me now; not only is he Jewish, but he's your homeboy, right? Well, not really, of course. I mean, he's American, and his parents grew up in England. But, you know, before all that.

Me (intrigued): Before all that, what?

Issa: Before all that, the family was Iraqi.

Me: You're kidding!

Issa: It's true. Both sides. But, I mean, we're talking about his grandparents.

Jacob's surname, Daniel, now resonated with me. Of course, the Daniel family! Menahem Daniel, senator in the Iraqi parliament, whose son Ezra followed in his footsteps. And how often had my mother the history teacher regaled me with the story of Salim Daniel, who became Iraq's first civilian aviator back in 1930 before moving to the UK a few years later?

Naturally, I wanted to talk to Jacob about this. But my preference was to do it in an informal way and without anyone milling about. My chance came when I espied him in the library one afternoon shortly after the school day had ended. I was there to return *The Curious Incident of the Dog in the Night-Time*, by Mark Haddon, which I had thoroughly enjoyed and wanted to suggest to Ms. Wilson as a novel we might incorporate into the middle school English curriculum (though I expected her to say no). The place was empty save for the assistant librarian on duty at the checkout desk. When I spotted Jacob browsing the Middle East history section, I ambled over and asked him what he was up to.

It turned out he had begun scouring the library for titles that might prove useful for his end-of-term presentation in social studies class. His subject, perceptions of guilt among various communities during the Lebanese civil war, struck me as inspired and quite grown-up. I was impressed.

And I saw an opportunity to ease into the conversation I wanted to have. Told him I knew a good deal about the war, and that, should he need any recommendations, I'd be happy to help. In a confident, non-committal manner, he said, "Cool. I'll keep that in mind." Then he added, "But I think I've got it taken care of. Already got a few books from here, and a couple others from my parents' collection at home."

This was my entry point. "By the way, about your parents," I said, "Mr. Sabra, whom you know from last year, tells me they're both of Iraqi origin. Is that right?"

Jacob (shrugging): Yeah, I guess.

Me: That's really something. I'm Iraqi too, you know.

Jacob (unimpressed): Yeah? Huh.

Me: Yeah, I mean, I didn't grow up there or anything, but I was born in Baghdad, and both my parents are Iraqi, so I was raised with that.

Jacob: Uh-huh.

Me: What about your parents? Also from Baghdad?

Jacob: Well, not really. They were born in London and grew up there, 'cause my grandparents from both sides of the family had left Iraq—yeah, Baghdad—in the early '50s, when things got bad for the Jews. So my mom and dad still sort of have a British accent. They met in college over there and got married. And then, when they came to the States for my dad's PhD, they just stayed. So I grew up in Columbus, Ohio.

Me: Right. So, tell me, do they speak Arabic at all?

Jacob: Not really. They understand some, my mom more than my dad. Growing up in London, she was part of this, like, close-knit Iraqi Jewish community.

Me: That's really interesting. You know, Jacob, the Jews of Iraq have a long and illustrious history. King Faisal I called them the life and soul of Iraq's citizenry.

Jacob (rolling his eyes): Yeah, I know. My grandparents always remind me of that when we visit them in London.

Me: Well, tell me, do you consider yourself Iraqi at all?

Jacob: No, can't say that I do. I mean, no offense; I don't consider myself British, either. I'm American.

Me: But what about your family's history before your parents moved to the States? Doesn't that mean anything? Haven't you kept some of that?

Jacob: Sure I have. The Jewish part. I'm American, but I'm also Jewish.

He had made it clear. No room for Iraqi in his identity package. Disappointing. Yet perhaps unsurprising, given the dismal end of the millennia-old Jewish community in

Iraq—including his grandparents. At any rate, I saw an opening to communicate something that had long played on my mind. Coughing a little even though I didn't have to, I said, "Well, speaking of the Jewish part, Jacob, tell me, are Hadi and his lackeys still giving you a hard time about that?"

He turned back to the books on the shelf just above him. I peered down at my feet so that he wouldn't feel my eyes on him. Quietly, he said, "It's not a big deal. I can handle it."

"Oh, I'm sure you can," I replied, looking at him again. "But listen. If, at any point, you want some backup, just give me a sign."

Without turning to face me, he cocked his head, catching my eye. I held his little sidelong glance of appraisal until, a split-second later, he redirected his vision to the books before him.

## 12

Samer responded to my email with one of his own. It confirmed what I had suspected but hoped against; he wouldn't be coming to Lebanon for Christmas. For one thing, he hadn't put in enough work to earn vacation days. And for another, he wasn't Christian, so requesting time off for religious reasons wouldn't fly. There was the Islamic holiday of Eid al-Adha coming up around the time of New Year's Eve, but just as he hadn't thought it worthwhile to buy a ticket to come to Lebanon for no more than a couple of days for Eid al-Fitr back around the end of October, he figured the sensible thing would be to hold off once again.

Otherwise, Samer told me that the job was bearable, though he bristled at the plaudits his paper constantly lavished on the Saudi government, and cringed at its ideologically rigid line on matters relating to Islam. For example, he found it pathetic that the paper's editor-in-chief had attempted to malign Irshad Manji's *The Trouble with Islam Today*, a book that Samer, like me, had read and admired— and known better than to fly into Saudi with.

He thanked me for my suggestion concerning handshaking and ass-wiping, which he said he had put into effect as soon as he received my email. And I got an update regarding his news. These days, he was recovering from trauma of the most severe kind. When Samer had come across a pseudo-scholarly, handsomely bound tome on the wickedness and perfidy of Rejectionists ("Apparently, that's what they call Shiites—including their own citizens—in this wonderful country") at his local Arabic-language bookstore, he decided that he had to have it. But knowing he'd feel uncomfortable spending any of his hard-earned money de Monet on such drivel, he swiped the thing.

Bad idea. He was caught. In line with the Quran's ruling on the punishment for theft, the authorities promptly chopped off his right hand. (At least he'd already practiced chowing down with his left, I told myself after taking in the shocking and repulsive news.)

"Fortunately, it was a *secondhand* store, so they gave me another one," he reassured me, "but I still have to pay for that stupid book."

So my friend hadn't lost his hand after all—nor, I was almost as relieved to discover, his sense of humor!

A few days later, I ran into Issa at the Cabin. It was a Friday night. The place was humming with activity, and a beaming Adnan tirelessly shouldered the deluge of orders. Issa's appearance there surprised me, but then I figured even the most devoted family man needed to step out on his own sometime. He saw me waving and ambled over, taking the seat next to mine at the bar. Got himself an Almaza, the venerable and ubiquitous local brew, and said he'd just come from a dinner at a nearby restaurant, where the family had celebrated the birthday of the elder of his two younger sisters. "She just turned 25," he told me. "Has a pretty good job at a computer software firm in Ashrafieh. We're all quite proud of her. My other sister is graduating—also from AUB—this year."

Me: Oh, so they both went to AUB? Then they must know this place! Do they ever hang out here, get a couple of drinks?

Issa (self-congratulatory sigh): No, we didn't raise them that way.

Me: Funny, I didn't raise *you* that way, and yet you turned into quite the busy bar-hopping whore-monger back in Dubai, didn't you?

Issa (wistful): Ah, yes. Dubai. Those were the days. Good times, Hunayn, good times.

He rambled on about his youthful indiscretions in that glittering desert metropolis. As always, he was at pains to explain that he didn't like Dubai itself or most of its people—foreign, local, and especially Lebanese expatriate —but that the Russian prostitutes and the high salaries made up for this. When, inevitably, he got on the subject of how much of a total whore he felt like that day, and for what reasons, my attention began to wane.

But then I heard my name. This was followed by, "How about you? When you heard that if they can convince the foreign teachers to return next year or get new ones instead, they're going to drag us back down to teaching assistants, didn't that make you feel like a whore?"

I should have expected this, I told myself. Not so much the school administration's plans, which the principal had informed us of via email the previous day, but Issa's putting me on the spot over whether some issue or other had whorified me. Still, it was annoying. I didn't want to pretend that I felt whore-like just so that he could register his point. Yet neither did I want to derail his entire argument by denying such a thing, especially as that might make it appear as though I were too self-important to come down to Issa's level, so that after confiding in me so many times about his whorishness and finally asking me to return the favor, he got snubbed instead.

"Well, the thing is," I began, "I'm not sure if when I'm underappreciated or slighted—"

Issa: No, really, Hunayn. I mean, doesn't what the school just told us make you feel like a cheap whore?

Me (stiffened resolve): Well, certainly not a cheap one. Moderately priced, I should think.

Issa (taken aback): Moderately pri—

Me: Yeah, the way I look at it, the price has gotta be commensurate with the physical attractiveness and the sexual repertoire of the particular whore we're talking about. Well, as you can see, the physical attractiveness part is right here and all up in your face, kinda like I just dunked on you and shattered the backboard Chocolate Thunder-style, leaving you all dazed and reeling and shit.

Issa: What?!

Me: Or maybe like one of your milfy Russian escorts back in Dubai, a busty babushka who Stalinistically mashes your face with her pendulous udders every time you incorrectly answer a question on her "Tolstoy or Dostoyevsky?" pop quiz.

Issa: What?!

Me: As for amassing sexual repertoire, let me assure you I'm no slouch in that department. Got some pretty tasty moves. Now, I admit this wasn't always the case, but today I can say with confidence that my cocksmanship is of a pretty high order.

Issa: What?!

Me: An order so high, in fact, that maybe your president should give me the National Order of the Cedar. If that shit comes in the form of a medal, I could wear it around the very thing it honors.

I half expected this to put his back up. But no; once he had digested the quip, he didn't seem offended in the least. I couldn't decide whether this was a good thing, in that I had a Lebanese colleague to whom I could say anything I wanted about Lebanon without fear of consequence, or a sad and disheartening one, in that it indicated the extent of his estrangement from his country.

At any rate, what I really wanted to talk about was Jacob, and how what Issa had told me about his Jewishness not having been an issue the previous year was no longer the case. But as soon as I began describing what the kid now had to endure, Issa seized the opportunity to engage in one of his favorite pastimes: ranting about "the dumbfuck Lebanese and their stupid mentality." I let him maunder on for a while before excusing myself and going home.

A few days later, I went to see Nariman again. Over the past few months, I had become pretty vigilant, keeping a hawk's eye on Jacob during the lunch break and recess, so that if the cruel treatment he was subjected to outside of my class ever reached the bullying stage, I'd intervene, irrespective of the embarrassment such a move might cause him. But when I thought about it, this didn't seem enough. I needed to find out more. What were Hadi and his cohorts getting up to in those classes—besides mine—that they shared with Jacob? Nariman might know; she was Jacob's homeroom advisor. Homeroom, of course, consisted of nothing more than a few minutes of roll call and the reading out of school-related news every morning before classes began. Yet a student experiencing problems of any kind was supposed to seek the counsel of his or her homeroom advisor.

Nariman was a twiggy brunette with a face so pinched that I often wondered if her undernourished body was eating into her cheeks to sustain itself. She tried to mask her chronic diffidence with a perpetual smile, but few people, including students, seemed fooled. Nariman told me that Jacob hadn't sought her assistance or confided in her about his in-class troubles in any way. But he didn't need to, she pointed out. After all, she was also his social studies teacher, and had witnessed his hounding at the hands of Hadi and company. Like me, Nariman had discerned that some of the things Jacob was getting flak for weren't issues his tormentors had previously seemed to care about.

"Like, for instance, the whole gay thing," she told me, hands raised with palms turned upward. For a moment, she looked as though she were going to pray, but then she brought her hands to her face and emitted a frustrated "Ughghghghghgh!"

Apparently, Jacob had at one point cited gays and lesbians as a marginalized group. This came during a class discussion of minorities that suffered discrimination in the contemporary US, a subject Nariman had decided to append to her lecture on the historical oppression of Native Americans and African Americans. Someone had ventured that these two groups continued to suffer various forms of bias and mistreatment, and Nariman had agreed. She then cited Arab and Muslim Americans, and asked for additional examples. That's when Jacob piped up about gays and lesbians. This elicited more agreement from Nariman, but prompted jeers on the part of certain of his classmates.

Following that discussion, Hadi and a few other guys took to hissing "Fag!" every time Jacob spoke in class. Nariman was finding it difficult to stamp out this ugly phenomenon, in part because a crafty Hadi soon stopped doing the heckling himself; instead, he deputized his stooges, who were seated in different parts of the classroom, to do it for him and disorient the poor teacher in the process. "I'm worried about the end-of-term presentations," she told me, blinking rapidly. "They're going to disrupt Jacob's as much as they can, I just know it."

When I offered to sit in on that class, Nariman stopped blinking. Now, her eyeballs bulged to such a degree—with those gray irises seemingly taking on a healthier greenish color—that I held out a cupped hand on either side of me, ready to catch one or even two inadvertent pop-outs. She thanked me profusely.

We agreed that, to offset the potential impression I was attending simply to watch out for Jacob, I'd sit in on all four sessions set aside for her 16 students' presentations, each of which was expected to take approximately 10 minutes. She had scheduled them for the first week of December. This way, anyone who flopped would get a second chance the next week, which was the last before Christmas vacation. (Though we were an American school, we called it Christmas vacation, not Winter Break, perhaps because no seasonal designations could be found to obscure Islamic holidays—which we also took off—determined as they were by the lunar calendar and therefore falling on different dates each year.) I looked forward to the students' talks. Unlike several of his class-mates, Nariman told me with evident pride, Jacob hadn't needed her help to brainstorm ideas; he knew from the start that he wanted to tackle perceptions of guilt during the civil war. And, as we were both aware, he had already started his research.

Sure enough, my presence ensured that Jacob, who spoke for a full 15 minutes, faced no heckling of any kind. And his presentation, in part an oblique commentary on his own travails, impressed me enough to tell Zaina about it. Of course, I knew that, provided I didn't reveal to her that he was the student who had delivered the talk in question, her SSNP-cultivated aversion to sectarianism would guarantee a positive response. So I didn't inform her that it was him. Not right away, at least.

"That's very perceptive," she commented once I had finished my brief account of a presentation by an unnamed student who cited specific massacres and sectarian cleansing operations as stemming from a tendency on the part of many Lebanese to view an entire community as responsible for the actions of some of its members, and consequently to situate it outside "the nation."

Then she added, "If our politicians had been more like this kid, we probably wouldn't have had a civil war."

We were sitting at the small circular plastic table in my kitchenette, sipping coffee I had just made. It was late afternoon on a Saturday, and we'd decided to soon set off for the Sofil Theater in Ashrafieh to watch a German movie called *The Lives of Others*, screened as part of the annual weeklong European Film Festival.

"Yeah, you're probably right," I said. "But what's funny is that if the SSNP had its way and convinced people around here to consider themselves part of a single Syrian nation, the guy who gave this talk wouldn't be allowed to join it."

Zaina: What do you mean?

Me (frisson of excitement): It's Jacob.

Zaina (setting her jaw): I see. Well, you already know what I think about that whole subject. It's not a mistake to say that the Jews aren't part of our nation, because that's something history shows us to be true. You see, saying that this or that group is not part of your nation isn't automatically wrong; it all depends on who you're talking about and what history says about them.

Me: History, huh?

Zaina: That's right. How else do you define your nation and figure out who's part of it? Without any regard for history?

I thought about this for a moment, and a delicious idea came to mind: *Why not use Saadeh and the SSNP's vociferous denunciation of sectarianism against them?* To begin with, Saadeh, a Greek Orthodox Christian, had cleverly drawn the borders of his desired Syria in such a way as to include virtually all the region's Greek Orthodox in a single country. But that was a minor matter. Something much bigger was at play here—an outright contradiction. And I knew my bringing it up would incense Zaina.

"Forget history for a moment," I began slowly. "If you absolutely have to have a nation, it should consist of all the people in that country. Unlike the SSNP's version, which excludes and vilifies a portion of those people. You guys are the most sectarian party around, you know."

"What?!" she cried, bolting up from her chair even as I remained seated. She looked horrified. "We're the ones who fight against sectarianism in all its forms, whether—"

"Except when it's directed against Jews," I interrupted calmly. "If someone says that any other ethnic or religious group around here isn't part of the Syrian nation, you reject that as sectarian. But then you turn around and discriminate against the Jews, a sect of people just like any other."

I paused—before moving in for the kill: "But how about I tell you the most ironic thing about all this, huh, Zaina? If the Jews of this region aren't part of your precious Syrian nation, why shouldn't they turn their backs on it? If you ask me, you're lucky that Antun Saadeh was a footnote in Lebanese history. I'm no Zionist, but if his views had been adopted by all those he considered Syrian, that would have justified the creation of a Jewish state, Israel, where all the Jews around here could have a country of their own."

Curling her lip upward as though to shield her nostrils from some fetid odor, Zaina bent down and brought her face close to mine. Her throat swelled with the bile that my words, indeed my very person, had forced her body to regurgitate. I drew back slightly, but managed not to blink.

"You know something, Hunayn?" she expectorated. "The Leader warned us about your kind. He called you domestic Jews. That's right, while we fight the Jews who stole Palestine, we have another enemy: Syrians who are Jews by choice, and who corrupt Syria from within. Like you."

Needless to say, we didn't end up going to the movie theater that night. Neither that night nor any subsequent one, as a matter of fact; Zaina and I broke up. This happened by mutual consent—funny how that argument proved the last straw for both of us—meaning that I felt no remorse about it. In fact, the twinge of guilt that had nagged me throughout our relationship, sometimes assuming the form of a voice in my head that grumbled "What the fuck are you doing with this totalitarian titillator, you pussy-whipped jabroni?" now went silent.

Of course, I knew loneliness would re-enter my life, and sexual frustration was poised for a comeback. However, I also knew I had done the right thing. Kept my cool throughout it all, too. In fact, when saying that if Jews in our part of the world were excluded from their countries, then they had a right to one of their own, I was thinking of Jacob. But I didn't insert him into that part of the argument, because I was sure that if Zaina badmouthed him again, it would enrage me.

On the Sunday before the last week of school that fall term, I decided to attend an ecumenical gathering at the Syriac Catholic patriarchate—over by the National Museum—bringing together Iraqi Christian refugees of all sects. Flyers I'd seen on the street had sparked my interest in the well-planned and event-packed day, and, as I was awake by mid-morning, I headed out. Lebanon's Iraqi Christian refugees, a few thousand, were far fewer than their Muslim counterparts in the country. However, as with Iraqis who'd fled to Syria and Jordan, the Christian percentage of the total was disproportionate to their actual numbers. The Lebanese state was doing precious little for these people—most of whom had entered Lebanon illegally or overstayed their visas—and did not permit them to work. They had to survive on handouts from the UN and Christian relief agencies, and perform menial labor on the sly.

I tried to time my arrival so that it would occur after the joint Mass, which I expected would pack the church with people. It was also my intention to avoid the hive of activity associated with the children's departure for their day trip. Several Christian aid groups had come together to sponsor a rare day of fun for refugee children, during which they'd take different groups to different places: older kids to the Jeita Grotto, younger ones to an amusement park, and both to the movies, presumably for separate films.

Sure enough, by the time I arrived, Mass was over and the parents had seen their kids off. Many of them had now returned to the church to listen to a planned series of speeches by religious figures from different denominations. I joined them and stood in the back. The pews were full, and I noticed that quite a few women had loosely covered their hair with white scarves, something that had caught my attention the previous Easter and Christmas at the Chaldean church in Hazmieh, indicating as it did the presence of Iraqis, who tended to be more conservative than Lebanese.

Meanwhile, the lightly bearded and ceremonially dressed head of the Syriac Catholic Church, small gold patriarchal cross in his right hand and long pastoral staff in his left, implored those present as well as the many others watching on local Christian TV channel Télé Lumière to work together across denominational lines so as to benefit the common good. Stepping up to the pulpit following the patriarch was a redheaded Syriac Orthodox clergyman who had come from Syria and whose accent marked him out as an Iraqi, just like the Damascus-based patriarch of the Church he was there to represent. He urged everyone to stand for truth and justice, but to refuse to hate their persecutors, even though the latter may hate them. Similar speeches by other figures followed, and although I didn't disagree with their content, I got restless and decided to step out for a walk through the grounds.

Even with the kids' departure, there remained a lot of people milling about. In one spot, smartly dressed young men and women were seated at several desks situated a few feet from one another. They represented various organizations offering assistance: the United Nations was encouraging refugees to register with its refugee-assistance arm; some NGOS said they could help with asylum applications at Western countries' embassies; others promised help with getting kids into schools; and Christian charities were donating clothes and other items. Quite a few people were lined up at these desks.

Although a Télé Lumière crew was filming the speeches in the church, I didn't see any correspondents conducting interviews out here. As I wasn't a journalist myself (and no longer even worked as an editor for the *Star*), it wouldn't do for me to go around asking people to open up about any recent trauma they'd endured in Iraq. What I had in mind was listening in on conversations tackling the upshot of all the terror and mayhem, and what it meant for the future of Christians specifically. In that sense, I had come to the right place. But how to gain entry, even just for the purpose of listening, to groups of people talking about this subject?

When I turned a corner and spotted Father Nameer from the Chaldean church in Hazmieh, whom I hadn't seen since last Easter, I knew that luck had crossed my path. He was talking to an attentive middle-aged couple who could have been his parents, the three of them standing just outside the patriarchate's "salon," or assembly hall, where a series of lectures on the history of Christianity in Iraq was scheduled to take place later in the day. When they finished speaking and parted, I walked up to him and introduced myself. Citing my parents' names caused a sign of recognition to flicker across his face. After I told him of my purpose in attending the gathering, he said, "Why don't you come along with me, Hunayn?" He was checking in on members of his flock as well as Assyrians and Syriacs he was friendly with. "I'll ask them additional questions so that you get some good information," he told me. This was what I had wanted. I thanked him warmly, and we proceeded to go around, with Father Nameer—an Iraqi himself—striking up conversations that gave me my first sustained view of the situation in Iraq through the eyes of my coreligionists.

From the start, it struck me as significant that although many people had harsh words for the US military for failing to protect them, they didn't hesitate to pinpoint Islamist groups, Sunni or Shiite, as their direct oppressors. This contrasted with much of the "analysis" from "experts" appearing on Arabic-language satellite channels following news broadcasts; they tended to spin conspiracy theories about the US and Israel orchestrating such outrageous acts.

Apparently, in Iraq itself, a similar approach was common. When Father Nameer asked a group of old-timers about Muslim religious and political figures' reactions to attacks on Christians, an energetic little man took a break from the game of backgammon he was playing with a friend to gesticulate—dice in one hand and rosary in the other—and answered the question. "They condemn them, but then they turn around and claim that the perpetrators aren't from their community," he lamented. "If they're Shiite, they say it's the Sunnis, and if they're Sunni, they say it's the Shiites. Witnesses and evidence mean nothing to them; it's all about point-scoring!"

His partner in the backgammon game, a bald and bespectacled man with a raspy voice, now chimed in. "They even do it when you ask them about attacks on the other community," he said. "So when Sunni figures are asked about an attack on Shiite civilians, they say that the Shiites themselves did it to make Sunnis look bad. And vice versa. Now, if both Sunni and Shiite leaders refuse to come to grips with the problem of radical Islam in their midst, what incentive could they have to fight it?!"

Most people were from Baghdad. Almost all, when talking about the lead-up to their departure from Iraq (a subject Father Nameer was probably familiar with in the case of the Chaldeans, but asked about for my benefit), described individual acts of kindness by Muslims—friends, colleagues, and others. For example, there was the neighbor who served as an unofficial real estate agent, a beard, for a family that wanted to sell its house. The family members, who lived in Karradat Mariam and had no income after closing down their liquor store in Al-Battaween due to threats from Muslim fundamentalists, didn't want to reveal to potential buyers that they were Christian for fear of being offered far less than the property was worth. And in an act of heroism that would have made Bonhoeffer proud, dozens of unarmed men and boys gathered in front of their Christian neighbors' homes in the Daura district and told a rampaging mob of infidel-hunting Islamists that they'd have to kill all these Muslims arrayed before them in order to get to the Christians. The Islamists left. But shortly thereafter, so did the terrified Christians.

The disturbing thing was that some of the refugees I met had experienced hate and discrimination from ordinary Muslims, as with the widow from Mosul whose neighbor began depositing his garbage on her little front porch shortly after the liberation. When she confronted him about it, he said, "You're a Christian; I'll put my trash inside your house if I feel like it." (Of course, such nasty behavior would soon become the least of her concerns; she ended up leaving Iraq due to the spike in overall violence.) Or the young couple from Baghdad's Ghadeer neighborhood that came home one day to find their furniture in the street. Their landlord informed them: "Saddam isn't here to protect you anymore." That was in 2003, a few years before members of the Mahdi Army, a Shiite militia that US intelligence said was receiving training from Lebanon's Hezbollah, broke into their new home in another neighborhood and warned them to leave Iraq because it was a Muslim country.

The sad truth was that, although terrorists and militias stood out from ordinary folk, the latter themselves included nasty people who weren't readily distinguishable from the decent sort among whom they mingled. Sure, the terrorists and militias were the worst, and most Muslims remained unaffiliated with them. But it wasn't as though the unaffiliated were all just and fair; some proved opportunistic and exploitative.

No one wanted to return to Iraq. This seemed noteworthy, particularly as it wasn't unreasonable to assume that the far more numerous Iraqi Christians who'd taken refuge in Syria and Jordan similarly balked at the prospect of going back. Most of the Iraqis who had sought sanctuary in those two countries were Sunni. According to news reports I'd read, they wished to return to Iraq as soon as the areas they had fled were no longer under threat from Shiite militias—some of which were in cahoots with the Shiite-dominated government. But the Christian refugees I spoke with were terrified at the thought of returning. It made little difference whether Sunni or Shiite militant factions held sway in their areas, as they all hated Christians, while certain Sunni terrorist groups took things a step further and wanted to kill them.

For those refugees languishing in Lebanon (as opposed to Syria or Jordan, where they faced fewer legal restrictions), remaining in place was untenable in the long run, given their murky legal status. At the same time, for Iraqi refugees anywhere, immigrating to countries in the West was proving exceedingly difficult. The US seemed to have the most exclusionary policies of all. Several men told me that their asylum applications were rejected because they had served in the Iraqi army under Saddam. (Of course, it wasn't their decision to serve—the military had drafted them—and in some cases their tour of duty was back in the 1980s, during much of which time the US was aiding Iraq in its war against Iran.) And if the head of the family couldn't go, the wife usually didn't consider trying her luck with the kids alone.

One entire household saw its members' applications rejected because, in order to secure their kidnapped 12-year-old son's freedom, the parents had paid his Sunni

Islamist abductors a ransom. For having provided financial aid to terrorists, they and their immediate kin, who had helped raise the funds for the ransom, would never gain entry to the US. "It's incredible," the haggard and enervated mother told us. "First, we have to pay money to the very people making life for Christians in Iraq a living hell, so that we end up funding the war against us. And now, to make matters worse, the Americans basically tell us that we have no choice but to go back and continue doing that!" She laughed a little maniacally and then brought her hand to her mouth, ashamed of how she sounded.

Meanwhile, churches in Iraq had stopped issuing birth certificates to members of their flock who needed identification, so as to stem the exodus. And still they left, hoping and praying that Jordan or Syria or Lebanon or Turkey would mark a brief stop on their way to a country far away from this accursed region.

At one point, as Father Nameer and I walked through the grounds, a woman who was about his age came up to him and touched his forearm. He paused and lowered his head a little, giving her his ear. The woman, who had short black hair and wore a formal-looking beige dress, said a few words to him and squeezed his arm before nodding at me and hurrying off. Father Nameer turned to me and explained that his wife had just informed him that his presence was required for something back at the salon. He excused himself, I thanked him for all his trouble, and he left to join her.

Moments later, a dour-faced, mustachioed Saddam lookalike clad in an olive green safari suit accosted me and said gruffly, "Why are you going around collecting people's stories? You're not a journalist."

I conceded that I wasn't, and tried to sound reassuring by informing him—in what would have sounded too explicitly worded in any other context—that I was an Iraqi Christian who lived in Lebanon. His face lit up, and I continued: "I just thought I'd come down here and get an idea of what you're going through."

"Tell me, son, do you speak Christian?" he asked eagerly.

I couldn't help but smile. In Iraq, the ancient language properly termed Aramaic, several modern dialects of which were spoken throughout the country, was referred to by some people as "Christian." After all, although not all Christians knew the storied Semitic language, an earlier version of which was spoken by Jesus, those Iraqis who did were almost exclusively Christian, the Jewish speakers having left the Kurdish region for Israel decades ago.

I told the man that no, to my regret, I didn't speak Christian. He said not to worry, and we carried on chatting in Arabic. His name was Sargon, and he was an Assyrian from Hayy al-Athouriyyeen, one of several neighborhoods in the capital's badly affected Daura area, though he had been born and raised in the town of Al-Habbaniyya. A taxi driver who had fled Iraq with his wife upon learning that his name was included on a list of "infidels" posted on the bulletin board of a nearby mosque, Sargon was passionate about music. It grieved him that, when he and his wife had packed up their belongings and left Iraq, he had had to leave behind his life's collection of records, cassette tapes, and CDs of Arabic and Assyrian music by hundreds of Iraqi artists. He mentioned a few of them to me and was shocked and pained to discover the extent of my ignorance of Iraqi music. No matter; he took it upon himself to educate me, then and there, about some of the greats.

So instead of attending the lectures on Iraqi Christian history at the salon, I listened to Sargon discourse on popular Iraqi music, as we sat side by side on two white plastic chairs in the courtyard. He threw a lot of information my way. Anecdotes, too. Some were engaging, some not so much. He talked for the duration of the lecture series—a few hours at least. When the salon eventually disgorged its occupants and they streamed out in all directions, his wife came over. We were briefly introduced—she said "I hope my husband isn't boring you" with a kind smile; I assured her that he wasn't—and she spoke to Sargon in Aramaic before stepping away. He told me that she'd said she was going to talk to some of the ladies she'd met, but would be back in a bit.

Sargon looked pensive for a moment, staring off into the distance. Then, turning to me, he said in a low voice, "Hunayn, there's something I'm very afraid of, and I know I'll continue to fear it irrespective of whether we move to Chicago to be with our grown children, which is what we're trying to do, or stay here, or, God forbid…go back to Iraq."

He proceeded to explain to me that, because most Jews who left Iraq in the mass exodus of the early 1950s went to Israel, previously renowned and much-loved figures among the emigrants all of a sudden found their names expunged from the annals of noteworthy Iraqis. Sargon cited examples of how this whole shoddy business played out in the realm of music. "When national radio played songs by brothers Saleh and Daoud Al-Kuwaiti, our best musicians, it stopped crediting them!" he cried. The two had become Israeli, after all, and Iraq was officially in a state of war with Israel for the sake of the Palestinians.

Yet Iraq's problem with Iraqi Jews ran deeper than that, Sargon continued. Because both Zionism and Arab nationalism had associated all Jews, regardless of nationality or political inclination, with Israel, none of the Jews who stayed behind could avoid the stigma that now attached to all things Jewish, even Salima Murad, the country's pre-eminent songstress. Sargon told me that when Murad's (Muslim) husband, the legendary crooner Nadhem Al-Ghazali, released a ballad in which he serenaded his Jewish wife, he addressed her as though she were a Christian, a "Samra' min Qaum Issa," as the title (and refrain) had it. That's how bad things got.

"And my fear, Hunayn, is that the extremists are winning in Iraq," Sargon said, his voice now a whisper. "And if they win, not only will Iraq's Christians suffer the same fate as the country's Jews, but the very notion of an Iraqi Christian will become as unacceptable as that of an Iraqi Jew."

For me, the most poignant exchange of the day was one I didn't participate in, and nearly missed. Sargon and I had said our goodbyes, shaking hands and then hugging. He released me only after I promised to look up the singers and musicians he'd regaled me with stories about. Then he added that, should we meet again, he'd give me a history lesson on Aramaic-language Iraqi music by Assyrian and other Christian artists, which he hadn't had a chance to tell me about. A few moments later, I was walking toward the front gate. That's when I happened to hear someone off to the side say, "Of course I'll go back. You should, too, when the time is right."

I stopped and turned to look at the speaker, a silver-haired man in a wheelchair with a pen sticking out of his crumpled white shirt's ink-stained front pocket and several folded newspapers in his lap. He was addressing a tall and angular guy who looked not quite out of his teens and was dressed in a billowing yellow T-shirt and brown corduroy pants that barely reached the top of his ankles. What he had said startled me because it differed so dramatically from everybody else's expressed desire. Here was this older gentleman insisting that he'd return to Iraq, and encouraging a young man to do the same. To say that I was curious as to how he could justify such a position would be a gross understatement; I desperately wanted to hear a convincing explanation for why these Iraqi Christians shouldn't give up on Iraq—and why, by extension, I shouldn't either. For although I had no plans to move there, a part of me wished to continue clinging to the possibility that I'd do so eventually.

The older gent continued, "Our identity is bound up with Iraq's, which is the most important Arab country. And although we're not Arab ethnically, most of us adopted Arab culture centuries ago and made it our own alongside our original culture, so in some ways we're just as Arab as the Arabs themselves."

Immediately, an exchange I had had with Khaled popped into my head, taking me back to Orlando.

We were driving around in his car and listening to music. So as not to interfere with his concentration as Marc Cohn crooned his way through "Walking in Memphis," I saved my admiring comment about the song until it drew to a close, when I said, "Great choice, man. Almost makes me want to go out and book a flight there myself, just so that I can walk down Beale Street like he did."

Khaled reached over and switched the radio off. I wasn't surprised; this happened often. But instead of asking me to fish out the small binder from the glove compartment, remove a specific CD, and replace the Cohn one with it, which is what I was expecting, he said, "I know how you feel, Hunayn."

After a pause, frowning and sounding quite grave, he added, "But there's something else that gets me about this song. Something that might help you if you ever find yourself an outsider who wants to fit in and be accepted. I've been waiting for that with Mindy or her parents or any part of society here, so that I can apply the lesson I learned from this song, but it's just not happening, because everybody already accepts me."

Me: What're you talking about?

Khaled: You remember what Muriel asks him after he accompanies her on the piano by singing with all his might?

Me: Yeah, I think it's whether he's a Christian.

Khaled: That's right. And guess what? Marc Cohn's Jewish.

Me: Awkward moment, huh?

Khaled: Well, *potentially*. And that's even though she didn't mean it in an intrusive way; she was just convinced, in her simple fashion, that you sing with such soul, you must be Christian, right?

Me: Which he handles with a nice touch.

Khaled: "Ma'am, I am tonight!" In other words, he's not a Christian, but while singing at Muriel's place, he is.

He's not Christian by religion, but he is by culture, you know? So he is and he isn't, and somehow he resolves that contradiction and achieves the impossible.

Me: Like a kosher cheeseburger.

Khaled: You could say that...But more like a formula to fit in without giving up who you are.

The younger guy's voice brought me back to the conversation at hand. He was saying something about it not making a difference. I focused as he elaborated. "We've left Iraq. That was the first step. Now we have to never go back and put it behind us for good."

Older Gent: But our roots are there! And I shouldn't have to tell you that those roots run very deep. We're descended from the original inhabitants of the land. Let nobody think that because we're Christian, we're Western or foreign in any way. We are authentic Iraqis!

Charity-Clothed Youth (shaking his head): That doesn't matter, either. The old mentality's no good anymore, can't you see?

Older Gent: Listen, young man. This "old mentality" is everything; it placed us in just the right spot in relation to both the past and the present. In a country with such an ancient history, we were the past's direct heirs. And, despite not being Arab ourselves, we were open to the Arab culture of the present. These two things guaranteed us respect.

Charity-Clothed Youth: Fine. But the new Iraq isn't based on Arab nationalism combined with pride in its non-Arab ancient history. The Baath party lost, and the new Iraq is all about Islam now.

Older Gent: I have no fear of the true Islam, the tolerant kind, and have always enjoyed the call to prayer that sounds five times—

Charity-Clothed Youth: That's fine. But what about your status as an authentic Iraqi, like you said?

Older Gent: What do you mean?

Charity-Clothed Youth: People like you and me, we remind the Islamists of Iraq's pre-Islamic history. So the very fact that we're authentic Iraqis is the problem. You see, we're all supposed to become Muslim. That way, the Islamists can pretend that the odd Iraqi Christian they come across is a convert—and then kill him. Otherwise, Uncle, just by being who we are, we bring them face-to-face with what they hate about themselves: their non-Muslim origins.

Shortly after I got home that Sunday evening, I stood before the Iraq rug up on the wall. This trusty tapestry had traveled far and wide. A couple of months following my graduation from high school, when the time had come for me to leave Beirut for Orlando and begin life as a UCF student, my parents gave it to me as a gift. Before that, it had hung from the living room wall of every home we'd ever had. Though small and in most respects nondescript, to me it was the most important item in our household, what with its map of our far-off country, and the careful delineations of major historical and archeological sites. As I had no memories of Iraq, any sentimental attachment I developed to the things (small religious icons, finely wrought jewelry, colorful traditional attire for the Akitu New Year's festival) that my parents had brought from that near-mythic place derived from my experiences handling them in Abu Dhabi, Rome, or Beirut.

When it came to the Iraq rug, however, the situation was almost the opposite. There was nothing for me to associate it with other than what it depicted. In fact, whenever the subject of Iraq came up, my imagination took me straight to the sketches and symbols woven with black warps and wefts into the tapestry's beige background. Sure, I had my parents' stories, televised footage, and textual descriptions in books. But the Iraq rug seared itself into my mind like nothing else. When I heard "Baghdad," I thought of the grand Abbasid Palace at the rug's center, right beside the city's name. Erbil? Citadel atop a hill, with a statue of turbaned and bearded historian of the city Ibn Al-Mustaufi, seated and reading, at its entrance. Najaf and Karbala? The weavers' rendition of the shrines of Ali and Hussein, respectively. Basra? Sindbad on a rickety raft, sailing down the Shatt al-Arab into a lifetime of adventure.

Of course, the rug itself got me thinking of Iraq. Just looking at it could prompt flights of fancy. I wanted to sprint up the steps and slopes of the Great Ziggurat of Ur, an Iraqi Rocky training early in the morning for his next bout. But that wouldn't suffice, so I'd scale the Ukhaidir Fortress near Karbala and run all along the top of its rectangular wall, skipping across its crenellations and leaping over the tower at each corner. After that, I'd need a break. Might hole up in the tiny space at the top of the soaring Malwiya minaret in Samarra and think of Rapunzel, or sit cross-legged before a cuneiform tablet in Uruk and contemplate the birth of writing. And at day's end? Well, I'd probably avoid contributing to making the mythical Tower of Babel, made real by my magic carpet, even taller. Not for a lack of arrogance, though; wandering through the

Hanging Gardens of Babylon, restored to resplendence by the rug, I'd go so far as to spurn paradise.

This time, however, as I stood before the Iraq rug, examining it for the umpteenth time, something was weighing on me. Back in Rome, thanks to Coalition airstrikes increasingly making Saddam's occupation of Kuwait look like a calamity, and what with my consequent travails at school, I had begun to wean myself off Baathist Iraq. Over the next few years, as I read up on the bloody outrages Saddam had committed against Iraqis, the process came to completion. But I never stopped considering Iraq my country. And later events didn't change my mind. Though the terror and chaos of each year since the 2003 liberation pushed back further and further any notion of actually relocating there, I hadn't sought to sever the psychological link to my motherland.

Yet the hideous news coming out of Iraq on an almost daily basis had worn me down. And a couple of hours earlier, my talks with Iraqi Christian refugees gave me a close-up of true agony and despair. The journalistic detachment I had studiously maintained in the face of the otherwise devastating stories I solicited began to crumble. That there was nothing I could do to help these people (not even write an article on them for the *Star*, as might have been possible during my time in the paper's employ) proved exasperating. But it didn't change the fact that I needed to reckon with their reality, as well as their future. And since Iraq didn't seem to figure in that reality or that future as anything other than hell on earth, surely—from an admittedly selfish perspective—this had some bearing on my situation. A notion that had remained inchoate thanks to my best efforts at mental resistance now materialized fully in my mind: *The time had come to roll up the Iraq rug. Maybe even my Iraqiness with it. The time had come.*

Before I took such action, however, I wanted to savor the rug's beauty for a few more moments. My gaze lingered on the image in its top right-hand corner, outside the contours of the map, where the famous statue of the Lion of Babylon trampling a man underfoot was reproduced with striking care for detail. Below it appeared my favorite thing about the rug: a note in Arabic that read "Made in Baghdad Prison, 1964." This sophisticated work of art was created by prisoners in Baghdad's central jail as part of a rehabilitation program!

Glancing leftward, I let my eyes settle on an area within the map. It was northern Iraq. Quite a bit to take in. Near Erbil, the enigmatic winged sun common to several ancient religions in Mesopotamia and beyond. In Nineveh, just east of Mosul across the Tigris River, a magnificent lamassu—the Assyrian deity with the head of a human, body of a bull, and wings of an eagle. And southwest of Mosul, of course, the imposing columns of the Parthian city of Hatra. I found it a great relief that, though I was making the wrenching decision to turn away from my country, these sites and their archeological treasures would forever remain in all their glory.

Meanwhile, I concluded, carving Iraq out of my heart might hurt now, but would almost certainly spare me future pain.

For the last day of school before Christmas vacation, I planned to dismiss my eighth-grade class as soon as we finished watching *The Pearl*, which I'd begun screening after I'd had the students read the book and take a test on it. (A poor 2001 film adaptation had to substitute for the reputedly far superior Spanish-language effort from Mexico back in 1947, *La Perla*, as I was unable to get hold of the latter in either DVD or VHS format.) Half an hour remained of the movie from the previous day's period, which meant that they'd have 15 minutes to spare before the next class. Although I knew that, like me, their other teachers were going easy on them this day, it was obvious that they were all impatient for it to end, so that they might start their vacation.

Yet things didn't go according to plan. We finished the film without incident, but just as I was on the verge of giving the students the good news that they were free to go, someone asked, "Sir, was Steinbeck Jewish?"

It was Akram, a Tupac aficionado with a penchant for calling his peers "niggas" (which he unsuccessfully tried to convince me was distinct from "niggers" when I called him out on it in class). I wondered if Hadi had put him up to this, or at least planted the notion in his head. The two didn't seem to be friends, and headstrong Akram wasn't the type to do something simply at a classmate's urging. Perhaps he was voluntarily taking his cue from the obsessed-with-all-things-Jewish Hadi. Or maybe the question was entirely his, in which case it might reflect nothing other than an innocent wish to know more about the author.

"I don't know," I admitted, "though you mustn't consider 'Stein,' which means 'stone' in German and is pronounced *shtine* in that language, indicative of anything. See, 'Steinbeck' just means 'stonebrook.' And I don't know what his mother was, which makes all the difference from a traditional Jewish standpoint."

Then, as casually as I could (I didn't want Akram to think I was faulting him for posing the question), I asked, "How would you feel if he was?"

"Dunno," he said. "Maybe a little…insulted?"

So it wasn't innocent after all. But this bore closer examination. "Why's that, Akram?" I probed. "Because of the recent war?"

"Well, yeah, that's part of it," he replied. "But also because of what they did to the Palestinians."

"Wait a second," Jacob interjected. "You think that because of what Israel did, we should stop reading books by Jewish authors?" He sounded incredulous.

"Other schools have already done that," Hadi jumped in. His breath catching, he seemed elated that such a debate was underway, as he could smuggle in his bigotry through the otherwise encouraged practice of classroom participation. "You heard about the whole Anne Frank thing, right, Jacob?" he asked, concealing his spite with earnestness. He was referring to the recent Hezbollah-driven media brouhaha that erupted when it was discovered that nearby IC was teaching Anne Frank's *The Diary of a Young Girl* in its middle school section; the administration promptly pulled the book.

I refrained from butting in, deciding instead to let the exchange take its course. After all, it was civil in nature. Plus, I didn't want to seem like Jacob's protector every time the Jewish issue was brought up, which would encumber him with an additional burden. And, of course, I was hoping that he'd tackle this subject effectively on his own, employing reason and logic to stump Akram and Hadi.

"That's just what I'm saying!" replied Jacob, still incredulous. "You want to punish all Jewish writers because of Israel?!" he cried, looking at Hadi.

Akram, perhaps trying to regain control of what was supposed to be his baby and set himself apart from Hadi, answered, "Not all. Just the ones who support Israel."

Hadi: No, all of them. Otherwise, we could get stuck with Israeli writers, not just American Jewish ones. Like if an Israeli author criticizes Israel, everybody would be like, "Oh, this guy's okay," and make us read him so that we come around to accepting Israel. Which is just what they want. See how clever they are, Akram?

Jacob: Well, all I can say is that if you ban all Jewish writers, you'd just be hurting yourselves.

Hadi: Yeah? Why's that? Because we'll miss out on Anne Frank's made-up stories?

Jacob (trying to control himself): Not just Anne Frank's *Diary*, but tons of other stuff.

Hadi: Oh, right, I forgot. You're not just the chosen people, but the best writers, too!

Jacob (enraged): Not just the best writers, but the best everything!

Akram (taken aback): I can't believe how arrogant you are!

Hadi (gleeful): Believe it! And it's not just him, either!

Jacob (composing himself): You don't have to take my word for it. Isn't it a fact, Mr. Hunayn, that Jews outscore everybody else when it comes to getting the Nobel Prize? And that's, like, in all the different categories? Isn't it true that if you add up all the Arabs or even all the Muslims who've won the Nobel, they don't come close to us, even though there's so many more of them?

He looked at me. Fierce, expectant. I wondered whether I was seeing my future. Or, more accurately, the future of my child, were I to ever have one. If one day I landed a wife, and if she bore me a child, would he or she grow into Jacob's Christian counterpart? Someone of Iraqi origin who didn't identify with Iraq or Iraqis, much less Arabs? Who, when speaking of his or her people, narrowed that group down to Chaldeans-Syriacs-Assyrians, or perhaps even only Chaldeans? So that, should our happy little family leave Moloch's favorite stomping grounds and immigrate to an America that by then is no longer Septemberland, my kid would become a Chaldean American, not an Iraqi American?

More than likely. After all, I had already taken the first step in that direction myself, what with my recent decision to roll up the Iraq rug—and my Iraqiness with it. Could I expect a child of mine to be more Iraqi than I was?

But that was the future. I had a more pressing issue to deal with. An opportunity to do what I had wanted to do for so long: help Jacob in a meaningful way. All the other stuff I'd managed—shutting Hadi down back when he'd taunted Jacob with "Yaakov" in class and made that nasty remark about his father, offering to help the kid procure books he might need for his social studies presentation, and then attending it so as to help Nariman maintain control of her classroom—consisted of deflecting or pre-empting attacks on him. Now I had the chance to enable Jacob, who had for once gone on the offensive, to fell his greatest foe. How? Affirmation. Public affirmation of the value of his Jewishness.

Yet he had chosen a most distasteful way of trying to assert the value of that Jewishness. Distasteful and ironic. After all, this was the guy who delivered the presentation on sectarianism and the absurdity of assigning guilt collectively. Wasn't doing the same with excellence just as stupid, and potentially just as dangerous?

I certainly thought so. I didn't consider myself implicated in the crimes of the Chaldean gangsters and drug dealers in Detroit whose activities and increasing national reach Lewis or some news outlet would occasionally tell me about back in Septemberland, nor did I puff my chest out when hearing of other Chaldeans' decidedly more constructive contributions to humanity. That just wasn't my style.

Indeed, with the exception of my moment of weakness with Joelle, I had over the past several years successfully resisted playing the related game of securing a measure of acceptability or even just safety through identity association. When I could have extracted Samer and myself from a tight spot in Lebanon just by telling our tormentors that I was Christian like them, I decided to keep mum. When a multi-pronged terrorist attack upended my life in the States, I could have worn my crucifix outside my shirt to debunk the common assumption that my Iraqi identity signified a Muslim religious affiliation, and might easily have harped on the fact that, as a Chaldean, I wasn't even Arab. I didn't. A couple of years later, I found myself at the bar in the middle of nowhere with a drink flung at my face, courtesy of Kevin, African American scourge of all "sand niggers." Meanwhile, as indicated by Brad's calling me "Osama" (which he obviously associated with Bin Laden and Islam even though the name wasn't Islamic) and his reference to my "terrorist religion" prohibiting the consumption of alcohol, he thought me a Muslim. Still, I didn't even consider correcting him on the point then or a few minutes later, when he began administering my "punishment" with a knee to the groin. A power beyond my control and not in the business of consulting me intervened to spare me the worst of what he intended to do, much like what would happen with the crowd of hopping mad Lebanese nationalists in Martyrs' Square a couple of years later.

Of course, it worked the other way around, too. After going soft upon realizing that a lusty Amazon had glommed on to me precisely because she thought I was Muslim, I could have taken a minute to adjust to the situation and then gotten back in the game in the guise of who she thought I was. Instead, I knowingly undermined my chances at sexual gratification by scuppering, at *the* critical moment, the association in Kendra's mind between me and all those strong Muslim men and their fucking prowess.

But I hadn't always been so principled, so rigorous. Back in Rome, not long after Danny and company humiliated me in the locker incident and he and a whole bunch of others took to rubbing in the groveling Iraqi soldiers bit, something happened. An opportunity came my way one fine day, and I seized it. I allowed myself to bask in Maysoon's lambent glow for a wondrous but evanescent moment, fooling everyone (myself most of all) into thinking that her spectacular achievement that afternoon lent me a certain luster because I too was Iraqi. Well? Wasn't Jacob, via crude one-upmanship, trying to do the same thing now with his Jewishness? Jacob, whose facial

308

expression appeared more beseeching with each moment I held off on answering his question. Need I browbeat him with logic, on top of all the illogic Hadi and his cohorts were clobbering him with?

"That's right, Jacob," I finally said. My voice was weary and resigned, but firm. I looked straight at him as I spoke.

His face unclenched, and he gave me a slight, almost imperceptible nod. Then, steely-eyed, he turned to his erstwhile nemesis, now vanquished. Hadi not only averted his gaze; in a rare loss of sangfroid, he gripped the sides of his desk and growled as his cheeks flushed with fury. Jacob allowed himself a satisfied "Mm-hm" before turning his attention to Akram and nodding in slow and somber fashion, to which this lesser tormentor reacted by looking down at his desk and gnashing his teeth.

Now well and truly bereft over my abandonment at the hands of a presumed kindred spirit, but really just a beleaguered kid, I repeated, "That's absolutely right."

When we finally reached the auditorium, having walked down long and drafty hallways that, unlike the classrooms, weren't heated (making me wish I was back in Dubai), it was packed with students chattering, laughing, and shouting. Not just high schoolers; middle schoolers, too. That's why we sixth graders were there; at ACS Rome, middle school consisted of sixth to eighth grade. The teachers had worked out a reasonable seating arrangement beforehand. As the youngest grade, we were assigned the horizontal row closest to the stage, with the next grade up getting the row behind us, and so on until you reached the seniors at the very back.

We were the last to arrive, and made our way up the middle aisle in a single column to the empty front row. By the time I reached it, the half row to my right was completely full except for the seat abutting the aisle—just where I stood—so I took it. Those of my classmates behind me now started turning left as soon as they reached the front, and began filling up that half row.

A few moments later we were all seated. I looked across the aisle to my left and noticed Danny sitting in the chair abutting it, about a yard away from me. He was picking at a cuticle, clearly bored. When he caught me looking at him, he gave me the finger and then pursed his lips and emitted a smacking sound in mocking mimicry of those boot-kissing Iraqi soldiers.

After informing us that we were in for a special treat to mark the onset of Winter Break the following day, the principal, a youngish and vain fop decked out in a royal blue three-piece suit and salmon-colored tie, strutted off the stage as the curtain rose. Before us stood the school choir in a horizontal line. Behind them, on a raised platform of some kind, was assembled the school band (seated) and its conductor, Ms. Sutcliffe (standing). We clapped politely. Ms. Sutcliffe turned her back to us, readying herself to conduct. She nodded at the band members, and the gray little bun of hair tied behind her head bobbed up and down. But the band's instruments remained silent. Instead, the choir started singing a cappella—slowly, with drawn-out syllables. A story about calling an operator, asking for information, and trying to get through to heaven.

Then Ms. Sutcliffe counted out "Two, three," the choristers parted, and who should step forward but that numinous embodiment of earthy womanhood, Maysoon.

"Operator!" she cried out, her singing voice robust yet controlled and mellifluous. The choristers repeated after her, and the band kicked in.

"Information!" she called. Again, the response in kind from the choir.

"Get me Jesus...on the line!"

She wore a body-hugging strapless black dress that accentuated her curves and left exposed her beautiful bronze shoulders as well as her legs below the knee, and a pair of comfortable-looking black leather flats. Belting out one verse after another, she swung her shapely body this way and that in step with the effervescent music. Despite the fact that the choristers, many of them her fellow seniors, stood in a line on either side of her, and although the band members and Ms. Sutcliffe remained visible on the raised platform behind them, it was as if majestic Maysoon were the only person gracing that stage. Not because the others' contributions weren't essential, but because, with her combination of talent and afflatus, she owned it. Singing and dancing at the stage's center, encased in her magnificent nimbus, Maysoon commanded the attention of everyone in the audience, and literally roused them to boot.

Indeed, when—with great difficulty—I tore my eyes from her and scanned the auditorium, I noticed as much. We had all spontaneously and perhaps unconsciously stood up, and were now clapping in rhythm with the music and swaying from side to side in time with Maysoon. I looked across the aisle to my left and saw Danny. He was still just a few feet away from me, but out of his chair, gyrating his deceptively unthreatening homuncular body and slapping his hands together with gusto. A moment later, drawn by the inexorable force of Maysoon's vocals, my gaze reverted to her up on the stage.

Just then, as she admonished the operator to connect her call to her savior, whom her mother had never had any difficulty getting on the line, an epiphany descended on me. I realized that by figuratively brushing against the incandescent Maysoon, I might spark my own little glimmer, however faint and flickering.

Some time following what I did during that mesmerizing performance, as reason regained the upper hand over my craving for respect, I would feel pretty foolish. Shame on you, I'd berate myself, for trying to burnish your miserably matte image by pilfering even a scintilla of someone else's light. Isn't this just a variation on the opportunistic strategy you employed earlier, hitching your pathetic self to a Saddamized Iraq bounding toward regional superpower status, so that when it arrived, you might share in its triumph?

Yet such sober analysis and merciless self-criticism would only come later. The immediate effect achieved by the pint-sized, improbably stentorian thrush from the Land of the Two Rivers was momentous. In that pulsating auditorium, as I sequined my chthonic, wretched, loathsome Iraqiness with a refraction of Maysoon's ethereal luminosity for a fleeting instant, exhilaration permeated my every pore, and pride swelled my caved-in bosom. *I had become something. I was somebody.*

Still standing, I leaned across the aisle to my left and said, "Danny. Hey, Danny."

He paid me no heed, eyes riveted to the stage as he

continued to rock out to the song, hands helping to generate the crowd-synchronized "smack" heard throughout the auditorium every second or so.

"I just thought you might want to know that she's Iraqi. Maysoon."

Half an expression of sheer terror now disfigured his facial profile, and he went still as a statue—mid-sway and mid-clap. As though participating in freeze dance, the children's game with the rule that when the upbeat music stops, you become immobile.

But the music hadn't stopped. The band continued playing and the choir chorused and mighty Maysoon brought the house down and onto her little orb-shaped shoulders.

Taking a deep breath, I leaned over again. "That's right," I said. Then, my voice quavering: "Iraqi…just like me."

## Acknowledgments

For encouragement and other forms of support, I thank my parents and late grandmother (the three people to whom this book is dedicated), brother Tameem, uncle Shafic Ali, and cousin Najib Kabbani. For reading and critiquing the manuscript, in whole or in part, I am indebted to my brother Laith, friends Rudi Heinrich, Badr Soukarie, Josh Squires, Charles McNair, R.P. Finch, Dima Younis, cousin Jamil Ali, Truthdig's Eunice Wong (who published an excerpt from the first chapter), as well as Diana Miller, Chuck Adams, Daniel Menaker, Robert Boyers, and Stephanie Steiker. For helping me turn the manuscript into an actual book—edited, handsomely designed, and well-promoted—much appreciation is due the following members of the Interlink team: Michel Moushabeck, Whitney Sanderson, Pam Fontes-May, and Meredith Madyda.

Just so you know, I gave myself license to tinker with chronology. For example, Osama Bin Laden's boastful acknowledgment of responsibility for the 9/11 attacks is made reference to here before the filmed statement went public, the beer called 321 (Osama's beverage of choice while watching porn in his Abbottabad hideaway-in-plain-sight, I'm sure) comes into existence in Orlando earlier than it actually did, and the Hezbollah-generated hullabaloo over Anne Frank's *The Diary of a Young Girl* being taught at a Lebanese middle school is moved up in time.

I should mention that I decided to render "Université Saint-Joseph" as "Saint Joseph's University" in English, because the official translation—"Saint Joseph University"—strikes me as awkward. (The university can thank me later; I visit Beirut often.) On a related subject, when transliterating names of people and places in the Arab world—principally Lebanon and Iraq—I did not adhere to any standard. Finally, the harrowing personal stories Hunayn hears from Iraqi Christian refugees at the Syriac Catholic patriarchate in Beirut are based in large part on my recollection of actual news reports I read over a period of several years.